Bingsu FOR Two

SUJIN WITHERSPOON

U

**UNION
SQUARE
& CO.**

NEW YORK

**UNION
SQUARE
& CO.**

NEW YORK

UNION SQUARE & CO and the distinctive Union Square & Co. logo are
trademarks of Sterling Publishing Co., Inc.

Union Square & Co., LLC, is a subsidiary of Sterling Publishing Co., Inc.

ISBN 978-1-4549-5402-6 (hardcover)
ISBN: 978-1-4549-5404-0 (paperback)
ISBN: 978-1-4549-5403-3 (ebook)

Library of Congress Control Number: 2023051844

For information about custom editions, special sales, and premium purchases,
please contact specialsales@unionsquareandco.com.

Printed in Canada

2   4   6   8   10   9   7   5   3   1

unionsquareandco.com

Cover and interior design by Marcie Lawrence

Cover illustration by Jen Keenan

For those struggling with the question of who they are.

Maybe it's not about the answer.

1. A LOT OF BAD DECISIONS LED ME TO THIS MOMENT, BUT IN MY DEFENSE, I MADE THEM REALLY FAST

When I woke up this morning with a feeling that this was going to be the Worst Day of My Life So Far, I brushed it off as the self-destructive voice in my head doing his daily affirmations.

I was wrong. This is turning out to be the Worst Day of My Life *Ever*.

I'm not usually this pessimistic, but I think I'm allowed to mope in the privacy of my own thoughts after what happened last night—or maybe I'm not, because this whole mess is my own fault. I'm just not going to think about it, because *that's* a healthy way to deal with your problems, River.

The dreadful symphony of test pages being flipped and scribbled on with #2 pencils snaps me out of my spiraling. I sit up a little straighter in these god-awful chairs, glancing around the cafeteria-turned-testing room. This probably isn't the best time to reflect on my mistakes, since I'm supposed to be taking the most important test of my seventeen-year-old life.

My blank Scantron and unopened SAT booklet stare at me from the desk. The clock in the corner of the cafeteria ticks in time to my rapidly beating heart. How has an hour already passed? I'm running out of time. And air—it's stuffy in here. Panic rushes up my esophagus and perches below my chin, ready to spew all over my test. At least then I'd have something to turn in.

I lean forward and hold my head in my hands, leg bouncing under the table. I should've prepared for this. There's no amount of last-minute cramming that could make up for an entire academic career of slacking off and barely scraping through grade levels on Cs and the occasional B, but I should have at least *tried* to study, or gotten a good night's sleep—or, hey, maybe not have dumped my girlfriend of almost four years out of the blue.

My eyes drift a few rows over, locking onto the back of a head of long, ash-blond hair. Cecelia Campbell tucks a strand of it behind her ear, exposing the side of her face. There are deep circles under her eyes that aren't usually there, but she's still beautiful, always is, even last night when those eyes watered as I told her *I just can't do this anymore. I'm sorry.*

As if she can feel me staring—or the universe just hates me, which would also make sense—Cecelia glances over her shoulder and meets my gaze.

Seeing her heart break for the second time in twenty-four hours, across the aisles of desks and students between us, snaps the last tether in my mind grounding me to reality.

I don't even realize I'm standing until the squeal of my chair against the linoleum floor echoes through the cafeteria. Hundreds of eyes are on me in seconds. Their stares peel the skin from my bones.

"Langston-Lee?" Mrs. Klug, the principal and proctor, sits up from her perch at the front of the room. "If you have a question, raise your hand and I'll come to you."

My lips part, but no sound escapes. The room spins. My teeth vibrate in my gums, making my jaw chatter.

"I have to go," I manage to say.

"No one's allowed to leave the testing room. Please, sit down."

But my legs are moving on their own. I need to get out of here, get away. Mrs. Klug yells something as I pick up my backpack and thermos of coffee and sprint out the doors.

I flee the musty confines of Summit Sierra High School and find myself on the busy streets of Seattle. The cool, misty air helps regulate my system, and after a few blocks, I feel almost normal. Well, not on the verge of a panic attack anymore, which is an improvement.

A desperate laugh bubbles out of me like an indigestion burp. Raincoat-clad strangers passing by on the busy sidewalk glance at me before scuttling away. I duck my head and hold my thermos of coffee closer to my chest as I continue walking. Home certainly isn't an option right now, not unless I want to explain to Umma and Dad why I'm not at school, so I head to work. Going in a few hours early can't hurt.

For the first time in a long while, I'm not dreading my shift at Cafe Gong, my family's quaint coffee shop turned corporate caffeine hell. The way the business has changed since the early days of helping my parents pour milk and wipe up spills for their few loyal customers is disappointing, sure, but it's not the *cafe* I'm averse to. It's my co-workers.

It'll be a good distraction, though, especially since it's the grand opening week for our newest store, the one me and my girlfriend—*ex*-girlfriend now, I guess—are co-managers of. I'll clock in, bear Jorge and Rosalind's torment, then clock out and go home.

At the intersection of Union Street and 4th Avenue is Cafe Gong's newest and biggest location, nestled on the ground floor of one of downtown's many skyscraping buildings. Being co-managers, Cece and I oversaw everything that went into opening it. By that, I mean *she* oversaw everything important, and let me choose the location. I picked this spot mostly because we're a stone's throw away from the water, and standing at the crosswalk now, I can see the Puget Sound from the top of the hill. It's nice to pretend the squawking of seagulls and sloshing of waves is audible over the traffic.

Before entering Cafe Gong, I pause to gain some composure. *I can do this*, I think, rolling the tension from my shoulders. *Just play it cool and no one will know you're two seconds away from hurling.*

I try to salvage my appearance, fixing the oversized circle glasses that cover my narrow, upturned brown eyes. There's no helping the unruly, dark hair wilting over my forehead, or what Cecelia calls my "dumb lost puppy who's just happy to be included" expression, which is apparently a permanent fixture of my face.

Thinking of Cecelia physically hurts. A dull, pulsing ache that ricochets through my core. I push the thought of her out of my mind, brace myself, and open the door.

The place hums with life, with customers packed on gaudy industrial-chic furniture that matches the sleek decor. Umma and Dad own a dozen of these cafes across Seattle and they're all the same, from the cloying smell of sugary syrup and toasted pastries wafting in the air, to the generic coffeehouse music drowning out the sounds of chatter, keyboards clacking, and the espresso machine grinding. Cafe Gong didn't use to be like this, tacky and sterile, but its homely appeal was sanitized when business expanded beyond the scale of a ma-and-pa shop.

This location is the busiest by far, which is good because according to Dad, if Cece and I are able to turn this store into a success, they can start franchising nationally. And: *It'll look great on your guys' college applications.* Whoop-de-do.

I spot a head of corkscrew curls tied up by a purple ribbon across the cafe, and my anxiety eases. Thank *God*. Isabette Tucker is one of my two best friends, and the only decent human being working here. In fact, she's probably too good for this place, but I'm glad she lowered her standards enough to apply after we met at Comic-Con last year. She hasn't been able to shake me off since then despite going to a different school.

She looks up when I approach the counter, doe eyes widening in surprise.

"River!" Isabette says. The fluorescent lights shine on her warm brown face, creased with concern. "What the hell happened?"

I fish my manager badge from my pocket and clip it on. "I'm glad you asked. Remember that fan fiction I was telling you about? The one that hasn't updated in five years because the author's beta reader went to jail? Well, they're out, and she posted a note saying the next chapter is coming soon."

"Oh shoot, really?" Isabette pulls her phone out and starts tapping away before she catches herself. I grin. "Hey—don't change the subject. I heard what you did."

"How? It's been like, half an hour."

"What are you talking about?"

"Wait, what are *you* talking about?"

She looks worried that I left my head on my pillow this morning. Which *would* explain what just happened in the testing room at school.

"Hello? I'm talking about Cece?" Isabette whispers. "Rosalind said you dumped her last night."

"*Oh.* Yes, that," I say in the coolest tone of voice I can manage. I rub my chest, suddenly constricted by my hoodie. "I thought you were talking about something else."

"What else did you do?" she says, like she knows I'm capable of worse. Which is fair.

"I may have walked out of a certain test."

"Please don't tell me it was your SAT."

"Maybe."

"What?"

"I don't—forget it. Uh, yeah, about Cece. We broke up."

Instead of asking why, in true Isabette fashion, her voice lowers into the sincerest tone and she says, "Are you okay?"

Which is a harder question to answer.

I sip from my thermos to quench my suddenly dry mouth, when a hand slaps my back and makes me choke. Behind me is Jorge

Sanchez, Pain in My Ass Number Two. Who, despite my begging, Cece insisted be relocated to our new store with us. We've never had the same taste in friends.

"Sorry, boss. I forget you're jumpy," he says, leaning against the mop he was using. He's short enough that the handle reaches his chin, but he's on the wrestling team at Isabette's high school and could fold me into a pretzel without disturbing a single hair of his quiff. I know because he's tried enough times in the back room. "That's my nice way of saying you're a pu—"

"Hi to you, too," I cut him off, wiping the coffee dribbling down my chin. "You surprised me, is all. It's hard to see you down there. I guess the Axe body spray should've been a dead giveaway."

Jorge "accidentally" whacks my shin with the mop handle. My yelp is covered up by a nasally laugh. Pain in My Ass Number One, Rosalind Huynh: as muscled as Jorge but twice as terrifying. She steps up to the counter beside an uncomfortable Isabette, flinging her ombre hair behind her.

"You've got some nerve showing up," she says.

Here we go. "To my own job?"

"Yes, the one Mommy and Daddy handed you on a silver platter. Do us all a favor and keep your ugly mug at home. Cecelia won't want to see you."

"Can we please not argue in front of the customers? At least not during grand opening week," Isabette says.

I clench my fists. Rosalind and I have never gotten along, but when Cece and I were chosen to run this location instead of her, it didn't exactly sweeten our "friendship." "Don't pretend you give a shit about Cecelia."

Jorge grins, all teeth. "Neither do you, apparently."

I smile, eye twitching past the red in my vision, considering how to respond. The possible options blip calmly through my mind like a Top 10 Photos Taken Seconds Before Disaster compilation.

Photo 1: Me cramming a stack of the gift cards we keep next to the register into Jorge's mouth to shut him up for the first time in his life.

Photo 2: Me stealing the coffee from the soccer mom sitting behind me and giving Rosalind's perfectly styled hair an iced caramel macchiato salon treatment.

Photo 3: Me in the back, shoving my hand into the coffee grinder as punishment for not quitting the second Cecelia transferred my least favorite co-workers to our store—

That's enough of that.

Jorge and Rosalind hated me long before I broke Cecelia's heart or became co-manager—something I never asked for, by the way. Umma and Dad tasking me with running Cafe Gong isn't them sliding me a silver platter of success, contrary to Rosalind's belief; it's more of a lifeline. If they didn't think I could be successful outside of the family business before, skipping out on the SATs will be the final nail in that coffin. Which means I'm stuck with Jorge, Rosalind, and my ex-girlfriend for the foreseeable future.

I guess I have no choice but to resort to violence.

The bell chiming above the door stops me from acting on that intrusive thought. A feminine voice lets out an emphatic *"Ugh!"*

Two people enter the store. The first is a short girl with long black hair, copper-toned skin, and heavy-lidded eyes that scan the room. I hear Isabette make a panicked, garbled noise and run into the back, but I don't turn around, distracted by the second person.

Standing in the middle of the cafe is one of the prettiest girls I've ever seen. The kind of pretty that's startling to see in real life and not in a fashion magazine, or wherever else beautiful people spawn from. She's short, chubby, and dressed in an ensemble of sheer stockings, a black and teal plaid skirt, and a cropped shirt layered over a black neck sweater. The girl crinkles her pierced nose, a look of disgust on her heart-shaped face complemented by dark makeup and neon green, choppy bangs.

Rosalind huffs. "Halloween came early."

Green Hair doesn't bother lowering her voice as she approaches the counter. "*This* is their newest store? How are they our competition? Who could put up with this cheesy music? Holy shit, look at the prices. No one in their right mind should be charging that much for an espresso that's probably burnt."

My lips purse. Cecelia set the prices.

"We won't be here long," Green Hair's friend reassures her. "And we sure as hell aren't ordering anything."

The two girls reach me, Jorge, and Rosalind. The friend smiles lazily. "Hello. Cozy place you've got. Does someone named Betty happen to work here?"

Jorge and Rosalind exchange a not-very-subtle bitch face. "Nope, no Bettys here," Jorge says. "Anything you'd like to order?"

Green Hair barks out a laugh. "No."

As manager and resident idiot of the place Green Hair is shitting on, I feel like it's technically my responsibility to defend it. I turn on my best customer service voice. "If you're looking for something good on the menu, I can help."

She does a double take like she just noticed me, expression smoothing out, but then her eyes catch on the thermos in my hand, then my badge. "I don't think I'll take recommendations from a manager who doesn't drink the shit they're trying to sell."

Rosalind and Jorge snicker, and my neck heats up. This is the worst possible morning to deal with an annoying customer, but years of working a stupid food industry job means I can keep up my smile.

"I'm just trying to offer advice, since it seems like you have some issues with rational judgment." I glance at her highlighter-colored hair.

Without missing a beat, she nods to the hoodie I'm wearing: fan merch from my favorite (but objectively bad) book series, Son of Sin. "You can't be all that rational if you think wearing that out in broad daylight is a good idea."

"The cold brew here is great for digestion, which would really help in pushing that stick out of your ass."

A nearby table gasps, and some part of me realizes that half the cafe has stopped talking to watch us engage in the most passive-aggressive fight in the history of fights. I don't care; I've never been this riled up. I consider myself pretty laid-back—despite the last twenty-four hours proving otherwise—but for some reason, this baby-faced goth girl is pushing all my wrong buttons.

Green Hair smiles cutely. She has dimples. My eyes linger on them.

"Is your coffee still hot?" she asks.

I blink. "No?"

She gingerly grabs the thermos from my hand, pops the lid off, stands on her tiptoes, and dumps the coffee over my head.

The lukewarm liquid cascades across my scalp and over my face, shielding her from sight as a river of bean juice coats my glasses. The whole cafe goes dead silent besides the horrible elevator music coming over the speakers.

Only one thought runs through my mind: This is *now* officially the Worst Day of My Life Ever.

"What a waste of coffee," I say drily.

She shrugs, still showing off her dimples. "Worth it."

On any other day, I would let this slide. But today, I turn to her friend, who looks torn between amusement and exasperation, and gesture at the bags of whole coffee beans behind her. "Could you pass me one of those, please?"

Both Green Hair and her friend watch as I open the bag. The rich aroma of roasted beans wafts into my nose, though that could be the coffee dripping from my bangs. I take a step toward Green Hair. She doesn't move away. I hook one finger into the neckline of her sweater, pull the fabric back, and dump the entirety of the bag down the inside.

Her friend bursts into laughter, while Green Hair and everyone else in the store gapes at me.

I toss the bag to the ground and smile. "Worth it."

"Oh my *god*," Rosalind says with glee. "Your parents are *so* going to fire you for that."

I give her the middle finger. "I'll save them the trouble. I quit."

I don't look at anybody as I walk away, not even the pretty goth girl with coffee beans falling out of her sweater. The grating music and my rapid heartbeat thumping in my ears follow me out, the chiming of the bell above the door a sweet closing note.

Well, I tell myself, too high on adrenaline to regret anything that just happened yet, *at least it's literally impossible for it to get worse from here.*

2. IT GETS WORSE FROM HERE

As the coffee soaking into my clothes cools, so does my temper, and now all that's left is trepidation gurgling in my gut like I drank one too many americanos. I can't run from the inevitable forever, so I head home.

Our apartment building is a few streets down from Cafe Gong. It's nestled between an aging cinder block structure from the forties and a Safeway whose daily thefts and robberies boast anything *but* a safe way to pick up groceries for dinner. I punch in the code to be buzzed into the building, then climb the stairs to the gloomy fate that awaits me in apartment 614.

The instant I step foot inside, I'm bombarded by the spicy aroma of kimchi jjigae and Dad shouting "River Langston-Lee!"

He rounds the hallway. Matthew Langston-Lee is a tall, lean man with cropped brown hair and a long goatee who's got the hipster, white dad look down to an exact science, which is only fitting given he operates one of the most hipster-magnetizing coffee chains in the city. Looks, unfortunately, do deceive, because the amount of anger Dad keeps bottled inside of him is potent enough to knock three *real* e-juiced hipsters on their ass with a single, heavy sigh of disappointment.

"Hi," I say lamely. "What part did you hear?"

He pinches the bridge of his nose with the hand not holding his phone. "You walked out of your SATs? Why would—wait, what do you mean 'which part'? What else did you do?"

It's not like I can hide it from him.

Dad's resting state of tired irritation heats up to full-blown rage as I keep talking—but he doesn't explode. It would be better if he did, if he just got it out and screamed everything I know he's thinking: *You're a disappointment. You're tanking your future. You're wasting every opportunity we worked so hard to give you.* But instead, he just gets this look in his eyes like he doesn't know where to start with me, or where he went wrong, and what to do with the son dripping coffee all over his welcome mat now.

It stings so much more than being shouted at would.

I mean it, I'm really not a confrontational person. It's why I took two years of Rosalind and Jorge's shit, dated Cece for so long, and didn't say anything when Dad turned Cafe Gong from a family shop into a soulless corporate chain. Today's interaction with Green Hair surprised me; I've never acted like that with anybody. I don't like arguing, and I especially don't like letting my parents down when I know the bar for them is pretty much six feet under for all things concerning me. So I take Dad's loaded, heavy sighs with my head hung and my hands in my pockets.

"I just don't understand you," Dad says, volume increasing with every word. "You know how important this new location is for the business. You *know* the risk we're taking on to open it, all to give you and Cecelia the opportunity to prove yourselves by managing it. How could you do this, River? To yourself, *and* to your family?"

"I'm really sorry," I utter.

"I don't want an apology; I want an explanation. Why? You used to—" Dad cuts himself off, eyes closing. His nostrils flare as he strains to speak calmly. "You used to love Cafe Gong. It used to mean as much to you as it does to your mom and me. When did you stop caring?"

Something sharp and double-edged lodges itself in my throat. I *never* stopped caring. My earliest memories are coffee-stained; I spent more time inside Cafe Gong's first walls than in our apartment. I remember doing my homework in a booth in the corner while Umma rang out our then few customers and Dad served drinks. How we celebrated Cafe Gong's first year together in the store after closing, how Umma let me cut the cake she baked. How, when we were strapped for cash and time in the early days, Dad always let me practice brewing coffee even if it meant wasting cartons of milk on failed attempts at latte art, and Umma would teach me how to use the till. I remember it all: the excitement of our first customer, the years of tense, hushed conversations I overheard my parents having about the bills, the pride we all felt when our hard work resulted in a second store opening in Capitol Hill, then a third in Fremont, a fourth in International District, a fifth in South Lake Union . . .

I grew up as Cafe Gong grew out. Of course I care. It's my home. But somewhere along the way, Dad forgot home isn't company expansion and revenue growth at the cost of scrubbing every trace of your family from its walls.

But I didn't know how to say that to him years ago and I still don't know now.

Umma deems it time to intervene and steps out of the dining room.

"여보, 그만해.[1] We can talk about River coming back to work later."

Dad's anger deflates. "Yejun—"

"Later."

He purses his lips, but Umma's will wins. Dad looks me over from head to toe and shakes his head. "Fine. I don't know what to say to him anymore," he spits, then slinks toward their bedroom. My stomach turns.

"Thank you," I say.

Umma offers me a smile. I'm told I look more like her than my dad, with her long face, high cheekbones, and kind, flat eyes. Her auburn-dyed hair is tied neatly back. I'm closer to her than Dad these days, but there's a wall between us that's a different kind of impenetrable. With Umma, I think I let her down a long time ago. I know I'm not the ideal son she must have imagined when she left her life behind to immigrate from Seoul to Seattle. She would never say that, but I hear it in the pauses when she searches for words in English that I can't understand in her Korean.

"Mrs. Campbell told me that you and Cecelia broke up," she says gently, surprising me by changing the subject. "I don't know what you two argued about, but whatever it is, I'm sure you can fix it. You've been together a long time. She'll forgive you."

---

1.   Honey, stop it.

Now if this isn't the icing on my You Are the Worst Person Alive cake.

"No, Umma, *I* broke up with her."

Her worry lines smooth out. "Oh."

"Yeah."

"Why? I thought you loved her."

I did. I *do*. Cecelia always has a smile on despite a long day at work, she gets along with everybody, and she's the single most driven person I've ever met. Her eyes are more beautiful than any sight Seattle has to offer, and her freckles are like a sprinkling of cinnamon on top of latte foam. And sure, we weren't perfect, but we had a lot of love for each other. In fact, we never even fought. Mostly because I did what she told me to and said what she wanted to hear, and that was . . . okay. I *thought* it was okay. Everything else with her was so perfect.

Last night—or if I'm being honest, when we were chosen to co-manage Cafe Gong together—proved to be the breaking point.

"I don't know, Umma."

"You don't know?"

"I don't know."

"How do you not—"

She cuts herself off. She's making the face I hate most, the I'm So Disappointed in You I Can't Even Express It in English So I'm Not Going to Say Anything at All face.

"I'm going to go to my room," I mutter, slipping past her.

My bedroom is small, but the clutter of my favorite books and graphic novels stacked on every flat surface and the posters covering the walls is a solace. In one corner of the room is my recording station: a desk, laptop, microphone, and web camera angled *just* perfectly so that when I'm sitting in the chair making videos, nothing above my neck is visible. Like *hell* I'd ever show my face online.

I change out of my sticky, coffee-soaked clothes and collapse into the chair, folding my long legs up to my chest. In the silence, the swarm of guilt-slickened thoughts and feelings buzz like flies in my head.

I open my laptop and halfheartedly respond to comments on my last YouTube upload: "Why the Villain from Son of Sin Actually Has Some Good Points." I can't feel like shit if my one brain cell is focused on something else. Usually it's my fandoms, or Cecelia, but tonight, defending a fictional antagonist will have to do. It's a sufficient distraction until timid knuckles tap on my door.

Holy fuck, go away. "Come in."

My younger brother, Jace, lets himself in, carrying a plate of fruit and a bowl of the kimchi jjigae I smelled earlier.

"Umma told me to bring this for you."

I doubt that, since Umma only brings me fruit when she's apologizing. The misshapen slices further confirm it's not from her. I accept the food and set the plates down on my table so I can ruffle Jace's shaggy brown hair, smothering a smile so I don't embarrass him. He takes more after Dad and is already almost as tall as I am despite only being fourteen.

"Thanks. You're not so bad," I say as he plops onto my unmade bed. "So, how much did you hear?"

Jace reaches for one of the apple slices and pops it into his mouth. "All of it. You really fucked up today, didn't you?"

"Watch your mouth or else you'll slip up around Dad."

"Nothing I do could piss him off more than you did." He grins, showing off his braces. "I've got immunity for the next two weeks, easy. Thanks, River."

Jace gets immunity either way as our parents' star child. He's at the top of all his classes, on the varsity soccer team, and speaks fluent Korean. I scoop up some stew and rice and shovel it into my mouth. It's good, and the comforting spices and silken tofu immediately tamper down the brief flare of irritation within me. I don't resent Jace at all for being the favorite. He's my favorite, too.

"So, what are you going to do?" Jace asks.

"What do you mean? About Umma and Dad?"

"I mean in general. You know, life. You dumped your high school sweetheart, you probably won't get into a good college next year, and you quit your job."

"Just because we are—*were* high school sweethearts doesn't mean we were going to get married. And I'll figure out college later. As for a job . . . I'd rather walk into the ocean than go back to Cafe Gong. *My* Cafe Gong, at least, and I can't imagine Dad will let me transfer stores."

"You're weird. I guess you'll just have to deal with Dad every day after school."

Damn it. He's right. I won't have any excuse not to come right home if I'm unemployed, which means prolonged exposure to Dad's sighing and Umma's frowns. Plus, being newly single equals a lot more free time, which translates to a lot more time to think about how royally, utterly, ridiculously I screwed everything up. I don't even have school to keep me busy, because failing the

SATs means I can't apply to any universities this year, so there's no real reason for me to care about my grades or classes or . . . *oh god.*

"I'm sure things feel like they suck," Jace says, either ignorant to my angsting or ignoring it. "But it's pretty cool you had the guts to quit." He rolls over to smile at me, making me momentarily forget that he's the one who's three years younger. "I know you hated working with those guys, and you didn't seem stoked about being a manager. So, good for you. I don't think I could have done the same in your position."

I blink, then blink again, this time to cool the prickling heat behind my eyes. "Will you bite me if I try to hug you?"

Jace takes the last apple slice and the plate with him as he stands. "Yes. I'll leave so you can spiral in peace. Good luck."

He closes the door on his way out. My phone pings, burning a hole in my pocket. I've been ignoring it all day.

Reluctantly, I take it out and check my messages. The newest one is from Isabette.

Isabette :)

River!!!!

Are you ok? When did you leave?

Jorge and Rosalind said you got into a fight with one of our customers

Did you actually quit?

Stop making me worry about you, jerk :(call me when you can

My thumbs hover over the keyboard, but I exit out of our conversation thread without replying. I hesitate before the last of my unread messages. *I don't want to.* But I can't put it off forever.

Cecelia <3

Hey.

Can we talk?

I'm sorry I yelled last night.

I know you're not in love with someone else. You can't be. I don't know why you would say that.

I don't understand why you're doing this. I'm willing to hear you out, though.

Will I see you tmmr?

Her texts get harder to read, and I realize it's because of the tears. I fling my glasses off to scrub at my hot face. The image of Cecelia's broken expression from last night is vivid behind my closed eyes.

I hate fighting.

I owe her a reply, at the very least, but I don't have one for her. I'm still not completely sure why I wanted to break up. That's why I lied about being in love with someone else, so she'd hate me, and we could break things off cleanly. That's easier for her to understand than *Sorry, I don't know either. I just want to end this.*

That's the problem. That was the problem last night, the one that got worse after we were promoted to co-managers, and if I'm being honest, it's been the problem our entire relationship, the tiny nagging at the back of my head. I never know what to say, never know what I *want* to say—so I say whatever I think she wants to hear.

She's right. I'm such a fucking piece of shit.

My phone rings, cutting off my self-pitying soliloquy right when it was getting good. The face of my other best friend, Kai Zhang, pops on the screen. I stare at his shaggy black hair and his I Know Every Embarrassing Secret about You and Will Use It against You at Any Given Opportunity grin, before accepting the call.

I clear my throat. "What's up?"

"River, my man." Kai's chipper voice rings through my speakers. "Thought I'd check up on you after this morning. See what's going on."

I squint at my phone. "Why do you sound like that? All . . . suspicious."

Kai squawks. "*What?* This is my normal voice."

"Cut the crap."

"Fine. I may have heard from a little birdie that you dumped a bag of coffee beans down a girl's shirt at work today. And then quit."

"Who did you hear that from? Isabette?"

"No. The best friend of *my* best friend is my enemy. Or like, a sister-in-law I've never met because she goes to a different school. Like I said, it was a little birdie."

I pinch the bridge of my nose. "Your bird is correct, that happened."

"Yikes. You'd tell me if you're spiraling or something, right? Or will I see you in class one of these days with an eyebrow piercing and a shaved head?"

"I'm not spiraling, Kai."

"I don't know. I mean, I get why you quit, and the SATs are stressful for anybody, but you also dumped Cecelia out of nowhere. Don't get me wrong, I'm glad you finally did, she was terrible for you. And for the general population at large."

I usually ignore him when he talks about how toxic he thinks Cecelia is. "'Dumped' sounds harsh. We broke up."

"Sounds like you dumped her and lied about why. I know what that's like."

"Dario didn't *dump* you—"

"Yes, he did. He dumped me because he's tired of me and wants to sleep with different guys at his fancy D1 university next year."

This is a conversation we've had a handful of times over the last month, but I still feel the need to reassure him since his voice gets small and thin whenever Dario is mentioned. "You know it's not that, or at least, not in those words. You don't date someone for years and suddenly decide you're bored of them."

"Yeah? What about you and Cecelia, then?"

"That was—"

"Different?" Kai asks sarcastically. "You sound like Dario."

My stomach twists and I say nothing else. Maybe he's right.

Kai sighs. "Sorry, I didn't mean to make this about me. Seriously, are you good?"

"I think I regret quitting today."

A pause. "But you hate Cafe Gong."

"Not quite, I just . . . hate what it's become. But without a job, I'll have nothing to distract myself with," I say. "I ruined my relationship with Cece, my parents can't even look at me, and it's not like I'm going to get into college now. I'm a seventeen-year-old with

nothing to my name besides a semipopular fandom account and—
wow, is *that* depressing to say aloud. Holy crap, I can't even stand
listening to myself. How are you still on the line?"

"I've been your friend for too many years for some doom-spiraling
to scare me off. Besides, I follow your account. I've seen your lows,
buddy, this isn't the worst of it," Kai says. "And let's be real—nearly
fifty thousand YouTube subscribers is more than 'semifamous.'"

"Thanks," I say drily. "But quitting definitely tops the list of
'Times I've Made an Asshat of Myself.'"

He hums. "It's up there. If you're looking for something to keep
you busy, why don't you get a new job?"

"Who's going to hire me? The only thing I'm good at is making
coffee and talking about books."

"You make the *best* coffee, and we're in Seattle. Apply to one of
the billion cafes around here."

I sit up in my chair, a seedling of hope nudging its way between
my rib cage. I squash the bud and shake my head. "No place will
hire me when the only thing I have on my resume is my family's shop
I just walked out of. Besides, I doubt my parents would give me a
glowing reference to go work for their competitors."

"I know a place that wouldn't give a shit about your resume.
And they're hiring."

"Where?"

"You know where."

I blink. It hits me like a truck. "I'm not applying to your job, Kai."

"Why not?" he whines. "The Shithole is a cool place! Wouldn't it
be fun to work at a Korean cafe with your best friend?"

"A place you've nicknamed 'The Shithole' is not one I'm interested in. I've heard enough horror stories about your co-workers to stay away. Why do you think I've never visited you at work?"

He goes oddly quiet. "My co-workers aren't *that* bad. Besides Dario, but you're familiar with his level of douchebag-ness. Come on. Think about it. You have two options: stay jobless, single, and miserable at home, or work at a super sweet cafe with your outrageously good-looking best friend. What'll it be?"

Damn, I think as I lean back, staring up at my popcorn ceiling, *it's annoying how convinving Kai can be.* He's right, though. My options are limited here. I doubt I could find another cafe to work at that wouldn't also be a corporate crap hole, and the thought of doing nothing with my time makes my skin crawl.

With a sigh, I let myself smile and say, "Could you get me an interview with your manager?"

"Tomorrow after school, you got it."

"Thank you. Seriously. What's the place called? I'm not sure you've ever referred to it by name."

"I don't think about work when I'm not getting paid to," Kai says. "It's called Bingsu for Two; it's not that far from where your new store is."

Something at the back of my mind itches. "Huh, sounds kind of familiar."

"Can't imagine why, it's not popular. Chin up, River. You won't regret this."

True—but only because it's physically impossible for my body to hold any more regret at this point.

3. THE MOST UNFORTUNATE INTERVIEW IN RECORDED HUMAN HISTORY

I'm going to kill Kai.

Not really. Maybe. I'm considering it.

Kai :P

> Sorry man! There's this new fabric store downtown and I lost track of time finding stuff for my latest designs. You'll have to go to the interview without me

> You'll kick ass tho, i believe in you!!!!!!

> Here's the address to Bingsu for Two, good luck

I shake my head, pocketing my phone as I hop off the bus and onto the street Kai sent me. Huh. He was right, it *is* close to Cafe Gong, just a few blocks down in an alleyway, says my GPS. That itch in my brain starts up again. It does seem familiar, but I've never been here.

I turn the corner of 6th Avenue and peer down a crack between two buildings. Cautiously, I venture through the sketchy, musty alleyway. No way a cafe's down here. The hot, sweet stench of garbage juice makes the entire street uninhabitable for human life.

But there, tucked into the side of the building to my left, is a window and a chalkboard sign advertising a BOGO deal on drinks. The dim sign above the storefront says BINGSU FOR TWO.

And then it hits me, why this cafe looks so familiar. My legs almost give out into a puddle of dumpster juice.

Cece and I tried to put this place out of business.

When Dad made us co-managers, he let us take charge of opening the new Cafe Gong. That meant running the numbers, hiring staff, ordering inventory, and everything else. He called it "resume building," which is a weird way to pronounce "child labor." Cece took point on all of that, and I was happy to let her—she's good at that kind of thing, scarily good, which makes sense given she's gunning for UPenn's business program. She only tasked me with one thing: scouting the location for our new store.

"Oh god," I mutter to myself and the rats. *I* tried to put this place out of business. I chose Cafe Gong's storefront two blocks away because a quick Google search told me the only nearby competition was Bingsu for Two: a small, family-owned Korean cafe with less than a two-star rating. They *weren't* competition, to put it straight.

My throat tightens as I remember a conversation with Cece. She'd been so proud. I didn't always make her proud.

"No way they stay in business for more than a year," I had said. *"Six months tops if we open next to them. It's perfect."*

27

"No, no, no," I mutter, pacing in front of the storefront. I can't believe my best friend works here, at the place I *knew* would suffer if Cece and I opened Cafe Gong nearby—which we did.

I turn around and take two steps toward the street, then freeze. Kai's words ring in my head: *You have two options: stay jobless, single, and miserable at home, or work at a super sweet cafe with your outrageously good-looking best friend.*

Fuck. The first option still doesn't sound great.

I smooth down my dress shirt. *You can do this, River. It's just an interview at the place you tried to run out of business. But probably don't mention that to them.*

The bell above the door chimes as I slink inside. There's no one else in the shop—not even a worker.

"Hello?" I call out.

The smell of burnt espresso only barely conceals the wet odor of sanitizer and rain-warped wood. In the corner near a weathered sofa is a half-flickering LET'S EAT! sign whose lit bulbs now unfortunately proclaim TEAT! The brick facade walls and poor lighting are more grunge than cozy, which is fitting for Seattle, but combined with the scratched oak floors and mismatched furniture, it feels more like someone's basement than a place that could pass a health inspection with anything above an okay.

I approach the counter, peering past it for any sign of life. A fly buzzes around the untouched pastries in the glass case.

Something in the back room rustles. A lady leans out of the kitchen doorway, holding the floral curtains to the side.

"Hi—" I start.

"Can I help you?" she says, her voice low and drawling.

"I'm River. I'm here for the interview."

The lady blinks at me. "What interview?"

. . . Huh.

"Uh, Kai—Kai Zhang, he works here, he said you guys were hiring, so he set up an interview for me?"

The lady doesn't stop scowling, but she approaches the counter. She's more of a girl than a lady, I realize. She must only be a few years older than I am. Early twenties, maybe. Nearly as tall as me, with razor-sharp cheekbones, inky black hair to her chin, and blue eyeliner that pops against the suspicious glare she's giving me.

"Kai didn't say anything to me about an interview. And we're *not* hiring. Little shit's just probably trying to get Dario fired." She mutters the last part to herself.

Okay. I take it back. I *am* going to kill Kai.

Before I can scramble together a semi-cohesive response, the girl taps her manicured fingers on the counter. "Sorry for the confusion, kid. Now, did you want to order something before you leave?"

Could I smooth-talk her into giving me the job? God no, I have the charm of an empty clamshell. Just my luck. They're not hiring, *and* my dumbass best friend forgot to mention me.

"Well, no," I say, "but I would really love to work here, and I have experience with—"

"Nah." She cuts me off with a waving hand. "See yourself out." Then she turns her back on my gaping mouth.

"I'd be a good employee," I plead, rounding to the other side of the pastry case to follow her. "Please. I need this job."

She stops at the handoff counter, and she's close enough that I can read her name tag: 조하늘. Haneul Cho. Thank God I can at least read Korean, even if my speaking skills are worse than a five-year-old's.

Haneul gives me a tired look from beneath her perfectly straight bangs. "Look at this place. You see any customers? We barely get enough business to keep the staff we *do* have, especially as of late. There's a ton of other coffee shops in Seattle, I'm sure you can find a gig at one of them," she says. "Like Cafe Gong. There's a new one at the end of the block. I'm sure they're hiring."

I wince. Yes, I'm sure they *are* hiring, considering I just left them with an empty co-manager position.

"Please. I'll do anything," I utter pathetically.

My dumb-lost-puppy face must finally be doing the trick because Haneul's icy expression softens a degree or two.

"Ugh. Fine. You can have an interview."

I perk up. "Really?"

"Yeah. Tell me about yourself."

An eloquent "Uhhhhh" slips out as I drop onto a barstool. "Okay. My name is River Langston-Lee. I'm a senior in high school, and I'm going to study business next year at—well."

I play with the battered edge of the countertop to avoid Haneul's eyes. "I was going to study business at the University of Washington next year like my dad did, but that's not happening anymore since I flunked my SATs. I walked out of the test, at least, so that's probably flunking. Sorry, I should be talking more about job experience. I was a manager at another cafe up until yesterday. Yep. Walked out of the SATs, showed up to my shift, dealt with a very fun customer, then decided I'd had enough. I wish I had planned it more. Everybody dreams of telling their co-workers to go to hell and setting the place on fire, right? I didn't light anything on fire, I'm not—I'm not a pyromaniac, or any type of maniac. You don't have to worry about that. You can trust me with an open flame. I mean—"

I bury my hot face in my shaking hands. The last two days are finally sinking in. What have I done?

Congratulations, River, you've proved to yet another person what a massive fuckup you are. And it didn't even take five minutes.

Sitting up, I give Haneul a grin and hope she's not paying attention to how red my eyes are behind my glasses.

"So, any questions?" I ask.

Haneul blinks. "Plenty, but none related to the interview."

The bell above the front door jingles.

"Sorry I'm late! I didn't want to come."

"Shut up, Kai, that joke got old ages ago."

I jump. Walking into the cafe, skateboard under one skinny arm and fit in an oversized shirt he designed, is Kai. My earlier kill-on-sight plan is interrupted, by the pretty girl dressed in black at his side. The neon green hair and choppy bangs are instantly recognizable, and when she lifts her face, there's no doubting who she is.

"Holy shit, it's you. What are you doing here?" she says.

I turn to Haneul. "Does she work here?"

"Don't ignore me!" Green Hair retorts. I ignore her.

"That's Sarang, my sister," Haneul says. "Yeah, she works here, unfortunately."

Her name gives me pause. 사랑, the Korean word for love, which is funny because she looks like she's never loved anything in her life. "Cool, cool," I say, nodding. "Thanks for the opportunity, but I'm no longer interested in the job."

Kai intercepts me on my way to the door, using his skateboard as a shield. "Slow down. You know Sarang?"

"Don't play dumb. That's *Coffee Bean Girl*," I hiss.

His face does Olympic-worthy contortions as he feigns surprise. "*What?* Oh my god, Sarang is—no way. What are the odds?"

"*Kai.*"

He deflates. "Okay, fine, I may have forgotten to mention that the girl who dumped a cup of coffee on you is my co-worker. From the bottom of my heart: my bad. Let's look on the bright side, now you get to work with your best friend."

Haneul raises her eyebrows. "I haven't offered him a job yet."

"And you won't," Sarang interjects, glaring at me. "He works at Cafe Gong, the one stealing our customers."

"He was a manager—great transferable skills," Kai chips in.

I return Sarang's glare. What is her problem? It's like she's had a vendetta against me before we ever exchanged words. "Is this because I poured coffee beans down your shirt? Because that was justified, you have to admit."

"No, it's because you and your chain coffee house have been pushing small cafes like ours out of business for years. I looked you guys up—your parents own Cafe Gong, don't they? How do we know you're not some corporate spy sent over to steal our family recipes?" She huffs. "And yes, I also don't like you because of the coffee bean thing."

I throw my hands up. There's no point trying to talk sense into her. "Don't worry. I'd rather eat a sock than work with you."

Kai steps between the two of us. "You sure about that, River?" he asks. "You sounded *real* desperate for a job last night."

Damn it, Kai's right. I need . . .

Need what? A lifesaver as I drown in my own self-driven nothingness? Okay, that's dramatic, I know my life isn't completely screwed to hell, just halfway there. I'm not sure what I'm looking for, or if I ever did. If I came searching for stability after tearing everything safe in my life to shreds, I won't find it here. Stability was Cecelia. It was my job at my parents' place. And I left it all.

"Come on, Haneul," Kai urges. He approaches her at the counter. "It's October. Sarang and that asshole Dario will be leaving in a few months for college. We'll need someone to fill their spots."

"No we won't," Sarang says.

Haneul hesitates. Kai presses on.

"Unless you feel like waiting until the last minute," he taunts. "I can picture it now. It's June, our AC is still broken, and we get our once-a-year rush for bingsu. You're all alone with only me and Vanna to help. I'm your best worker usually, but once it gets hot, I'm out. And you know Vanna's too busy with her other jobs to step in." Kai leans forward, continuing to talk even as Haneul puts her hand over his face and tries to hold him back. "You can't run this place with the three of us. You need River."

"You are *so*—" Haneul grunts and succeeds in pushing Kai out of her space. She throws her head back and groans at the ceiling tiles. "*Fine.* It's not worth arguing about all day." She turns to me, scowling fiercely. "You got the job, you annoying brat."

"Really?" I ask.

"*Really?*" Sarang yells.

Haneul pinches the bridge of her nose. "Are you taking it?"

I gnaw on my lip, weighing my options here.

1. Go home—jobless, futureless, single—and face the combo of Dad's anxiety outbursts + Umma's disappointment and do nothing to distract myself from my inevitable withering into nonexistence.

     a. *No thanks. There are kinder forms of death than this, like swallowing batteries or playing with an electrical outlet.*

2. Return to Cafe Gong even though I pretty much told all my co-workers to go to hell in a pastry bag.

     a. *The batteries sound appetizing compared to this.*

3. Suck it up and work at Bingsu for Two, the place my ex and I plotted to strategically run out of business, with the green-haired goth bane of my existence.

     a. *Fuuuck. I have to do it, don't I?*

I plaster on a smile. "I'll take it."

Sarang groans. "This is going to suck so hard."

That's an understatement. But whatever, nothing can bring my mood down because I have a job now.

Wait, I have a *job* now. At the competitor's cafe.

What am I going to tell my parents?

4. JUST ONE MORE LIE—AS A TREAT

The door to our apartment slams despite my efforts to come in quietly. I wince, begging the house to be empty. Obviously, it's not.

"River," Dad says from the living room. "Would you come here?"

Hopefully Dad has calmed down since yesterday, but there's no way to predict how this awful intervention will go.

In the living room, he and Umma are situated on the couch, but the other sofa is empty: Jace is at soccer practice, which means I don't have a buffer to save me. Wearily, I sit down.

How am I supposed to tell them? *Hey, guys, sorry for letting you down again and throwing your hopes for me to have a semi-successful life after high school out the window. I know a lot was riding on our new store doing well and I may have doomed it by quitting, but good news, guess who just got hired at our business's competitor!*

Umma's mouth twists into a frown. "Your dad and I are worried about you, River."

"Worried about your mental state," Dad snaps.

Umma gives him a look I don't understand, and he sighs, rubbing his forehead.

"We're not going to punish you," Dad says.

"You're not?" I ask, stunned.

"What's done is done. Let's make this as painless as possible. Try again for the SATs in the spring and focus your time now on Cafe Gong. I understand you've been under a lot of stress trying to run the store, but that's why you have Cecelia to help. It's *your* store, River. *Your* future. Doesn't that mean something to you?"

For a while, all I can do is blink at him. A familiar, heavy feeling hollows itself into my chest. I wish it didn't surprise me—that all they think I'm capable of is continuing the family business, that I don't *have* a future outside of what they carve out for me—but it still does. And it still hurts.

I want to tell them everything. I want to confide in them about this cocktail of insecurity and imposter syndrome I've been chugging since I was a preteen. I know Umma loves me, but she doesn't always understand me. And Dad . . . well, he's Dad. We used to be close, the kind of close where I *could've* been honest with him, but the stress of the business has changed our relationship and wound him up to the verge of fully losing his shit at all times. Some days I feel more like his employee than his son. Today's one of those days.

"I can't go back to Cafe Gong," I blurt.

The second the words are out of my mouth, there it is, that *look* in both their eyes. All confidence zaps from my body. I've never stopped being the little kid afraid to let down their parents.

"Excuse me?" Dad says.

"Because . . ." *Be brave. Please, just this one time.* "Because I'm . . ."

The vein bulges on Dad's forehead. Umma's shoulders fall.

"I'm going to be too busy. Getting tutored. For the makeup SATs."

I hate myself.

But the thought of how Umma and Dad would feel if they found out I betrayed Cafe Gong—betrayed *them* and everything they've put at stake—for a different family's business? I hate that more.

Dad and Umma do a simultaneous double take. "Tutoring lessons?" Umma asks. "*You?* After years of us trying to get you signed up?"

"Yeah," I lie on the spot. "I walked out of the SATs because I knew I'd fail. Haven't been doing so hot in my classes, as you know. It'd be humiliating to try my best on the test and not get a good score, so I quit before that could happen. Yesterday was a wakeup call. So, uh, after school, I walked over to a tutoring center and signed myself up for SAT prep. *Intensive* SAT prep, so I can take them in the spring. But, you know, the thing is, the tutor said I'm going to have zero free time after school now. Meaning I won't be able to work at Cafe Gong—or anywhere, for that matter, because for the next five months I'm going to be doing algebra and learning what an adverb is."

I suck in a huge breath, feeling dizzy. My parents scrutinize me, and I can nearly see the little cogs in their heads getting stuck because *River is voluntarily studying?* Yeah, not my most credible lie.

"Is that so?" Dad asks, doubtful.

"Yep."

"Where's the tutoring center?" Umma says.

"It's in Fremont. Isabette recommended it to me—she got me a discount, too, so I can afford it with what I have saved up. She said her cousin's friend got tutored there and was accepted to Stanford."

Dad runs a hand over his beard. "I don't know about this. We need you at Cafe Gong."

"No you don't," I say a little too desperately. "Cece's got it covered, and she's a better manager than I am anyway. Please, *this* is my future. How am I going to get into the Foster School of Business like you if I can't even get a thousand on the SAT? I can come back to work afterward."

Ugh, I'm going to vomit, but I think my lie is working. They exchange another one of their looks, with a few eyebrow wiggles and pursed lips thrown in, while I watch the silent charade act with sweat dripping down my hairline. Finally, they both sit a little straighter.

"Fine," Dad turns to me and says. "You can do your tutoring. But once you take your SATs in spring, you're coming right back to Cafe Gong. Okay?"

"Sir, yes sir," I mumble.

"What was that?"

"I understand."

I allow myself a small smile. They believed me. Maybe not forever, but it's a temporary fix until I figure out a better way to keep them from finding out about Bingsu for Two. I just have to keep this lie up until spring. I can do that.

Umma leans forward and rests her hand on my knee. "Are you sure you don't want to stay at Cafe Gong? I know you broke up, but won't you miss working with Cecelia?"

And that's my cue. I stand, walking backward out of the room. "I'm sure she'll manage on her own. All right, thanks, love you guys, bye."

One problem down, I think to myself as I walk away, *only one annoying, green, goth problem left to go.*

5. WHY MAKE A LATTE WHEN I COULD MAKE YOUR LIFE HELL?

For someone who insisted they didn't have the hours to spare, Haneul wasted no time in putting me on the schedule. My first day at Bingsu for Two is the next day—which is not nearly enough time to prepare emotionally and mentally for working with the green-haired bane of my existence.

"Green-haired bane of your existence? Really?" Kai says as we walk toward the cafe after school. "Since when did you become so dramatic?"

"I'm not sure. It's been a weird few days," I say. We pass Cafe Gong, and I avert my eyes, trying not to think of Cecelia who must be inside right now, scrambling to adjust without a co-manager. "Maybe I'm just stressed, but there's something about Sarang and her smug face that brings out this side of me that makes me want to—" I strangle the air. Kai snorts.

"I feel like under different circumstances, you two would've hit it off."

"Your blind faith in your friends is infuriating."

We step down the alleyway, and I swallow past the sudden guilt rising in my throat. I glance at Kai. I can't believe I unknowingly tried putting my best friend's cafe out of business, and now I *work* there. I make a vow to clean up every spill I see, brew the best coffee, and show up on time to my shifts as reparations. It still doesn't feel like enough.

We walk in. Haneul is behind the register. Before I can say anything, she tosses a wad of black fabric at me. An apron.

"Right on time. Put that on and leave your stuff in the back room. Kai will show you." Haneul turns and yells Sarang's name in the direction of the kitchen, then speak of the devil, her round face pops out between the curtains a moment later.

"What—ugh." Her eyes land on me, features twisting in disgust. "It's him."

"You're training him," Haneul says.

"Like hell."

"No thanks," I say.

Haneul says something in Korean with too many clauses and nouns for someone with an elementary schooler's understanding of Hangul—aka me—to comprehend, but I do hear my name. I shift awkwardly, feeling all too reminded of when my aunts and uncles visit from Seoul and I'm the only one at the table who doesn't quite get what's going on. Not for the first time, I wonder what I'm doing at a place called Bingsu for Two with my white-passing features and my American mouth that pronounces vowels too round and low.

Sarang whines in the universal language of defeat. Haneul tuts. "That's what I thought. Now both of you, get to the back and clock your sorry asses in."

Me and Sarang glare at each other for a few tense seconds, but I cave first and follow Kai into the kitchen. I made my choice to work here; I can't afford to get fired now.

Parting through the curtains, the first thing that surprises me is how small the back-of-house is. It's almost the same size as the dining area but split evenly between a tiny kitchen and a make-shift breakroom consisting of a ratty couch, long wooden table, and a few plastic chairs. There's a door labeled Restroom, a storage closet, and beside that, an opening in the wall with an ascending staircase.

"Where does that lead?" I ask.

"Our apartment. Don't go up there," Sarang grumbles.

I'm about to tell her I wasn't planning on it, when the bathroom door creaks open and a familiar-looking girl steps out. Her heavy-lidded eyes snap to mine. Then a toothy grin splits her lips.

"Holy crap, it's Coffee Bean Boy," she says.

She strides forward, offering her hand that I shake warily. Her fingers are adorned with rings that match her silver earrings, septum, and eyebrow piercings. "Vanna Kaev. You're my hero."

I recognize her then: Green Hair's friend, the one who was looking for Betty.

The curtains rustle behind us. "What's a Coffee Bean Boy?"

Sarang sighs in relief. "Finally, the only other sane person that works here."

Dario Lopez walks in, six feet of lean muscle and "a face like a marble bust if they made marble busts out of beautiful Filipino guys" if you asked Kai. Which I didn't, but he told me once anyway, and it has since lived in my head like a curse.

41

Dario stops when he sees me. "River? What are you doing here?"

"I work here now."

"Really? Well, cool, it'll be good to have you around." He offers me an awkward but genuine smile. "I saw you walk out of the SATs yesterday. You good?"

We're in the same grade, plus he and Kai dated for so long that we were friends by default, but we haven't talked since their breakup. Besides Kai, we don't have a whole lot in common: he's more into sports and photography than small talk, but he's a nice guy nonetheless. Kai was the only person who could crack a lively side out of him. The realization that I'll have to work with them both, in the same room, hits me then. This isn't going to be pretty.

"I'm fine. Thanks," I say.

"You know Coffee Bean Boy, too?" Vanna asks.

"Can I be referred to as River?"

"I'm referring to you solely as 'asshole,'" Sarang says, her arms crossed over her chest.

I close my eyes and remind myself that I'm a good person, and good people don't consider fighting their new co-workers on the first day. After a week? Possibly. More importantly, I can't keep letting her rile me up like this, or else I'll have to face the reality that maybe I take more after Dad than I'd like to admit.

"Look, I know you're not happy I'm from Cafe Gong, but I promise I'm not a corporate spy or whatever, okay? We're going to have to work together, so let's try to get along," I say gently.

She does an impressive job conveying how much she wants to kill me with her eyes alone. Then she turns on her heel and walks back out into the cafe. Huh. More levelheaded than I remember the girl who dumped coffee on me being. Maybe she's also giving the one-week-trial-before-I-fight-you thing a chance.

Kai helps me clock in, and when I'm finished, I go meet Sarang at the drink station out front. It's a modest setup, with a grinder, knock box, espresso machine, scale, and tamp. Stacked against the mint-checkered tile wall is an array of sauces and syrups.

"So," Sarang says, leaning against the counter and making a face like she's swallowed a shot of burnt espresso. "I have to train you on how to make a latte."

"I know how to make a latte. You *saw* where I used to work."

She snorts. "Exactly. You worked at that corporate chain. The kind that uses one of those machines with a grinder, tamper, and pulls shots all in one." She shakes her head. "You don't know coffee."

I'm aware that's the pettiest thing to get irritated about, but it *does* irritate me. I've been making pour-overs and using a French press since I was tall enough to stand at the kitchen table. Besides creating content and running fandom accounts, coffee is the one thing I can confidently say I'm good at. And sure, Cafe Gong doesn't have the most authentic equipment anymore, and a lot of our syrups are bullshit instead of homemade like they used to be, but at one point we were the size of Bingsu for Two, and I got to take my time making each cup of coffee like it deserved to be made.

I snap myself out of it. That place doesn't exist anymore.

"You're right, Sarang, I don't have a *clue*." I gesture to the coffee machine. "Please. Grace me with your wisdom."

Sarang tucks her short green hair behind her pierced ears and pulls the portafilter from the group head of the espresso machine, emptying the puck of coffee grounds into the knock box beside it.

"Pay attention, because I hate doing things twice."

I lean on the counter beside her and put my chin in my hands, a perfectly pleasant expression on my face. "Oh, don't worry, you have my full attention."

She glares. "This is a portafilter. It's where the coffee grinds go." Sarang flips the machine on, and it fills the metal scoop with finely ground espresso. Then she picks up the metal tamp to the side, which looks like those stamps used for wax seals. "Add enough pressure to the grinds to smooth it out and give it a twist."

Kai walks up to us, Vanna at his heel. "Sarang, River knows how to tamp grinds, he was manager at—"

I put my finger up. "Apparently, I don't know. Let's hope I learn anything at all."

"I seriously doubt it, smart-ass," Sarang grumbles. "After you do that, stick the portafilter back into the group head: this part right here—are you looking? Good."

She reaches into the mini fridge below the counter, pulls out a carton of milk, and pours some into a metallic frothing pitcher. Then she fiddles with a couple of dials on the machine, and the nutty, caramelized aroma of espresso perfumes the air as the liquid trickles into the cup.

"Pour the milk, then while the shots are going, froth it." She jabs her black-manicured finger in my chest, tapping twice. My breath hitches at the sudden contact. "*Pay attention* to this part, because it's the hardest."

"I couldn't look away if I wanted to," I drawl.

A flip of a lever envelops the metal wand on the side of the machine in steam. Sarang wipes it before inserting the frothing wand into the pitcher of milk. Twisting the knob on the side makes the wand whir to life, and the milk sounds like paper ripping as it's aerated. When she's finished, she wipes down the wand and taps the bottom of the pitcher on the counter, popping any air bubbles. She swirls the milk gently around the cup to groom it, showing off the smooth micro-foam.

Of course she froths milk perfectly.

Kai *oohs* behind me, and I step on his toes.

Sarang tilts the cup with the espresso and pours the milk in a high, wide arc of cream. As she draws closer to the cup, she shakes the mouth of the pitcher in gentle side-to-side motions, creating a flawless foam heart.

She beams up at me, dimples indented in her cheeks. I glare at them.

"Go ahead and make one, and try not to screw it up, okay?"

I nudge past her, emptying the espresso puck into the knock box. I grab another clean pitcher and begin pouring milk, when Sarang lets out a loud sigh. I stop.

"What?" I ask.

"Don't pour the milk before you grind the espresso."

"*I* pour the milk first."

"Okay? But I didn't ask you to make me a latte the wrong way, did I?"

"No, you didn't, but you showed me how to."

"The most efficient way is to—"

"Efficient? How is this not efficient?"

"It takes *longer*. Even a second wasted could cause the shots to oxidize, the foam to fall, it could hold up a customer—"

I set the milk down and scoff in disbelief, turning toward her fully. "Customers? Where?"

"Maybe we'd *have* more if you made a quicker cup of coffee!"

"This is my first day!"

Kai fiddles with his thumbs. "We're not supposed to pour the milk first?"

Dario chooses that moment to exit the kitchen and join us. "No. Don't you remember when I trained you?" he says.

"I don't want to hear it from you, Mister 'the espresso machine doesn't need to be sanitized twice a day,'" Kai accuses.

From her place sitting on the counter, Vanna says, "You guys sanitize the machine?"

I finish pouring the milk, shaking my head. "No one's going to die if I pour the milk first."

Sarang squawks indignantly, the sound halfway between a choke and a yell that makes me believe *she* might die.

The other four watch me, practically breathing over my shoulder as I tamp the espresso and froth the milk. Pushing past memories of doing this elbow-to-elbow with Isabette during a rush, and flirting with Cece after the customers were gone, I pour a modest but perfect rosette pattern in the latte.

"That's the sexiest thing I've ever seen," Vanna states in her deadpan tone.

"You're really good," Dario says.

Smiling, I lock eyes with Sarang, and try very hard not to give her an *I told you so* look. I *will* be the bigger person here.

Sarang purses her lips. "It's a good first attempt, I'll give you that."

"Just good? Come on."

"What? I'm not going to lie and say it's perfect. Look at that." She holds the bottom of the cup over my hand and points at the glossy surface of the drink. "This micro-foam isn't smooth enough. You pulled the shots too early and they're not as fresh as they should be. And while the latte art is okay, you didn't fill the drink up to the top. There's a centimeter of space left—"

"A *centimeter*?" I say. "You're getting on my back for a centimeter?"

"It's the details that are most important."

"Then pull out a ruler. Measure it."

"You are so—" Sarang groans and pulls on her short hair, looking up to the ceiling for patience. "I'm feeling charitable today, so I'm going to show you one more time."

Vanna slips the cup out of my hand and takes a long slurp. Dario murmurs something about making himself busy.

I purse my lips. "I don't need to be condescended to like—"

"Just watch. I'm your trainer."

I shut my eyes and count to three in my head. No one has ever riled me up so much before, not even Jorge and Rosalind. "Fine."

She begins prepping her station. "Take a video, that way you can review it when you get lost, and I don't have to keep teaching you."

"Yes ma'am," I grumble, pulling my phone out of my pocket. I'm deleting this as soon as I get off work.

INT. "BINGSU FOR TWO"/COFFEE BAR — DAY

SARANG CHO is emptying the portafilter with violent fervor, giving the impression that she'd prefer to smash it *over RIVER'S head instead of the knock box. The camera shakes as River films carelessly.*

SARANG

Are you recording?

RIVER (O.S.)

Yes, I'm recording.

Sarang scowls and looks generally unpleasant as she turns to the coffee grinder.

SARANG

Once again, the first step in making a latte is to fill the portafilter with grinds—

RIVER (O.S.)

Technically the first thing you did was empty the portafilter.

Sarang turns to the camera with a blank expression, silent.

RIVER (O.S.)

Uhhhh.

SARANG

(returning to the grinder and grabbing the tamper)
Anyway, I'm going to fill it, tamp it—

RIVER (O.S.)

If you're trying to teach me how to do this, you're not being very thorough. What's tamping? Elaborate.

SARANG

(monotone)
You're telling me you don't know how to tamp?

RIVER (O.S.)

I told you I know how to make a latte but apparently
what I know doesn't matter.

SARANG

Because you made it wrong.

RIVER (O.S.)

Just because I make mine differently than you do does
not make me wrong.

SARANG

Yes, it does.

RIVER (O.S.)

Says who?

SARANG

Says me, your trainer! Now shut up and learn.

*River makes unhappy grunting noises behind the camera
but relents.*

SARANG

(louder and angrier)

After you tamp it, you put this in the group head and
pull the shots—

RIVER (O.S.)

Last time you showed me, you poured the milk first
before pulling the shots.

*Sarang swings her arm around and accidentally smacks a tin
of metal spoons off the counter, which clatter when they
fall to the ground. The camera briefly pans to the mess
before flicking back up to frame Sarang's tomato-red face.*

SARANG

So you were paying attention last time and just did it

the opposite way to piss me off.

RIVER (O.S)

The order clearly doesn't matter as much as you said it

did if you're not even following it.

A terrific CRASH and SPLOOSHING sounds from the other end
of the cafe, interrupting them. The camera jerks toward
the dining area. DARIO is flat on his ass in a puddle of
spilled soapy water, a kicked mop bucket nearby.

DARIO

Kai, what the hell?

KAI

(offended, but clearly guilty)

Me? I didn't push you.

DARIO

You pushed the bucket.

KAI

How was I supposed to know you were going to fall

with it?

DARIO

You're a little piece of shit.

KAI

Aw, stop. You know I love it when you talk sweet to me.
Dario lets out a sigh, visibly regretting all his life
choices that have led to him soaking in a pool of mop
cleaner. He holds his hand up.

DARIO

Just help me up.

KAI rolls his eyes but grabs Dario's hand. Dario yanks, and Kai slips, falling next to him.

DARIO

(grinning)

Like a newborn deer.

Kai scrambles onto his hands and knees and lunges for Dario, but Dario grabs the nearby mop and uses the handle to hold him back.

SARANG (O.S.)

God—stop it, you two! Hey, River!

(her head pops in and out of frame as she tries to jump in front of the camera)

Pay attention. Oh fuck—the shots sat out too long and oxidized. Thanks a lot.

The camera pans back to Sarang staring at the burnt espresso mournfully.

RIVER (O.S.)

(mocking)

Maybe if you poured the milk at the beginning and had it ready . . .

CRACK!

The camera zooms back to Dario and Kai, one half of the snapped mop handle in both of their hands incriminatingly. They look up at Sarang with matching expressions of "Oh shit." Sarang storms toward them, yelling

incoherently as Kai and Dario both shout over each other
about whose fault it was.

River pans the camera slowly, hesitantly, toward VANNA,
who's been lounging comfortably on the counter this entire
time. She slurps her latte obnoxiously.

VANNA

Welcome to Bingsu for Two, River.

River sighs. The camera drops to his shoes as he turns
his phone downward.

RIVER (O.S.)

(muttering to himself)

I hate this job.

I end the video there. Sarang, Dario, and Kai's voices are a cacophony of sound that doesn't seem like it'll be reaching a conclusion anytime soon, so I lean back against the counter and open my fandom account on Instagram. I pull up the video and type a caption: #IHateMyJob.

The share options are *Post*, *Story*, or *Reel*. I swipe to add it to my Close Friends list on my story, so only Isabette, Kai, and a handful of other fandom creators I'm close enough with online can watch the video. It's so awful it's funny; Isabette in particular would get a kick out of this. I click post then tuck my phone back into my pocket, waiting for the chaos to de-escalate.

6. THE MORTIFYING ORDEAL OF BEING KNOWN (AND YOUR CO-WORKERS FINDING OUT ABOUT YOUR SECRET FANDOM ACCOUNT)

A steady buzzing under my face wakes me up the next morning. For a second I panic, thinking I'm late for school, but then I remember it's the weekend. Groaning, I shield my eyes from the sun seeping in through the half-slanted blinds and fumble for my phone.

"What?" I mumble.

"Dude! You finally answered." Kai's voice rings through my speakers, shocking me into alertness. I check the time on my alarm clock: not even eight.

"Why are you calling me this early on a Saturday?"

"Have you heard?"

"Heard what?"

"The—just—everything! Oh my god." An orchestra of chatter chimes in the background, like he's somewhere busy. "Shit, I gotta go. Check the group chat, man."

"What group chat?" I ask, but Kai hangs up.

I sleep with my phone on Do Not Disturb. Warily, I turn on my notifications to see what messages he's talking about.

My screen *implodes*.

New notifications pop up quicker than lightning, a flashing, rotating pinwheel of *New follower! New like! New comment!* They come in so fast I can hardly read them. What the *hell*?

Scrambling to sit up, I struggle to unlock my phone with the influx of notifications flooding the screen. The first app I open is Instagram.

Last night, my fandom account—a secret that I'll take to my *grave*—had around twenty-five thousand followers.

Today, it has ninety-three thousand.

For a long time, I stare unblinking at the *93K* right next to my username: AtlasSaitoApologist.

Oh my god.

Ninety-three thousand people now follow my account. Ninety-three thousand people have seen every edit, fan art, and unhinged thought I've posted here. Ninety-three thousand people know I'm an apologist for the villain in what's known in the book community as one of the cringiest series of all time.

Holy crap. How many of these people do I know from school?

Mortification perches under my chin like a teakettle ready to boil over. "No, no, no, it's okay, it's fine," I tell myself, holding my head in my hands. No one knows I run this account, I've always kept it anonymous. I don't have any pictures of myself up and I've never mentioned my name. I don't even show my face when I live stream. Only Kai and Isabette know it's me—not even Cece knows.

I'm about to swipe out of the app to text Isabette a panicked keyboard smash when my eyes drift over my profile, where there *isn't* a green ring around my picture indicating that a story has been posted. My thumbs lock in stiff horror, hovering above the screen.

Looking further down my page, there's a new post. A new *reel*. Dread folds over me like a weighted blanket.

Warily, I tap on it.

"Are you recording?" "Yes, I'm recording" echoes out from the speakers.

I'm going to die.

The video I took yesterday at the cafe plays across my screen. I accidentally uploaded it. *All of it.* And to my feed for all my followers to see, not just the dozen people in my Close Friends story.

There are nearly a million views. How?!

I shut my phone off and fling it at my pile of laundry on the ground, staring blankly at the wall ahead of me. My brain whirs like a worn-down blender as it tries to comprehend a number as large as 798,743 and counting. Numbers that big aren't real. Why did this even get picked up by the algorithm?

A second, worse realization hits me. Sarang said my name in the video. They *do* know who I am.

I leap up and snatch my phone, shaking as I delete the video from my feed, but it's too late. A quick scroll through my notifications tells me it's been reposted hundreds of times by separate accounts, and—is that a Twitter screenshot? *Why?* I open Twitter in a panic. My username is the same there, and even though I have a smaller following than on Instagram, the follower count has also ballooned overnight.

My eyes catch on the *What's Happening* bar in the explore page. Trending in the United States at #14 is Bingsu for Two.

I'm so shocked that I almost miss a hashtag a few spots up: #Ihatemyjob. I click on it and see hundreds of tweets and videos of people at work. Some are funny, some are sarcastic, and some are sweet, featuring selfies of people with their co-workers. My video is sprinkled throughout. At the top of the feed is a short summary of the hashtag:

> *A latte tutorial gone wrong at a Seattle cafe has spurred a trend of workers telling their own minimum-wage job horror stories.*

I groan. That explains why my stupid video is blowing up beyond a one-off viral Reel. My misery is interrupted by a different, brighter ping of my phone: a text message. I open my messages and see a new group chat with fifty-plus notifications that weren't there the night before.

STOP CHANGING THE GROUP CHAT NAME, KAI

Unknown number 1:

woah, the store is swamped today

Unknown number 2:

lol

Unknown number 1:

I'm not joking. I came in to open at six and there were people outside waiting

Kai:

you're lying

Unknown number 1:

I'm not lying, brat

Unknown number 4:

is it still busy, Dario?

Unknown number 1:

yes. Can someone come in and help me?

Unknown number 1:

there's literally a line out the door

Unknown number 4:

mf i s2g if you're lying

Unknown number 1:

I'M NOT

Kai:

I don't trust it. I'm coming in to see

Unknown number 1:

no not you

Unknown number 4:

Sarang go down and check

Unknown number 3:

why me? You're upstairs too

Unknown number 4:

because I'm the manager and your older sister. Go.

Unknown number 3:

ugh I'll look out the window

Unknown number 3:

WHY IS THERE A LINE OUT THE DOOR?

Unknown number 1:

I SAID THAT

Kai:

no one believes you

Unknown number 1:

ARE YOU OR ARE YOU NOT COMING IN
TO HELP KAI

Kai:

say pretty please

Unknown number 1:

no

Unknown number 1:

pretty please

Kai:

i'm on my way~

Unknown number 4:

damn it fine I'll go down to help, too

Unknown number 4:

why do we have customers?

Unknown number 4:

this is unsettling. I don't like it

Kai:

I asked somebody and they said they found this place
on TikTok???

Unknown number 2:

the Ke$ha song?

Kai:

Vanna dear god how are you eighteen

Unknown number 2:

my body may be eighteen, but my spirit is a fit
mid-thirties MILF

Unknown number 4:

get off your phone. we're still busy. Vanna can you come in or are you at one of your other jobs

Unknown number 2:

I'm not but no

Unknown number 4:

come in or i'm never giving you another shift when Betty's here

Unknown number 2:

I'll be there in fifteen

Kai:

Is no one going to question why we've apparently blown up on TikTok?

Unknown number 1:

no one uses TikTok except you

My phone rings again, *Unknown Caller* flashing across the screen.

"Hello?" I say.

"Hey." It's Haneul. "I know it's your day off, but can you come in?"

"You guys are *that* busy?"

"Yes. It's awful. Please hurry."

Haneul hangs up. I blink. My room tilts to the side. Maybe I'm in a dream.

But I get up, shower, dress, and head to the cafe. *Everyone* stares as I step onto the street. Okay, no they don't. That's my anxiety talking. Nobody in Seattle even makes eye contact with each other. Everything's fine. The video didn't go *that* viral. Well—it did. Oh god it did. What am I going to do? *Stop it. It's fine. Act cool.*

I get to the alley of Bingsu for Two and halt in my steps. The line spills out onto the sidewalk. Over the noise of the crowd, I hear Haneul's voice.

"Go home, everybody. We're out of product."

"Out of product?" a guy shouts. "It's ten in the morning!"

"We've had over three hundred sales in three hours. You guys wiped us out of inventory for the rest of the week!" Haneul yells back.

I peer over the sea of heads and see Sarang hurry out into the alley, shoving Haneul back inside. She turns to the crowd with a smile that's too cutesy for the girl I know.

"Thank you all so much for coming by to support us. Bingsu for Two will be reopening on Monday, so please come see us then."

That gets the line to backtrack, grumbling disappointedly as they leave. I squeeze through and knock on the door just as Sarang closes it. Her lips part in surprise.

"What are you doing here? You don't work today," she says through the glass.

Haneul reaches above her and pushes the door open, then locks it and flips the sign to Closed once I'm inside. "I asked him to."

"Did you guys seriously run out of product?" I say.

Dario is half-collapsed against one of the tables. "Yes."

"What are you out of?"

"Everything."

"Everything?"

"*Everything*," Dario mumbles into the countertop. "You name it. Espresso, brewed coffee, milk, tea, sauces, syrups—we even sold all the pastries Sarang baked last night."

Vanna moans pathetically behind the counter beside Kai. "I haven't worked this hard since . . . actually, I've never worked this hard."

"You literally have two other jobs," Kai objects.

"I don't understand how this happened, but I'm not going to look a gift horse in the mouth," Sarang says. She has a splatter of whipped cream on her apron, and her green bangs are slicked to her forehead with sweat, but this is the happiest I've ever seen her. Happy is a good look on her, I begrudgingly admit.

Kai props himself up on his elbows. "I told you, somebody said they found us on TikTok. And another person mentioned they saw us in a video on Instagram."

"That makes no sense, we don't have any socials for the cafe," Vanna says.

"Well, *someone* posted a video."

"Who?"

My ears burn, but I keep my mouth shut and stay very still. That way, maybe they'll forget about me and I can blend into the puddle of spilled milk on the ground.

Kai and Dario both pull out their phones. I'm about to lose my shit. What do I do? I don't want them to find out about—

"I found it," Dario declares.

"You know," I blurt, "I'm sure it isn't important. We don't need to—"

"Are you recording?" "Yes, I'm recording."

Dario plays the video on his phone, speakers on full blast. The others crowd around and watch. I consider crawling inside the mini fridge to slowly thaw to death, but I don't think I could fit.

"Oh my god, look at Sarang's face! She looks like a fussy toddler!" Kai exclaims. Vanna cackles in delight, and Sarang squeaks like one of those rubber chickens that let out ungodly screeches when you squeeze them.

I duck my head and shield my eyes as they finish the video. Me mumbling about how I hate this job is the last thing that sounds before silence fills the cafe. Chancing a peek through my fingers, I find them all staring.

"Sorry?"

"Don't apologize, it's funny," Haneul says.

"Funny? What about this is funny!" Sarang grabs Dario's phone and shakes it around like it helps her point. "This is—this is humiliating! This is a stain on our public image. The store's, and all of ours."

A cold tendril of guilt slides into my stomach. I'd been so preoccupied with how the video reflected on me, I forgot to consider how the others might feel about being uploaded online and viewed by over a million strangers without their consent.

I try for damage control. "Bad publicity is still publicity?"

"You're just saying that to save your ass."

"Hey," Kai interrupts, putting a hand on Sarang's arm. "It's not bad publicity. I mean, you and River's bickering is embarrassing *and* hilarious, but look here." He scrolls through his phone. Curiosity piqued, I approach to see. He's under the comments of a repost on Instagram that's gotten a couple hundred thousand views.

Likelysalami: this place looks chaotic. I'd go here

MarkIsBadAtUsernames: lmfao I love their vibes

Ripe.cornflower: the two guys arguing in the back are so cute HAHA

SupportLocalIndieAuthors429: I like the short one's shirt. Does anyone have the link?

Sophie_338: omg I ship green girl and the camera guy, the sexual tension is so real

Concernednugget: FR she wants him bro

Camilla.R22: did someone say enemies to lovers coffee shop AU?? <3

I glance over at Sarang, who's quiet. Her cheeks are pink with a rising flush, and she's nibbling on her bottom lip as if she's embarrassed. No, "flustered" is a better word. I blink a few times at the sight. Then, trying to be reassuring while not sounding like an asshole, I say, "See? The video doesn't make you look bad at all."

"That doesn't make up for the fact that you posted a video of us without permission."

I open my mouth, a million explanations on the tip of my tongue, but before I can say any of them, a memory of Cece's silky voice chastises me like she's breathing into my ear.

All you do is make excuses.

The shame inside me sloshes over. Not just because I've avoided her text messages for three days now, but because she's right.

"I'm sorry. I really am. I shouldn't have shared it with anyone" is all I say, because it's true.

I think she's surprised at my apology, which is—okay, fair, given the fact we haven't been exactly cordial to each other. Her mouth pops open, but she snaps it shut and crosses her arms, glancing away.

"Whatever. I guess it brought us some business."

Dario taps on his phone screen. His thick eyebrows knit together. "What's an Atlas Saito Apologist?"

Fuuuuuckk.

Kai goes "Er—" and looks at me, which draws everyone's attention my way. I wish the floorboards would finally give out and drop me into the Earth's core.

"That's . . . me?"

Vanna raises a brow. "Are you asking?"

"No. That's my, uh, account."

"Account for what?" Sarang says.

This may be a solid contender with the Single Most Humiliating Day of My Existence. "My . . ." I trail off and mutter the rest. "Fandom account."

Sarang blows a raspberry so powerful that spittle flies into my face.

"Fandom account? Let me see that."

I groan as they scroll through it. Why didn't I take it down? I could've. My heart wouldn't have been able to handle it, though.

Vanna represses laughter. "This is . . ."

"Embarrassing," Sarang finishes.

"Aw, leave River alone. He could have weirder hobbies. Like tree shaping. Or beetle fighting," Kai says in my defense. He shoots me a thumbs-up.

I have to turn this situation around before—*oh god they're still scrolling.*

Think. What's the best way to save yourself from an embarrassing situation?

A. Pretend you didn't do it.

B. Pretend you *meant* to do it.

C. Curl up like a roly-poly and hope you make such a pathetic sight that they take pity and leave you alone.

D. There is nothing that can save you from this. Accept your fate and the shame you've brought upon yourself and your descendants for a thousand years.

All these options suck. I'm going to use the only thing I learned for the SATs: when in doubt, choose B.

"Look, guys," I start, hoping the smile on my face is more disarming than it is pained. "I'm sorry for posting the video without your permission. I should've known it would make some of you uncomfortable—*I'd* be uncomfortable if somebody did that to me. But I thought it'd be a harmless way to get some attention for the cafe."

Haneul's eyebrows rise and disappear behind her curtain of bangs. "You planned this?"

Nope. "Yep."

Amusement lights up Kai's face, his eyes narrowing with delight in what I recognize as his This Is Such Bullshit expression. But, like I mentioned, Kai is always down to go along with things, especially if he thinks it'll end up as a disaster.

"See?" he says to Haneul. "I told you hiring him was a good idea." He turns to me. "Now it's like we have a fandom for the cafe, right, River?"

The word inflates a bubble of excitement in me. "You're right, it *is* like we're creating a fandom. People are reacting to us like fans do." A smile stretches across my face. "You know what? We should keep going, seize the momentum while people are still talking about Bingsu for Two. Marketing firms can only *dream* of organic engagement like this."

"What are you saying? We should make more videos?" Vanna asks.

I nod. "YouTube, Twitter, TikTok, Instagram. Everything. Bring this cafe out of the Stone Age. It could be great for business. See what one video did for us? And if people are interested in *us* as content creators, they'll stick around. Look at the fan base some of these huge influencers have."

"No," Sarang says, affronted. "You want to film us like the cafe is a zoo?"

"Yeah, I don't know how I feel about that." Dario rubs his neck sheepishly. "That's a lot of attention. Plus, just because this video started trending doesn't mean the rest will. There's no guarantee people will care about anything else we post."

"We'll make them care," I reply. "I already run a fandom account. This isn't too different."

Kai, ever the enabler, says, "I'm in. It's a great idea. You've got the PR brain and the social platform to make this work. Sarang, you said it yourself: we made more today than we have in the last month, and it's thanks to River."

"No. No way." Sarang stands and shakes her head, short green bob whipping back and forth. "It's a cheap sellout. It's—it's *weird*. We don't need the internet or River's stupid posts to save the store. We can do it our—"

Haneul flicks the side of her head.

"That's your problem," Haneul scolds. "You think your way is the only way. How are we going to save the store, Sarang? What ideas do you have that haven't already failed? More flyers taped around the city? Another sale? Appa's business is going to run itself into the ground unless we do something new." The impassioned look on Haneul's face dissolves, and she collapses back onto a chair. "Though it won't be your concern if the cafe shuts down, since you'll be off at Johns Hopkins next year, riding out of this flaming disaster of a family business on your full-ride scholarship."

My chest concaves into a pithole. I steal a glance at Sarang and immediately regret it. For a second I think she'll cry, and the thought is so disconcerting, because what do you even do when a person like Sarang cries?

She doesn't, though.

Kai clears his throat, painfully loud in the gloom of family drama hanging over the dining area. "Hey, just because I'm not a Cho doesn't mean I don't care about this place as if it was my own folks'."

"Me too," Dario agrees, glancing at Kai and then away. "I've been here so long it feels like I'm part of the family." He sits up and looks at me. "I changed my mind. I support River's idea if it means it'll save the store."

"Same. I'll do anything to help." Vanna smiles, and it's more authentic than any of the sharp, sly smirks I've seen her wear. "I owe Mr. Cho."

A lump the size of an espresso puck lodges in my throat. I hadn't realized how important this place was to them, the same way Cafe Gong used to be important to me. *This* is what I miss, the *family* in family business. They've sowed their hearts into the cracks in the ceiling and the scratches on the countertops, and now they're counting on me to save their store—the one I almost sacrificed for my own—because they think I'm some savvy marketer and not just chronically online.

I wish I could join in and chime that I also love the cafe. But I don't—not like they do, not yet. But after hearing them, I *want* to. If running a fandom blog is what helps keep Bingsu for Two alive, then I'll take pride in it for once in my life.

Turning to Sarang, I tell her, "If you don't want to worry about this place falling apart when you leave for college, let's work to make sure it doesn't. I promise—you can trust me with this. I know what I'm doing."

She gnaws on her bottom lip for a long time, teeth wearing at black lipstick, before her eyes flick up and catch mine.

"Fine. Let's hope you're a better social media manager than you are a barista."

7. DON'T TELL THE INTERNET YOU EAT BITCH CHEERIOS, COME ON

By Sunday night, I've made an Instagram, Twitter, TikTok, and YouTube account for Bingsu for Two.

The next day after school, Kai and I head to the cafe, bracing ourselves for another busy shift, but to my surprise and relief, there are only three lingering customers in the lobby and one at the register.

"I guess our fifteen minutes of fame are up," I say. Makes sense. After I got over the mortification of having so many new followers, I went back to my regularly scheduled fandom posting and a good chunk of people unfollowed after realizing the cafe content was a one-time thing. Not for long, though.

"Nah, this is still—how many people are in here?—four more customers than we usually have." Kai thumps me on the arm as we head into the kitchen. "It's up to you to get us back to a hundred customers, though."

Sarang and Dario are in the kitchen. She's smoothing non-existent wrinkles out of her apron while he's watching UW's football game from last night on his phone. As I'm clocking in, Vanna arrives, and all five of us squeeze around my laptop on the table.

"Our accounts are up. Now we just have to figure out what to post," I say.

"I thought that was your job," Sarang says. Today she's wearing her hair half up in a way that frames her face. That combined with her off-the-shoulder black top and long, flared denim skirt, it's hard to pay attention to her snark.

And yet, I manage.

"Well, yeah, but I want everybody's input, too."

"You've got no clue what you're doing, huh?"

"I know more than *you*—"

Dario pulls us apart, and I realize belatedly that we had leaned halfway across the table. Sarang huffs as she drops back into her chair.

"Enough bickering," he says. "How about we brainstorm? River and Kai, you guys are most online. What makes something go viral?"

Kai does jazz hands. "Sex appeal."

"I don't know what I expected from you. River?"

"Our last video probably went viral because people liked"—I gesture at everyone—"us. You know, having fun."

Sarang barks out a laugh. She eyes me up and down, and I know it's in disdain, but her gaze is so intense it makes me squirm anyway. "Trying to teach you to make a latte was not *fun*."

"I didn't need to be taught."

"Yes, you did. You still do, we never finished."

"You are so"—*pretty*—"annoying. Moving *on*. I think it's our interactions that get people invested," I say, clearing my thoughts.

"We should approach this like we're content creators catering toward a fan base. Or, you know, some piece of media that people are obsessed about."

A mischievous look lifts Vanna's features. "Viewers seemed to *love* all that tension between you and Sarang."

"Ooh, what's the word for that, River?" Kai says. "They 'ship' you two?"

"What's 'shipping'?" Sarang asks.

I cut them off before they can fall too far down that rabbit hole. "Vetoed. How about we make another video? We can introduce ourselves and do some promo for the store, and hopefully ride on the tail of our last video's success. I can figure out what hashtags to use, the best time to post, that sort of thing."

"You know a lot about this. It'll be helpful," Dario says approvingly. I rub my neck. Nobody needs to know how much research I did as a preteen when I first launched my fandom accounts. There was a lot of trial and error, and dozens of now-deleted failed accounts.

Everyone agrees except Sarang, who furrows her half-shaved brows at me. "I don't like this. It's an invasion of privacy, and more than that, it's a sellout. We aren't actors or characters like in your precious fandoms."

"I didn't realize you had such high standards about honesty," I drawl.

"I *do*. I hate when people hide their real intentions. It's just as bad as lying," she says pointedly.

My hands go cold under her cutting stare. It's as if the secret I'm keeping from them was tattooed on my forehead. But it's impossible. The only people who know the role I played in choosing

Cafe Gong's new location are Cece and my parents—not even Kai or Isabette.

"Let's consider this a test run, huh?" Kai says. "If it works and gets the shop some sales, we'll keep at it. If not, we'll figure out another way. How's that sound?" He looks at us both.

"Fine," Sarang grits out.

I release my clenched fists under the table. "Peachy."

After the cafe closes at seven, we get to recording.

EXT/INT. "BINGSU FOR TWO"/
ENTRANCE — NIGHT — TRACKING

A nondescript storefront. The neon sign above flashes Bingsu for Two, a pink glow against the swath of dark-ness blanketing the alleyway. The glass door swings open, revealing KAI ZHANG, who is attempting what is supposed to be a dazzling smile.

KAI
(with bravado)

Hello there, I didn't expect to see you. Come on in,

get out of the cold.

RIVER (O.S.)

Oh my god, Kai.

The camera follows Kai into the cafe. Kai takes a seat at a barstool and gestures to the unimpressive setup of the cafe. The camera follows his movements, catching SARANG, DARIO, and VANNA ducking in the corner beside the bath-room. Vanna flashes a peace sign as Dario flaps his hand to redirect the camera back at Kai.

KAI

Welcome to the luxurious and exclusive Korean cafe,
Bingsu for Two. Home of Seattle's richest espresso and
its iciest bingsu, it's a cozy alcove for the city's
biggest stars, like—

RIVER (O.S.)

Why are you talking like that?

KAI

Like what?

RIVER (O.S.)

Like you're some swanky middle-aged doorman at a
five-star hotel. It's weird. Act normal.

KAI

You're so boring. How are we supposed to get views if
we're not spicing it up? You and Dario already vetoed
going for sex appeal. What am I supposed to work
with here?

RIVER (O.S.)

Just tell us your name, a bit about you, and, I don't
know, your favorite thing on the menu. And a cool fact
about the place.

Kai grumbles something about lacking vision.

KAI

Fine. Hi, everyone, my name's Kai. I'm the resident eye
candy and I've been working here since I was fifteen.
I like skateboarding, Taiwanese dramas, and
designing clothes. My favorite thing to order
here? I dunno. The menu's meh.

> **SARANG (O.S.)**
>
> Don't blame the menu for your terrible taste.

> **KAI**
>
> Ignore that, it's the pipes creaking. Anyway, I'd say my favorite thing is our honey toast.

> **RIVER (O.S.)**
>
> Give me a fun fact about the cafe.

> **KAI**
>
> For the past month, I've been trying to make this as *hostile* a work environment as possible so my ex will quit. The last thing I did was sandpaper the bottom of his nonslip shoes.

> **DARIO (O.S.)**
>
> No, the last thing you did was tip the mop bucket over and make me slip.

> **KAI**
>
> (laughing)
>
> Oh yeah. Good times.

> **RIVER (O.S.)**
>
> Rough start.

INT. "Bingsu for Two"/ DINING AREA — NIGHT

VANNA KAEV *lounges on the beaten sofa underneath the* TEAT! *LED sign. The glow illuminates her striking features and multiple facial piercings.*

RIVER (O.S.)

Okay, introduce yourself.

KAI (O.S.)

(whispering)

Sex appeal.

Vanna sits up and shimmies her shoulders. Her face remains impassive.

RIVER (O.S.)

Please stop?

VANNA

What was I supposed to say again? Oh, oh right. What's up, internet. I'm Vanna. I'm eighteen. I don't have a whole lot of time for hobbies these days, but I do like astrology and that kind of thing—my younger sister introduced me to it. The best thing we have on our menu is the Khmer mung bean pudding. We added it at my suggestion.

SARANG (O.S.)

It was your only contribution to the menu.

VANNA

(repeating sagely)

It *was* my only contribution to the menu.

RIVER (O.S.)

Cool, okay. And a fun fact?

Kai bursts into frame, taking up nearly three-quarters of it. His grinning face is blurry as the camera struggles to focus.

KAI

I have one for her. She schedules most of her shifts around when one of our regular customers comes in, so she can flirt with her and act cool.

VANNA

(blushing)

Shut the fuck up, Kai. I have a reputation to protect.

INT. "Bingsu for Two"/DINING AREA — NIGHT

DARIO LOPEZ leans against the pale-yellow wall beside the windows, arms crossed, his dark Henley shirt rolled up to his sleeves.

SARANG (O.S)

(muttering)

Poser.

RIVER (O.S.)

Okay, Dario. Please don't get sidetracked like the other two.

DARIO

Hello. I'm Dario Lopez. I'm a senior in high school, and I enjoy photography and sports, especially basketball. I'm going to be playing D1 basketball at Florida State next—

KAI (O.S.)

(yelling)

No one likes jocks.

DARIO

You did.

KAI(O.S.)

It was a phase. I'm tired of grade A beef with
no brains.

Dario's steely face contorts in interesting ways, shift-
ing between irked and something quieter—before settling
on annoyed.

RIVER (O.S.)

(whispering)

Kai, didn't you flunk chemistry last year?

SARANG (O.S.)

Kai has no beef *and* no brains.

VANNA (O.S.)

Look at these noodle arms. He's vegetarian-friendly.

KAI (O.S.)

Stop it! I don't need to know chemistry to design
clothing anyway.

DARIO

(clearing his throat)

What were the other questions?

RIVER (O.S.)

Favorite menu item and a fun fact.

DARIO

I like the citron tea and the kimchi pancake. Fun fact,
I'm aware of Kai's efforts to try and get me to quit,
but I'm going to get *him* to quit first.

RIVER (O.S.)

(muttering)

Here we go again.

KAI (O.S.)

Ha! I'm never going to quit.

DARIO

Neither am I.

KAI (O.S.)

I'm persistent.

DARIO

I'll get you to throw down your apron

before January.

KAI (O.S.)

Like hell. I'm going to *die* in this cafe.

SARANG (O.S.)

No dying in the cafe. It'll lower our health score.

RIVER (O.S.)

I'm going to die in this cafe first, because none of you

know how to answer simple questions without

getting offtrack.

SARANG (O.S.)

Go ahead. I'll make an exception for you.

RIVER (O.S.)

(under his breath)

It hasn't been a week yet. No fighting her.

You promised.

DARIO

What?

RIVER (O.S.)

What?

INT. "Bingsu for Two"/BAR — NIGHT

SARANG CHO leans against the handoff counter, arms crossed. Her pouting face is turned away, glaring at something offscreen.

SARANG

I refuse.

RIVER (O.S)

Oh my god. Do you wake up every day and choose to be a problem?

SARANG

Yes. I set an alarm for seven so I have enough time to get dressed and eat my Bitch Cheerios. That way I'm ready to make your life hell by eight o'clock sharp.

River makes a low garbled noise like something caught in the garbage disposal.

RIVER (O.S)

This is going to help *your* business, so I don't see why you're giving me such a hard time.

SARANG

(incredulous)

You work here now, too. Why shouldn't you be in front of the camera telling thousands of strangers about your life? In fact—

Sarang lunges for the camera. River shouts in surprise. The camera shakes. Glimpses of hands and the ceiling tiles dart across the frame while they scuffle. A whack!

The camera settles to capture River, cradling his hand to his chest. His eyes widen upon seeing the camera pointed at him, and he lunges off the stool to duck beneath the counter.

RIVER (O.S.)

I don't like my face being on camera.

SARANG (O.S.)

(mockingly)

You don't like being recorded and broadcast on the internet? Wow, I can't even imagine what that must feel like. Get up.

Probably realizing he's a hypocrite, River reluctantly climbs back into view and settles onto the stool. It squeaks as he shifts on it, fidgeting with the sleeves of his hoodie.

SARANG (O.S.)

Get on with it.

RIVER

Okay . . . Hi. I'm River. I'm new here. I started a few days ago, so I haven't tried much on the menu. I mean, I've had some stuff like tteokbokki and bingsu before since my mom's Korean, but not—I haven't had them *here*, so I don't know if they're any good.

VANNA (O.S.)

Holy crap. He's a total disaster.

DARIO (O.S.)

Maybe he has stage fright.

SARANG (O.S.)

No, Vanna's right. He's a disaster.

KAI (O.S.)

Stop rambling, man. Get to the good stuff,

you got this.

River buries his face in his hands, slumping on the counter.

RIVER

This sucks. Why'd I suggest this?

SARANG (O.S.)

Suck it up, pretty boy.

RIVER

You think I'm pretty?

SARANG (O.S.)

What? I—no—shut up. Favorite thing on the menu.

Come on.

RIVER

The sweet potato latte.

SARANG (O.S.)

And a fun fact about the cafe?

RIVER

Like I said, I've only been here for a few days.

I don't know that much about it . . . but this place

has the worst trainer in the world.

Record-breaking horrible.

SARANG (O.S.)

Eat shit.

RIVER

Give me the camera now. It's your turn.

SARANG angles the camera toward herself, an unimpressed

expression on her up close face.

SARANG

If you want to know what my favorite thing on the menu
is or a fun fact, come visit Bingsu for Two and order
something. I'll tell you in person.

She puts her hand over my phone camera and ends the video there. I shake my head.

"We're not going to get fans if you act so cold," I say.

"We're not looking for *fans*. We're looking for customers. This is a business relationship."

She doesn't get it, a fandom is so much more than just a business transaction; it's about building and finding community, it's a place where you don't have to dilute your passion or interests to avoid making others uncomfortable. I can imagine the face she'd give me if I tried explaining that to her, though, so I don't even try.

I stand and tuck my phone into my pocket. "I think that was a good enough start. I'll go home and upload it to our YouTube and TikTok accounts and use my fandom blog to promote the video. Any volunteers to run the other socials?"

Crickets.

I sigh. "Kai, post on our Twitter account that we have a new video up, and make sure to quote-retweet our other video that went viral. Dario and Vanna, can you guys co-manage our Instagram? Since you like photography, you can take the photos, Dario, and Vanna can upload them. I'll send you both some more instructions about hashtags, posting at the best times of day, that kind of thing. And Sarang—"

She narrows her eyes in a withering glare at me, and a shiver runs up my spine. Why are short people so scary?

"Uh, never mind. Good night, guys." They chorus their good-byes as I slip out of the cafe.

The night air is chilled with the tinge of ocean water, and blacker than the Seattle basin—which I can spot from the top of the hill as I start walking.

Both Umma and Dad are already in bed by the time I get home, Jace having told them I was at the tutoring center. I slip in my room and get to work editing the footage. It doesn't take long.

Before I go to upload it to YouTube, I hesitate, rewatching my part. My stomach curdles. It's so embarrassing. But more than social humiliation, if someone I know watches it and recognizes me—especially someone from my old job—I'm screwed. They'd tell my parents, and then my cover of studying for the SATs is blown, and worse: they'll know I'm working for our business's direct competition. I can't even imagine how my dad would react if he found out, especially with so much riding on the newest Cafe Gong location. Should I cut my scene?

Oddly, Sarang's words from earlier today creep into the forefront of my mind as I hover my cursor over the upload button.

I hate when people hide their real intentions. It's just as bad as lying.

Irritation smothers the ember of anxiety glowing in my stomach. I *am* honest. Most of the time. About what counts, anyway. Who does she think she is? She doesn't know me.

Neither do you, Cecelia's voice pipes up.

Sarang *and* that other voice in my head are not helpful.

I press upload.

My stomach lifts and sinks in a decrescendo of relief, then worry. But it'll be fine. What are the odds of anyone at Cafe Gong stumbling across this video? I never told Cece about my fandom blog. Moreover, what are the odds they'll watch it to the end and see me? No one expects me to be working there. Still, I know I'll have to take stronger precautions soon.

I text Kai, Vanna, and Dario that the video is up and they can go ahead and share it on Twitter and Instagram, along with some tips about posting. Then I make a quick post on my own fandom accounts about it. Now all we have to do is wait and see if this works.

If it doesn't, I'm not sure—

Ping!

Ping! Pingpingping—

I pick up my phone. The video already has a hundred views in the last three minutes, and our subscriber count has now hit 40 . . . 43 . . . 50.

A quick glance at the cafe's growing Instagram and Twitter accounts confirms one thing: Bingsu for Two's fifteen minutes of fame aren't over yet.

Switching my messages—and doing my best to ignore Cece's yet unanswered one—I tap out a quick text.

Sarang

> Told you it'd work

> Shut up

8. PILLOW SHOPPING AND A CINNABON-SPONSORED TRIP DOWN MEMORY LANE

My next shift is two days later. I'm grateful for the distraction, especially after a long day at school hearing people commiserate over how hard the SATs were, dealing with the few brave souls who asked if Cecelia and I were really over ("and does that mean she's available now?"), and a very uncomfortable conversation with the principal and counselor that was basically, "So, what's wrong with you?"

I walk into the cafe to see Dario and Vanna helping a long line at the register. Nearly all the tables are taken up by chattering students and hipsters on their laptops. Sarang is working alongside them, glaring fiercely at some shot glasses she's polishing.

I tie my apron as I walk past her. "Hi, Dario and Vanna. Hi Sa—"

"Go to hell," Sarang replies distractedly.

"I'm already here. What crawled up your ass and died?"

Vanna speaks as she works the espresso machine. "She's pissed because some people are talking shit about the cafe online. Not a lot, but still."

My stomach drops. "What are they saying?"

Sarang slams a shot glass on the countertop with more force than necessary. "Somebody said that the cafe is ugly."

I blink at her. She glares back.

"And?"

"And what?"

"I mean, was that all? Because it *is* ugly in here."

I yelp and dodge the milk rag she tries to snap at me.

"It's not ugly!" Sarang says. "Just because we're not like other restaurants and don't have matching furniture and unstained walls doesn't mean it's gross in here."

"Is the bar that low?"

A second later, Kai exits the kitchen. "Why is Sarang angry-blushing again? Did you do something, River?"

"He said the cafe's ugly," Sarang answers.

Kai shrugs. "Yeah, that's putting it nicely."

"Hey!"

"Apparently we got some comments about how the place looks," I say. For as popular as our video was, though, I'm surprised that's the worst thing being said.

"The cafe is overdue for a facelift. Or at least a deep cleaning," Kai says, glancing around and inspecting the dingy dining area. "Maybe a fresh coat of paint on the walls."

I perk up. "This would make a perfect second video."

"Us painting the walls?"

"No, decorating the cafe. Revamping it. People love transformations."

Sarang looks less than unimpressed. "Since when are you a master of interior design?"

"I'm not—but I know someone who is. She'd love to help."

Kai squeezes her arm. "It could be good for business."

Sarang taps her knuckles to her lips, considering it. "Fine."

"I'll talk to my friend," I say. "I'm sure she'll have some great ideas."

"I don't know if I trust anybody who willingly befriends you to have good taste," Sarang mutters.

"What was that?"

"Go clock in."

"What's your opinion on BTS?"

I snort at Isabette's question. "They're cool."

"Oh, goodie. I'll bring some BTS posters to hang around the cafe then," she says brightly, linking our arms as we walk through the cold toward the Westlake mall. It's been a few days since we decided to redo the cafe, and tonight we're meeting the rest of my co-workers at the mall to start shopping. Obviously Isabette, the intended interior design major she is, was more than happy to help when I asked. I'm grateful for more than just her advice; I miss working together.

She hums in thought, her corkscrew curls flopping to one side as she tilts her head. "I've already made a list of things we need to get. Fairy lights, fake plants, vintage mirrors."

I grin down at her, bundled in her winter coat. "I knew you'd be the right person to ask. Bingsu for Two is going to look amazing."

"Yeah, I've always thought some decorating would fix the place up."

"Huh? You've been inside?"

Isabette tenses. Laughing awkwardly, she looks across the dark streets to avoid my eyes. "Just a few times."

"Why didn't I know that? Kai hasn't mentioned seeing you before."

"I've never run into him. It's always the same barista scheduled when I go."

"Really? Who?"

We turn onto another street and the Westlake mall comes into view down the block. I told the others to wait for us out front, but it's too crowded and dark to tell if they're there.

Isabette's voice rises a few octaves. "Can't remember her name."

I shake my head. "Well, whatever, you can ask when we meet them."

Isabette stops dead in her tracks, pulling us both to a halt in front of the mall. "What are you talking about? Are we meeting your co-workers?"

"Didn't I mention that?"

"No, you didn't!"

"What's the big deal?"

Someone calls out my name a few feet away. Isabette and I both turn to find the others near the entrance, and Vanna walking toward us.

"Hey, River. We've been waiting for . . ." Vanna trails off, her eyes popping wide. "*Betty?*"

"Betty?" I repeat, confused, turning to Isabette for an answer. She shrinks into her pink scarf, looking like she would sprint in the other direction if our arms weren't linked.

"Hi, Vanna." She winces, finishing with a nervous giggle. "I didn't know you'd be here."

Vanna *folds.* I've never seen someone visibly swoon before, and I wouldn't have expected her to do so. Her usual relaxed slouch straightens, and she fidgets from foot to foot while crossing her arms nervously.

"Hey there, Betty. You look—it's good to see you, don't get me wrong. Because you look so . . . pink's really your color. Brings out your eyes, or something."

The others approach us. Sarang steps beside Vanna. She's wearing a leather skater skirt with tights, but the giant puffer coat clashes with her usual dark and gloomy goth vibe, making her look like an angry emo marshmallow. She slaps Vanna on the back, cutting off her nervous babbling. "Didn't you say you have a reputation to protect?"

Dario nods at us in greeting. "Hey, Betty, you haven't come around the cafe in a while. Don't you know you're our only regular?"

I put my hands up. "Wait a minute, I'm still confused, how do you guys know Isabette?"

Sarang tilts her head. "Betty's full name is Isabette?"

My thoughts exactly. I gawk, glancing between Isabette and a bewildered Vanna as my brain fumbles to stitch together information. The pretty barista Isabette sometimes sheepishly mentioned when I prodded her enough; her odd reply of "You work *there* now?"

after I told her about Bingsu for Two; Vanna coming into Cafe Gong looking for "Betty" that one time . . . Isabette's known all along.

She laughs self-consciously and shrugs. "I really like their bingsu?"

Kai claps his hands. "Damn, small world. Well, since everyone's here, how should we do this?"

I gesture for Isabette to take it away. She clears her throat and pulls a long list from her pocket. "We need to buy paint, decorations, and furniture. Since there's six of us, why don't we divide and conquer? That might make it easier for you guys to film content for your next video, too. River told me all about that. I've seen what people are saying online, and they seem to enjoy certain . . . pairings. Maybe you'd get more views if we split up into those?"

"I should've known you were a fandom person too," Sarang mutters.

Dario purses his lips. "How do you want to split us up then?"

"How about you and Kai shop for paint, River and Sarang get the furniture . . ." Isabette twists her soft features into exaggerated contemplation. "Huh. Vanna isn't really shipped with anyone. I guess she and I can work together, if that's all right."

Vanna's normally passive face does impressive contusions. "For sure, yeah, definitely, I'm fine with that. Whatever."

My eye twitches. *Isabette, you sneaky motherfucker.* I don't even think I can be mad—her improvisation skills are too impressive.

Kai and Dario shake their heads at the same time.

"No way in hell."

"I'm not working with him."

"Me neither," Sarang spits. She and I lock eyes, then glare and look away.

Isabette lets her shoulders sag as she gazes forlornly at the ground. "Oh . . . I'm sorry," she says in a voice I've only heard her use to guilt-trip the Karens at work to stop yelling at us. "It was a dumb idea. I shouldn't have brought it up."

Glancing over at the others, I see they've fallen right into Isabette's sickly-sweet trap.

"No, your ideas aren't stupid," Sarang says. Realizing what she's committing herself to, she looks at me and groans. "Fine. I'll go with Bean Boy."

Kai and Dario still look upset, but not upset enough to argue with Isabette.

"Let's get this over with," Sarang huffs.

She takes off first, heading straight into the mall. I trudge after her, grumbling under my breath, "Yay, teamwork."

INT. "Target"/ENTRANCE — CONTINUOUS

A shaky camera follows RIVER entering the surreal, overly lit store that is Target. He pushes a shopping cart past the dollar novelty section.

RIVER

What's the cafe's budget for redecorating?

SARANG (O.S.)

I thought you were fronting the bill.

He glances over his shoulder to give her and the camera a weary look. Sarang snorts.

SARANG (O.S.)

My dad said two hundred.

RIVER

That reminds me, how come I've never seen your dad?

Don't you guys live right above the store?

Silence. The camera slows, not following River down the aisle, and pans to the floor before shutting off.

I turn around, confused. "Why'd you—"

"My dad is sick," she says, voice hard; no cracks for any hint of emotion to slip through. Her face is unreadable, too. "He stays upstairs when he's out of the hospital."

"Oh," I reply because I'm an idiot. "I'm sorry to hear that."

I don't know Sarang well enough to tell if that's the right thing to say, or if she's like me and prefers not to talk about it at all. Maybe hearing "I'm sorry" from the guy she wants to stab with a stir stick is like a slap in the face. I mean it, though. No one deserves to go through something like that.

But she doesn't get pissed or tell me to butt out. "You'll meet him eventually, if you stick around long enough."

"You're not getting rid of me that easily. I need this job."

"How come? Sounds like you had a pretty cushy setup at your family's cafe."

We turn into the pillow aisle, and I lean against the shopping cart, considering how forthright to be. "It used to be, but not so much these days. I couldn't stay, even if it hurt my folks. I was getting desperate."

She laughs so abruptly it makes me jump. "Yeah, I heard. Haneul told me at your interview you went on this embarrassing rant about how you're not a pyromaniac and—"

I grab one of the sequined throw pillows on the shelf and whack her over the head with it. Not hard enough to hurt, but hard enough that she stumbles and makes a great "*Eyack!*" sound.

A laugh bubbles from me, and I hold my sides when she looks up and her hair is a frizzy halo around her scowling face. She looks cute when she's disheveled like this.

Then she chucks the pillow at my head.

"Okay, okay! Truce!" I say, holding my hands up. Sarang lowers her down-feathered weapon, victory in her smile. Idiot. I grab another pillow and throw it at her.

We hear quickened steps hurry toward us, then an employee peers down the aisle with suspicion—good timing. A look at Sarang confirms that if the worker wasn't watching, my face would have a date with the *Home Sweet Home* pillow clutched in her hands.

We get back to work. She's quick to take over, obviously, so she hands me the camera as she picks cushions in shades of forest green and sage. I turn the camera in my hands before tucking it away in my pocket.

"What's he sick with?" I ask.

Her hand grasping toward the highest shelf freezes. She doesn't turn my way. "Congestive heart failure."

I'm surprised she answered.

She says nothing else, still struggling to reach the pillow. I walk up and grab it for her, tossing it into the cart.

"My uncle had a heart attack," I say. "I know it's not the same, but . . . I get it. It's scary."

Sarang's mouth thins into a straight line. "Who says I'm scared?"

"Nobody. But *I* was." I shake my head. What am I doing? I don't know how to make people feel better. I don't know why I'm even trying. "We've got enough pillows. Let's check out the coffee tables."

She catches up with me. "Is he okay?" she asks, looking ahead. "Your uncle."

"He died two years ago."

"Oh." I can see the fight on her face. She's not good with words, either. "I'm . . . sorry."

I spare her a smile, putting us both out of our misery. "Thank you."

Sarang looks like she wants to say something else, but whatever it is she swallows it down. She bumps her shoulder against my arm as she passes to lead the cart—so gently it must be an accident.

"Aren't you supposed to be recording?" she asks.

"I'm not going to subject the internet to the view you're giving me right now," I say behind her.

The shower loofah she flings at me is worth it.

While Sarang's ringing up at the register, I shoot the group chat a message.

STOP CHANGING THE GROUP CHAT NAME, KAI

> Are you guys finished? Me and Sarang are done

Kai:

> Wow, and you guys didn't kill each other?

> Not yet

Kai:

yeah, Dario and I are finished

Kai:

technically

What's technically mean

Kai:

don't worry about it

Dario:

we got kicked out of the store

Dario:

banned, actually

The cashier hands Sarang her mile-long receipt and I flash her my phone. "Kai and Dario got kicked out."

"What? How the fuck do you get kicked out of Lowe's?" She pulls out her own phone and taps away.

Sarang:

how the FUCK do you get kicked out of Lowe's???

Kai:

from the bottom of my heart—I don't know

Dario:

he spilled four cans of paint all over the floor

Kai:

HEY YOU SPILLED TWO

Dario:

not as bad as four

You guys spilled SIX cans of paint?

What's wrong with you?

Kai:

what started out as an innocent attempt to get Dario to quit his job and flee the continent resulted in a series of unfortunate events

Dario:

Haneul, this has to be the final straw. He got us banned from Lowe's. Fire him already

Sarang:

Haneul has this group chat muted

Kai:

hahaaa

Dario:

quiet

Please tell me you guys got it on camera at the very least

Dario:

unfortunately so

Sarang:

a miracle you managed to do one thing right

Vanna? How did you and Isabette do with the decorations?

Uh, hello?

Vanna:

oh hey

Vanna:

yeah, isabette picked some cute stuff out. It only took us twenty minutes

Sarang:

twenty minutes? What have you been doing all this time then?

Vanna:

talking

Sarang:

glad to see you're all taking this seriously

Vanna:

extremely

I exit the group chat, and my eyes catch on Cecelia's messages I've yet to answer. A chill snakes around my heart. I rub absently at my chest.

"Morons. I work with a bunch of morons," Sarang mutters under her breath. "Let's meet up with everyone outside. I think Haneul should be here to pick us up soon."

"Yeah, yeah . . ."

She looks at me quizzically. "What are you spacing out about?"

"Nothing." I pocket my phone, trying not to think about it. "Come on."

I push the cart out of the store, and we walk through the mall. Sarang is running a nonstop loop of why we should've gotten the black tablecloths, which I'm mostly tuning out. We pass through the food court. The fragrant, caramelized sugar aroma of fresh cinnamon rolls wafts in the air, unearthing a memory from last year.

"Here."

A blue Cinnabon box plops on my half-finished essay. I look up. Cecelia's standing in front of my table, the smile on her lips clashing with the worry between her knit brows.

I pop open the lid, and the scent of vanilla and brown sugar makes my mouth water. "What's this?" I ask.

She takes a seat at the table next to me. No one else is in the library, but she keeps her voice down anyway. "A cinnamon roll."

"I see."

"And an apology."

I frown. "What are you apologizing for? We didn't get into a fight."

"Didn't we?" She tucks a strand of her long, ash-blond hair behind her ear, glancing at the aisle of books. "Well, yeah, I guess we don't fight. But still, I owe you an apology for what I said the other day about your hobbies. Your fandoms and stuff."

I'm surprised she knows it upset me. I thought I'd done a good job of not letting it show. I close the box, pushing it back toward her. An inkling of irritation builds at the base of my skull. "You didn't need to do this or apologize. It is an embarrassing hobby."

"That's not the point," Cecelia says, finally piercing me with her eyes. "I hurt your feelings—I must have, you've been acting distant. I wanted to bring you something to make up for it."

I drop my gaze to the blue box so I don't need to keep up with hers. Something claws at the back of my brain, something left dissatisfied, an itch gone unscratched. I rub the nape of my neck to try to rid the prickling sensation, but it's still there.

Cecelia reaches over and grabs my hand, holding it in hers. "I know you said I don't need to apologize, so I hope this is enough. It's okay that we have different interests. Opposites attract. We've been through worse, haven't we?"

Yeah, she doesn't need to apologize. It was a dumb conversation and a dumb thing to get insulted by. I'm too sensitive sometimes.

Cecelia squeezes. "High school sweethearts to the end, right?"

I squeeze back, and her face lights up. That's better, familiar. "Why a cinnamon roll?"

"Don't you like them?" she asks, voice lifting innocently. She blinks twice, and her short, straight lashes bat elegantly. "You're always saying my freckles remind you of cinnamon."

She leans forward, and I can see her freckles better. They do look like a perfect sprinkling of cinnamon. I don't have the heart to tell her I'm not personally a fan of the taste, because she's right in front of me, and I'm closing the gap and pressing my lips to hers. Soft and warm, a taste I prefer over cinnamon. I pull back first, her smile having molded my own lips into one.

Yeah. High school sweethearts. It'd be stupid to let something as small as this get between us.

"Have half," I say. "I can't finish it myself."

Sarang snaps her fingers in front of my face.

"Earth to River." Her voice is like a bucket of cold water splashed over my head. My heart jogs in my chest, an unsteady *babump-a-bump.* "What's wrong with you? Are you hungry or something? Why are you giving the Cinnabon worker bedroom eyes?"

"*Bedroom eyes?* I was not—" I shake my head. "Uh, can you take this and meet the others?"

I push the cart toward her. Sarang sputters but grabs the handle. "Where are *you* going?"

I'm already walking away. "I have to talk to somebody. Sorry. I'll see you at work."

"What? River!" I hear her call out behind me. "Prick!"

As I head out of the mall, I pull my phone out. Before I can think too long about it and change my mind, I make a call. It rings four times before she picks up.

A beat. Then, "River?"

My stomach does weird things at the sound of Cecelia's voice. I can't tell if they're good or bad. Her voice is exactly the same as the one in my head.

"Hey," I say. The night air is a blanket of ice wrapped around me, seeping into my bones. "Can we still talk?"

9. HOLY CRAP, AM I EVER GOING TO SAY THE RIGHT THING?

Cecelia lives twenty-five minutes from the Westlake mall. It's not nearly enough time to collect myself before I'm standing in front of the familiar apartment building. I gaze up at it, shrouded in night, and consider turning around.

The lobby door opens before I can.

There she is. She's as stunning as ever, clad in loose pajama bottoms and a winter coat. Cecelia checks both sides of the street before crossing it to join me. The frigid wind and the sight of her steals my breath. I can't believe it's only been a little over a week since I last saw her—that's probably the longest we've been apart since getting together freshman year. Holy shit. My whole body is stiff. From anticipation or fear, I don't know.

"Hi," I say.

"Hey, River."

Now what?

I guess since I'm the one who asked to meet up, I'm in charge of the conversation, but that hasn't really happened before, plus I don't know what I want to say. So I stall. "Are you cold? Do you want my jacket? We can go inside."

"No, I'm fine. Are you cold?"

"No."

"Okay."

Well, that didn't buy me much time.

Cecelia huffs, that half-laugh, half-sigh thing she does when she wants to break the tension. "You were never one for small-talk, were you?"

"No, I guess not."

"Not one for *any* talk."

"I guess not."

"What changed your mind?" She gestures around us at the blackened streets, broken by the tinny orange halos of the lampposts. We're the only ones out here, save for the occasional passerby who doesn't spare us a glance. "Why do you want to chat all of a sudden after the radio silence?"

"Cinnabon," I answer.

She shakes her head. "I'm not following."

"I passed by a Cinnabon, and it reminded me of that time you brought me a cinnamon roll after . . . I don't know. I thought of you. I've *been* thinking of you. It's not fair to leave you without answers any longer so . . . ask away."

Cecelia crosses her arms, and her expression gives the nearly freezing temperature a run for its money. "I only have one question, and you know what it is."

Damn it. I was hoping she'd ask a different one. "I thought I answered that."

A harsh scoff. "All you said was some bullshit, River. You? In love with someone else? When would that have happened? That's not you. None of it makes any sense. It's like you didn't know why you were dumping me either." She steps closer, and I shove down the impulse to step away. Her eyes, narrowed in a glare, glimmer with tears. "So please, *please* just answer me now. Why'd you break up with me?"

My mind scatters in a dozen directions at once like a porcelain vase just dropped on the floor. I fight to pick up a single thought, to follow it to some sort of coherent conclusion. *Because I thought a relationship was too much work? Because "it's not you, it's me"?*

I can't say any of that, though, because it's not true. I'd be lying. Haven't I lied to her enough? No, I didn't cheat on her. No, I'm not in love with anyone else—but small lies can accumulate to something harmful, too. In fact, I don't even know if I can call them lies. They're stuck somewhere in the hesitant middle, the *maybes.*

Do you want to see a movie with me this Friday? Sure, I'd said. Instead of maybe.

Will you be my boyfriend? Yes, I'd said. Instead of let me think about it.

I love you, River. I love you, too, I'd said. Instead of I'm not sure yet, can you give me time?

Why? Why hadn't I allowed myself to teeter in the uncharted territory between yes and no? Black and white? What was so scary about gray?

I don't know. And *that's* scary.

My mouth opens. Shuts. The pieces of the shattered vase are too small to pick up.

I wet my dry lips. "I loved you, you know. I still do. It's just . . ."

"You broke up with me because you *love* me?"

"That's not what I—"

"We were perfect together," Cecelia interrupts. Her fingers are vises around her biceps.

"Yeah."

"We had a whole *future* together."

"Well—"

"And you just blew it all for no reason. You left me and Cafe Gong when we needed you the most, and the worst part is you don't even care—did you *ever* care? You know how much that management promotion meant to me. It was everything I needed for my application to UPenn. Cafe Gong was going to be *our* success story, it was going to take *both* of us to bigger, better places. If you didn't want that, why didn't you say anything to me or your parents? Do you not trust me?"

"Cece, please let me—"

"Let you *what*?" she shouts. It echoes like gunfire down the street, ricocheting off the buildings around us and piercing me in the back. My eyes fly open. Cecelia crumbles. She sobs, hiding her face in her hands. Her shoulders shake up and down like she's laughing, but the sound tearing from her throat is anything but happy.

My fingers twitch at my sides. Hesitantly, with a touch so featherlight she could swat me away and I'd be gone, I grab her shoulders. She falls into me. I hug her, tracing the knobs on her spine as she cries into my shoulder. Despite it all, the way our relationship has grown complicated since we began working together, holding her still brings me comfort.

"I'm sorry. This is humiliating," she sniffles, more to herself than to me. Her cries vibrate through me, rattling in my chest. "I love you. I loved *us*. Now I feel like I don't know you."

My skin prickles. I don't know who I am, either, so how could I have believed in an "us?" I never know what to do, what to say. I *never* know. But I do know that saying nothing, when I brought her out here for answers, isn't right either.

She pushes me away, ripping herself from my embrace. The phantom sensation of her palms on my chest singes my skin like her touch was embers.

"I'm just tired," she says, sounding as gutted as I feel. "No more excuses. Say something. Explain yourself."

A new turmoil broils in me, pushing words left to simmer to the surface. "I don't know what you want me to say."

"The truth."

That is the truth! I don't scream. *The truth is I don't know! Why isn't that enough?*

A familiar, unsettling feeling buds at the base of my skull. Something that begs to be examined, like the answer's right *there*, and I just have to look at it for one goddamn second.

My phone rings in my pocket.

Her eyes dart to it, then up. "You should answer that."

I shake my head. "It's not important. Cecelia—"

"It could be your parents."

Sighing, I pull my phone out and check. Sarang. Great timing. I decline the call. "It's work."

"Work?" Her head tilts to the side. "But you quit."

My throat closes around my breath, making me choke. "Oh. No, not work, I meant—"

"Your mom said you're too busy studying for the SATs to come back to Cafe Gong. Did you find a new job?"

My phone shakes in my grip.

For a moment, nothing shows on her face. Not disdain, or curiosity, or hurt. Then she ducks her head and shakes it, and I'm not sure what she's thinking.

"You lie to everybody, don't you? Me, your parents. You're lying to yourself too, River."

"I—"

I think she's right.

Cecelia turns on her heel, crossing the street toward her apartment. On the sidewalk, she looks back at me.

"Don't tell them," I plead out, voice breaking.

She shakes her head.

I feel sick.

10. WHY DO HUNDREDS OF PEOPLE WANT TO WATCH PAINT LITERALLY DRY?

Bingsu for Two is closed today, but I still have to drag my feet out of bed at ten in the morning and head over instead of reading through my saved fics on Archive of Our Own like I want.

I check my messages while walking to the cafe. Nothing besides the work chat chewing me out for ditching, though I'm only focused on Cecelia's contact. I think about tapping out a message but realize that's an awful idea. Fuck, I made everything worse. I didn't know that was possible. Something stirs in my chest, aching, yearning for a time when I used to make her happy. I'm an idiot to think that just because I was the one who ended things would mean I wouldn't have to grieve, or question every day if I made the right choice. Breakups *suck*. I never want to go through another one.

Everybody is already working when I arrive. My eyes snap to the main wall of the restaurant. Yesterday, it was a splotchy lime green. Now it looks like an installation at the Seattle Art Museum. The backdrop has been painted a matte black, with curving, abstract streaks of cadmium red and ultramarine blue popping off the mural. Lights and shadows are delicately painted into their crevices to give the impression that a wave of color could come crashing into the room at any second.

"Holy shit, who did that?" I utter, approaching. My eyes are glued to the mural, so I don't see the crouched figure on the ground next to it until I nearly trip over them.

"Hey, no touching, the paint isn't dry. Get your grubby fingers away from it."

The squatting lump unfurls, revealing Haneul, wearing an apron streaked with paint and her hair tied back.

I point at the painting. "You made this?"

"No, I just decided to douse myself in paint and sit next to it."

God, they really *are* sisters. "This is incredible. I didn't know you were a painter."

"Whatever. I'm more into animating and digital art. Sarang helped, too."

"She did?"

I hear footsteps from the kitchen, then "Hey, asshole!"

Speak of the devil.

Sarang storms up to me, but it's difficult to take her look of fury seriously when she's dressed like a toddler who's been finger painting. Her overalls are splattered with pastel yellow, pink, green, and blue. She wipes her forehead with the back of her hand, smearing white paint there. I don't mention it.

"What was that last night? Leaving us with all the stuff?" she asks.

I move around her. "I told you, I had to talk to someone."

"And it couldn't wait?"

I approach Kai brushing wood stain on to the tables. Sarang's on my heel, stomping around the pools of spilled paint on the plastic-tarped floor.

"No, it couldn't," I reply. "I'm sorry. But I'm here now, aren't I?"

Kai sits back. His bangs are pinned up and he's sweaty. He's wearing another hoodie he designed, this one with a collage of skateboard renderings. "Who'd you meet?" he asks.

Shit, he'll be pissed. I chew on my lip and glance away, over to where Vanna and Isabette are hanging art up on the wall, standing closer than necessary. Even from this far, I can tell they're both rambling awkwardly, nodding too enthusiastically, and smiling a bit too hard.

Kai jumps up into my periphery, looking—yep, pissed. "No fucking way."

"I didn't say anything."

"Are you for real?"

Sarang looks between us. "What's going on?"

I groan and pinch the bridge of my nose under my glasses. "Okay, yeah. Her."

"*Why?* Jesus, man!"

"Who?" Sarang exclaims.

"His manipulative ex-girlfriend," Kai answers with an eye roll.

"She's not *manipulative.*"

"She would literally gaslight you."

"You don't know what 'gaslight' means."

"No, *you* don't. Which one of us walked out of their SATs, River?" Sarang snorts. "Loser."

"It wasn't like that," I say, rounding on them. "I wasn't trying to win her back. We just needed to talk."

"And how'd that go?" Kai asks condescendingly.

My face twists like a dirty washcloth being wrung. Kai clicks his tongue.

"Can't say I'm surprised."

I shake my head. "Whatever. I don't know what I . . ."

Propped up on the table is a laptop, reflecting us and the rest of the cafe on its screen. The camera blinks red.

"Is that thing on?"

"Hmm? Oh yeah. Recording live."

"Live?"

I hop over an upturned chair to get to the computer. Sure enough, we're broadcasting live on YouTube, with 16,000 current viewers. Propped against a coffee mug next to the laptop is some-body's phone, where I see we're *also* streaming on TikTok. There's even live commentary.

PutTheOfficeBackOnNetflix: oooh work gossip

NellieParkson2: hey I want to hear more about the ex!!!

King_bowlingpin: can this guy get his face out of the camera? I can't see Vanna

I duck out of sight. Sarang and Kai look down at me with amusement.

"You're so embarrassing," she sighs.

"Yeah," Kai agrees.

I groan and throw my head back, accidentally knocking it against the table and making the laptop jump. "Thanks for the heads-up about the live."

"Not our fault you decided to spend the night with your ex and come into work late," Sarang says petulantly.

"I wasn't spending the night with—ugh, never mind."

I don't have it in me to talk about Cece any longer. I stand to join Vanna and Isabette on the opposite side of the cafe.

They've done good work so far. Or Isabette has, I assume, if all the fandom posters are anything to go by. The wall adjacent to the counter is decorated with gold-framed photos of local art, poetry, and pictures of K-pop stars.

I point to one of Felix from Stray Kids without a shirt. "Really?"

Vanna shimmies her shoulders with a grin. "Sex appeal, remember?"

"We don't need sex appeal to sell coffee."

"It wouldn't hurt."

Isabette giggles and adjusts a hanging potted plant. "There will be more tasteful photos, don't worry. I printed some of G-Dragon, Blackpink, and Monsta X. It'll be cute."

She shoos me away to draw the new menu board, dropping a dozen paint markers in my lap and telling me to get to work. Somebody connects their phone to the speakers and starts playing K-pop, so I settle myself into a corner as Loona bumps through the cafe and the others continue their tasks.

WELCOME TO BINGSU FOR TWO!

ESPRESSO 에스프레소

AFFOGATO 아포가토 3.25

AMERICANO 아메리카노 3.00

CAPPUCCINO 카푸치노 4.25

LATTE 라떼 3.75

MACCHIATO 마끼아또 4.25

MOCHA 모카 4.25

NON-COFFEE/TEA 논 커피/차

HOT CHOCOLATE 코코아 2.95

GRAPEFRUIT ADE 자몽 에이드 3.75

HERBAL TEA 쌍화 차 2.75

CITRON TEA 유자차 2.75

SWEET POTATO LATTE 고구마 라떼 3.50

BINGSU 빙수

FRUIT BINGSU 과일 8.00

RED BEAN INJEOLMI BINGSU

　팥 인절미 8.00

MANGO BINGSU 망고 8.00

OREO BINGSU 오레오 10.00

TARO BINGSU 타로 10.00

COFFEE BINGSU 커피 10.00

BUNGEOPPANG 붕어빵

RED BEAN 팥 1.25

CUSTARD 커스터드 1.25

NUTELLA 누텔라 1.25

SWEET POTATO 고구마 1.25

BRUNCH/DESSERT 브런치/디저트

HONEY TOAST 허니 토스트 7.95

INJEOLMI TOAST 인절미 토스트 7.95

WAFFLE WITH FRUIT 과일 와플 6.95

KHMER MUNG BEAN PUDDING

　캄보디아 녹두 푸딩 5.75

ENTREE 메인 요리

KIMCHI PANCAKE 김치 전 9.95

TTEOKBOKKI 떡볶이 7.50

BULGOGI SANDWICH 불고기 샌드위치 6.50

"Smile."

Dario stands above me, holding a camera, his muscle tank damp with sweat. I throw up a peace sign as he snaps the picture.

"For the accounts," he explains. "Menu's looking good."

"Thanks. What have you been working on?"

"Sarang put me in charge of deep cleaning and reorganizing our drink station."

I stand up and peer over the counter. "Wow, it looks like it might pass a health inspection now."

But Dario's attention has wandered. He's watching Kai and Sarang, who are finishing up the chairs. Sarang seems pissed as usual, and Kai's cracking up, holding onto her shoulder as he throws his head back and laughs. I catch the way Dario's eyes soften, the twitch by his lip. It's not something I was meant to see, so I avert my gaze and pretend I didn't. Kai's laugh echoes through the cafe and rings in my ears.

"Hey," I say, changing the subject to something that's been burning in the back of my mind. "You've met Mr. Cho, right?"

Dario blinks, dragging his eyes away from Kai. "Yeah, a handful of times. More often when I first started working here. He even came to a few of my basketball games when he was healthier."

"Really?"

"Yeah. He's nice, you'll like him." He smiles a little. "He made sure Haneul scheduled Kai and me together most days when we were dating, and that I could get time off to visit my brothers whenever I wanted."

The mention of his brothers reminds me of how Kai would rave about Dario's parents and siblings. Kai and his mom moved here from Taiwan when he was little, just the two of them, so I think the idea of a big extended family always appealed to him—especially having older siblings to lean on. It's funny to imagine Dario as the youngest, and Kai an only child; you'd assume it'd be the other way around given their personalities. They always had an opposites-attract kind of thing, though. Complementary.

As if he fell down the same line of thinking, Dario asks quietly, "Do you know how Kai's mom and grandma are doing? I haven't talked to Aunty since we broke up."

I muster a weak smile. "His grandma's dementia is getting worse, unfortunately. He said his mom picked up a second job so she can fly over soon to take care of her."

"Kai already gives her most of what he earns here. He barely has time for his design and fashion stuff because he's always picking up shifts . . ." Dario trails off. He chews his lip, glancing back at Kai.

A shrill whistle slices through the air. Haneul claps her hands.

"Looks like we're done here. Start cleaning up."

Dario looks lost in thought. I pat him awkwardly on the shoulder, intending to give him some space by joining the others.

The place looks good. Really good, like something off Pinterest. All the tables and chairs have been painted, the mural is finished, and Isabette and Vanna have most of the decor up.

Kai waves everyone over toward the laptop. "We've got to say goodbye before ending the live."

"You act like we're FaceTiming relatives or something, and not a bunch of faceless, nameless strangers on the internet," Sarang mumbles as we approach. She squints at the screen, reading the comments. "They didn't like that, did they? Well, too damn bad, skimmilklover425."

I not so subtly nudge the back of her knee with my foot, and she folds like a deck of cards. Waving at the screen, I say, "Thank you guys for watching and supporting the—*ack!*"

Sarang kicks *my* knee, and I topple over, taking a freshly painted chair with me and collapsing on top of her.

The others close out the live before Sarang or I can get back up, but when I finally untangle myself from her thrashing limbs, they're still staring at the screen. Kai is scrolling through the comment section.

Ilovealiens42_069: this cafe is Chaotic Good

Pampamkazam: Sarang and River arguing at the beginning omg! they're so cute together

MisaMoxley: I ship LoveLee!!!

> Solomon.salamander: What's LoveLee?
>
> X_yoonie_X: it's Sarang and River's ship name
>
> MisaMoxley: yeah, Sarang means love in Korean, plus River's last name = LoveLee!

I startle. "How did they find out my last name?"

"Everyone on the internet is an idiot if that's what they think of us," Sarang says, ignoring me. Her nose crinkles with distaste at the word "us," which stings. Sure, we don't even like each other, but her pure disgust at the thought of being associated with me isn't *great*.

Isabette smiles at me. "Your idea of making the cafe famous through fandom is working."

Sarang grunts. "We've had a few *okay* days of business."

"Would it kill you to admit I was right?" I ask, turning to face her. She's closer than I expected. Sarang barely comes up to my sternum; I bow my head while she cranes her neck back. The height difference makes me feel flustered for a second, but I push that away. How can such a short person contain so much evil inside them? Maybe it's more concentrated that way.

Haneul pops her head from behind the kitchen curtains again. "Can you annoying shits be a little quieter? Appa's trying to sleep."

Sarang shakes her head and turns to follow her sister into the back. Before leaving, she shoots me a look over her shoulder. I think she might say something, but all she does is grimace and walk away. Strikingly, I'm reminded of the expression Cecelia made last night.

Disgust.

My innards do a weird clench, curdling in on themselves.

The feeling is mutual, apparently.

11. HACKING INTO MY EX-GIRLFRIEND'S PHONE BUT NOT IN A TOXIC STALKER WAY, I PROMISE

I can't get it out of my head, that comment we got on our live stream the other day: *LoveLee.*

On the one hand, the logical, rational part of me (yes, that part still exists) cringes at the idea of people pairing Sarang and me together. Shudder. But the fan boy in me has to admit that *LoveLee* is one hell of a ship name.

But what's really been eating at me is, how did strangers online find out my full name? I was careful not to reveal too much personal information in our videos, and *definitely* not on my fandom accounts, so how?

It was a wake-up call. If a random person on the internet can figure out my government name, it won't be long until Cece or my parents find out about me and Bingsu for Two. It's a miracle they haven't already, even given the fact that Umma and Dad don't really use social media and I know Cece is too busy writing her college application letters to monitor her accounts 24/7, but it's only a matter of time unless I do something.

And when I say *I* do something, I mean employ my little brother to help.

A good way to butter Jace up is by treating him to his favorite meal: burgers at Dick's Drive-In, a quick, greasy Seattle staple. So, after his soccer practice, we ride the light-rail to Capitol Hill, where he takes advantage of his brother's kindness and orders three burgers, fries, and a chocolate shake.

"What's this about?" Jace asks, shoving a handful of limp, oily fries into his mouth. We sit shoulder to shoulder on the curb in front of the restaurant, ignoring the people passing on the sidewalk behind us. It's the ideal way to enjoy a Dick's burger. "Did you finally realize I'm the best brother ever and you should be spoiling me more?"

"Uh. Yes, and I have something to tell you." I take a sip of my strawberry milkshake as I gather my nerve. "You know how I said I'm getting tutored, and that's why I can't come back to work for Umma and Dad? Well, I'm not. I lied and got a different job. At another cafe . . . the one that's down the street from Cafe Gong."

Jace's jaw falls, and a few chewed-up fries tumble out.

"Oh, you are *so* fucked," he says.

"Listen, I know I'm screwed if Umma and Dad ever find out—"

"*If?* You're working two streets down from them, of course they're going to find out! How long have you kept this a secret?"

I try not to feel embarrassed about getting lectured to by my little brother, because he's unfortunately right. "A few weeks. It all happened so fast, I didn't exactly stop and think through the logistics." I rest my elbows on my knees and lay my forehead against my arms. I turn to him. "I work with Kai now, though, so that's fun."

Jace perks up at that. "Really? Can I visit?"

"I don't know why you think he's so cool, but sure—if you help me with something first."

He looks down at his burger, then at me suspiciously, realizing the price for his meal is a big, fat favor. "Am I going to regret this?"

Yeah, probably. "Of course not," I say.

The first Wednesday of the month is inventory day at Cafe Gong. Since this is the new location's first time, Umma and Dad will both be here to walk Cece through it. Inventory usually takes about an hour, which means I don't have a lot of time for my plan. I have to do this *now*.

Jace and I huddle around the corner of Cafe Gong, out of sight of the windows. He wrings the hem of his sweaty jersey, still in his soccer uniform. "You sure about this?" he asks. "If you get caught, you're in big trouble."

"That's why you're here. And I know, but I have no choice. If they find out about Bingsu for Two, it's not just trouble for me, but my co-workers, too."

At his silence, I look away from the store and back at him. Jace is staring at me with an unusual, quiet expression, like he's reconsidering some of his worldviews for the first time. I raise my eyebrows. "What?"

He shrugs and drops his gaze. "It sounds like you care about that other place a lot, unlike Cafe Gong. I haven't seen you so passionate about something besides your books in a while."

I stutter, trying to find a reason that justifies my decision to essentially betray the family business, when Jace knocks his shoulder into me, flashing his braces in a disarming smile.

"You don't gotta worry about me saying anything to Dad and Umma. If Bingsu for Two means something to you, then I think it's cool you're trying to protect it. I'm glad I can help. Hey, *hey*, are you tearing up? Stop it!" Jace groans, his face turning pink. "Let's just get this over with. I'll go first."

He beelines it to Cafe Gong's entrance, flashing me a peace sign. I scrub my eyes and make a mental note to treat him to lunch more often, then head the opposite way toward the back entrance.

I asked Isabette to send me the schedule earlier, confirming my suspicion: only Cece is on the closing shift today, since my parents are in. Meaning, if Jace successfully distracts the three of them like I asked him to, the back of the cafe should be clear.

I fish out my manager keys I never returned, pray for the best, and unlock the back door. I don't hear anything besides the buzz of the fridge room and the customers up front. Then Jace's voice drifts in from the lobby.

"What? I can't visit my parents at our own cafe? I didn't know it was a crime to *care*. If so, then slap some cuffs on these wrists and lock me up, because guess who has two thumbs and a big heart. *This* kid."

Some muffled response that sounds like Dad's voice.

"I'm not disturbing the customers!" Jace yells loud enough to disturb me all the way in the back. "Right, Cece? Hey, did you get a haircut? It looks great. Oh, you didn't? Let me see, come here, let me look at your ends. Wow, smooth. Hey, don't leave, I'm not done. Umma, come look."

He's too good. If soccer doesn't pan out for him, Jace has a bright future in community theater.

While he has the three of them distracted up front, I dart to the breakroom.

If there's one thing Dad's a stickler for, it's about putting phones away at work. There's a special basket for them in the back near the fridge and cubbies. To my relief, three iPhones are inside when I check.

I take them from the basket and put them down on a table. The sound of commotion up front has me glancing over my shoulder constantly. I don't have much time. All the phones are locked, but Umma and Dad's passwords are easy: the date we first opened Cafe Gong. They use it for everything. I stare a bit longer at Cece's phone, stomach clenching with guilt. Is it better or worse to snoop through someone's phone when you're together or broken up? There's no time for ethical dilemmas on boundaries within relationships right now. What would her password be? She used to have mine, but I didn't bother asking for hers.

I try her birthday: 100506. October 5, 2006.

The phone vibrates in an angry response. *BZZRT!* Wrong password.

My eyebrows furrowing, I try her cat's name: Olivia, 654842. *BZZRT!* Also wrong.

Goddamn it. I should've been a more insecure boyfriend and gotten her passcodes for everything. I run my fingers through my hair, flipping the phone over in my hand nervously. On the back of her case, there's a Polaroid of us. My breath hitches.

I remember exactly where it was taken. Back in sophomore year, we visited a pumpkin patch for the first time. Fall is Cecelia's favorite season: the changing leaves, scary movies, hot apple cider, she loves all of it. In the picture, we're crouched next to a huge pumpkin in the middle of the patch. Cecelia's hugging it proudly, beaming at the camera and bundled in a red scarf and beanie that made her blue eyes stand out like crystals in comparison. I'm behind her, wearing her favorite flannel of mine with an arm around her shoulders, but I'm not looking at the camera. I'm watching her. That soft, unguarded expression on my face, glowing with love, adoration—it looks like it belongs to a stranger.

Hesitantly, I flip the phone back over. I try 020321—February 3, 2021. Our anniversary.

Her phone unlocks.

I have to pause for a few long and still moments before I'm able to continue.

With the three phones laid out, I open Twitter first. I start with Dad's account, going into the privacy and safety section of his settings. Under "Muted Words," I type *Bingsu for Two, River Langston-Lee, LoveLee,* and *#ihatemyjob*. Then I search up Bingsu for Two's account and block it, making sure to clear my search history afterward. Next is Umma's phone, then Cece's; then I start the process over with Instagram and YouTube.

I'm sweating by the time I finish. The lobby is starting to sound quieter, so I dump the phones back in their basket and hightail it out of the breakroom. As I exit and lock the back door behind me, I text Jace:

Jace

All done. Out back. You're the best

I lean against the building, stomach twisting from more than just the adrenaline pumping through my veins.

At least that's taken care of.

12. THIS IS WHAT I GET FOR NOT CALLING OUT OF WORK

As much as Sarang will try to claim otherwise, it's undeniable: social media is bringing in business for the cafe. I was *right*. I'm exhausted after my shifts and my fingers cramp from pouring milk, but it's worth it to see Bingsu for Two thriving. It's nice to see physical proof that my fandom and social media knowledge have real-life benefits for the people around me. *Take that, Dad and Umma—scrolling Instagram all day* is *a skill.*

After a long week of school and hacking my ex's phone (yikes), I decide to pick up Haneul's opening shift the following Saturday since she got a job painting a mural downtown. After the one she made for the cafe went viral, she's been getting commissions left and right from local businesses and is hopeful the exposure will lead to an animating gig.

Kai and I are trying to pry the lid off a metal whipped cream canister when we hear someone running down the stairs in the back. Barreling through the kitchen curtains comes a suspiciously cute Sarang: frizzy haired, still in her pajamas, and a look of shock on her face. God, she's unfortunately attractive. I hate her. I can do both; I'm a very multifaceted individual.

"Morning, sleeping beauty," I grunt as I try twisting off the top again. No luck.

Her lips part, then close. No words come out. She shows us her phone screen. There's an email.

Hello Cho family,

My name is Lani Kapule. I'm a local reporter for KING 5 News here in Seattle. My team and I recently caught wind of your cafe's viral video, and I would love to do a segment with you and your employees. If you are interested, please give me a call at my number below and we can set up a time for our camera crew and I to meet you at your establishment.

Kind regards,
Lani Kapule
Reporter for KING 5 News

Kai looks up. "Holy shit."

"Holy *shit*," I repeat.

"Holy shit!" Sarang exclaims. "The news wants to interview us. *Us*, our tiny Korean cafe that no one knew anything about until two weeks ago. The actual news."

Something about that is more immediate, more real than the attention we've gotten online. Those are, to borrow Sarang's crude words, nameless, faceless strangers on a screen. Real, but not real like a crew of anchors and journalists. The situation flushes through me, at first exhilarating, then terrifying. Dad has KING 5 running on the television every single morning—*that's* real.

Wait.

Dad has KING 5 running on the television every single morning.

"This is incredible. Hurry up, reply to her before she changes her mind," Kai urges, trying to manhandle Sarang's fingers onto her phone's keypad. He elbows me in my ribs. "Isn't this great?"

Yeah, Umma and Dad finding out that I lied about SAT tutoring and abandoned our business for the competitor's is fantastic.

"This is it," Sarang says breathlessly before I can come up with anything to derail this whole plan. She looks up from her phone, and my breath stalls at the sight. I haven't seen her look this happy since . . .

Oh. I've *never* seen her look this happy. Her inky-black eyes glisten, the corners crinkled with joy. She's smiling so hard it must hurt. Her dimples may never smooth away.

"This is *it*," Sarang repeats. "This is the cafe's insurance. Even if a million strangers know about us online, it means nothing if they can't support us in person, but this will put us on Seattle's radar for good. This will make sure the cafe doesn't go under when our internet fame dries up. Even when I leave for college." She whispers this last part, eyes trailing back to her phone's screen and glazing over.

A fist reaches inside my chest and squeezes my heart. No. No, I can't take that away from her, from all of them. What if Umma and Dad got an opportunity like this? What if some new hire ruined it for them? I can't forget how I tried to sabotage Bingsu for Two in the first place, and what I still need to do to make up for it.

"You should tell her to bring her crew around tomorrow," I say. "The cafe's closed on Sundays. It'll be perfect."

Sarang blinks. Her eyes—not lined with makeup today—flick up and down my face. Then she nods. Unsure at first, but then with gusto. "Yeah, tomorrow. I'll tell her she can interview us then."

Kai cheers, and despite how glad I am for the store, I can't help the lingering tendrils of dread swirling in the pool of my gut.

But it's fine. I just won't show up tomorrow. Problem solved.

Problem *not* solved.

Around noon, the door jangles with a customer. I turn around. "Welcome. What can I—"

Three guys squeeze through the door, wheeling in two hefty video cameras. A woman follows them carrying boom mics, and three other crew members barge into the cafe on their tail. Finally, a tall woman with wavy black hair framing a striking face walks in. From the look of her navy blazer and pencil skirt, she's a reporter. Her heels make clicking sounds as she struts toward me at the register.

"Hi there, I'm Lani Kapule with KING 5 News. Thanks so much for having us—what an adorable place. Unfortunate location, for sure, but the interior makes up for it." She extends her hand and I shake it in a daze, still focused on the absurd amount of crew people crowding into our lobby. The customers gawk at them.

"Hi," I remember to say belatedly. A beat. "Uh, what are you doing here? I—I mean, how can I help you?"

Ms. Kapule laughs heartily. "You're precious. You're the one who was filming the video that went viral, right? I want you up front when we do a full interview with everyone who works here. Speaking of, where are your co-workers?"

"My only other co-worker here today is on his lunch break. I'm sorry, I still don't understand. This is about the segment you're doing on the cafe, right? I thought that was tomorrow."

The curtain rustles behind me. Sarang walks out of the kitchen with her hair curled, makeup done, and wearing this black dress-thing with puffy sleeves that slide off her shoulders. I swallow past the sudden dryness in my mouth.

Ms. Kapule peers around me and beams. "Ah, you must be Sarang."

"Hi, that's me. Thank you so much for coming down here."

I nearly strain a muscle in my forehead with how fast my eyebrows shoot up. Her voice drips like syrup, an artificial sweetness clinging to her words that isn't usually there. The smile she gives Ms. Kapule is friendlier than normal—hell, she's even wearing a modest red lipstick today instead of her familiar black gloss.

I hold back a scoff. And she was telling *me* that honesty is the most important thing.

"Hey," I whisper to her. "What is this? I thought they were coming tomorrow?"

Sarang flaps her hand dismissively. "I suggested Sunday, but Lani said they could do it today, so why not?"

I can think of a hundred reasons why not, Sarang.

"What about the others?" I ask, smothering my panic.

"They're on their way. Except for Haneul, she's still at her commission job."

"Don't you want her to be here? She can take my spot."

"I already called her—she won't leave her mural. I don't blame her, she's spent years trying to get a job like that."

My eyes dart to the front. Maybe I can sneak out while everyone is distracted? Pretend there was an emergency?

But of course, that's when Kai, Vanna, and Dario walk in.

"Celebrity life, here we come," Kai announces, hands laced behind his head. "We're going to be bigger than that girl on TikTok who does a review of each glass of milk she drinks."

Dario flicks Kai's head. "There's no way we're going to be more famous than her. This is just the local news."

Vanna walks past them both, fluffing her hair. "I don't care if we get famous or not. I'm here for the extra hours without having to do anything but sit and look pretty. Which is what I do most of the time for free, anyway."

"Can you guys please take this seriously?" Sarang snaps. She does a one-eighty and flashes Ms. Kapule a charming smile. "Sorry about them."

"No, no, this is perfect. The audience will eat you guys up." Ms. Kapule gestures to the dining area. "Can we start clearing out the customers? I'm thinking we have the five of you over on that sofa, yeah, next to the window, and . . ."

Somebody ambles out of the kitchen, their footsteps slow and faltering. An older Asian man, with a face wrinkled by age and smile lines, and neatly combed hair that's more salt than pepper. He's dressed in a crisp blue button-down and slim dress pants.

Sarang springs up and hurries to his side. She latches onto his elbow, asking him if he feels okay in Korean, to which he reassures her with a pat on the hand. He notices me standing awkwardly in the center of the room.

He blinks, and then recognition flashes through his eyes. "You must be River. My daughter said you're Korean, right? 와, 키가 정말 크구나."[2] He grasps my hand and shakes it, clapping my shoulder with his other hand. "I'm sorry it's taken me so long to introduce myself. I've heard great things about you," he says playfully.

I do a weird half bow, which is even more awkward because I'm a head taller than him. "No, it's totally fine. It's nice to meet you. Thank you again for hiring me, I appreciate it."

Ms. Kapule joins us. "This must be Dad, right? You've got a beautiful cafe here, very homey. Would you mind sitting down in front of the camera? I'd like to get an interview with you and your daughter first."

Mr. Cho squeezes my shoulder. "And then you're interviewing all the employees, correct?"

"That's right, everyone here."

He smiles at me. "Good. I'm excited to hear what you have to say in particular, River, given all this is possible because of you."

I cringe. "I'm not sure. I'm not really a fan of being in front of the camera."

"Wasn't it your idea to start making videos for social media?"

Damn it. Bad excuse.

Mr. Cho senses my reluctance. "Is there a reason you don't want to be on television?"

---

2.   Wow, you're so tall.

Yeah, my parents recognizing their son on the morning news will be hard to explain. But what would be harder is looking Mr. Cho straight in his kind, warm eyes and telling him about how I helped my family's business try to run *his* out.

"Nope," I say, forcing a smile. "Just nerves. But I'll do it."

Fuck it, I'll just figure out a way to prevent Umma and Dad from hearing about this later.

Part of me almost wishes they would, so they could see I'm capable of doing something without them. I shake the thought from my head. A tiny moment of "I told you so" isn't worth the fallout.

Kai, Vanna, and Dario are on the sofa already, and I join them as we wait for Sarang and her dad to finish filming at the other end of the cafe. When they're done, the cameras and Ms. Kapule situate themselves opposite the couch, and Mr. Cho takes a seat at one of the tables, beaming at us with pride. Sarang is directed by Ms. Kapule to sit next to me. My heart rate spikes when a blipping red light flashes on each of the cameras.

INT. "Bingsu for Two"/DINING ROOM — CONTINUOUS
The half-lit TEAT! sign flickers above RIVER, SARANG, VANNA, KAI, and DARIO all squished together on the couch. MS. KAP-ULE leans forward in her chair, an eager smile on her face.

MS. KAPULE

It's wonderful to get a chance to sit down with the baristas of Bingsu for Two. It's no secret that you guys have taken the internet by storm. Tell me about what inspired the video that rocketed your cozy, unassuming cafe to internet fame.

DARIO

It's all thanks to River, you should ask him.

RIVER

Well, what started all of this was a video I took
of Sarang training me when I was first hired.
It got . . . uploaded online, and things kind
of took off from there.

MS. KAPULE

You've all done a lot to grow that fame. Plenty of
videos go viral, but not everyone is able to harness
those fifteen minutes of attention and turn it into real
success. How did a couple of baristas become savvy
marketers overnight?

KAI

River's the mastermind behind that. He has a huge
following on social media for his fandom stuff. Videos,
edits, the works. He's a pro at understanding how to
cater to people online.

MS. KAPULE

I'd say so. You guys were an instant hit—how do you
feel about that?

VANNA

Shocked at first, yeah, but it's pretty cool to see how
many people are supporting us.

SARANG

I wasn't a fan of being so exposed online originally,
but it's been good for business.

RIVER

(mumbling)

Oh, *now* you'll admit it.

Sarang shifts in her seat to disguise herself discreetly elbowing River in the rib cage.

MS. KAPULE

Back to your online supporters, you've acquired quite the fan base in a very short span of time. It seems like people *love* the dynamics between you five.

VANNA

Can you blame them? Look at us. We're so lovable.

RIVER

Yeah! A fan base is a good way to put it. People are responding to us the same way a fandom reacts to their favorite creators. We think it's really neat.

MS. KAPULE

Exactly. And just like a fandom, there's been lots of interest in you and the individual relationships between you all. I want to focus on one rumor the internet seems to be especially fixated on. River?

RIVER

Yes?

MS. KAPULE

Did you and Sarang start dating when you began working here, or before?

River stares blankly at Ms. Kapule, a dumb smile still on his face, while the others simultaneously whip their heads to stare at him. He blinks, and makes a choking, gurgling sound that might be a laugh. A flush instantly colors his cheeks.

RIVER

I think there's a—

KAI

They started dating within River's first week here.

River conveys a look that says "I'm going to kill Kai" with a single twitch of his eye. He opens his mouth, only to be interrupted again.

VANNA

Isn't it adorable? Real meet-cute.

KAI

I'd call it love at first sight.

VANNA

I would have to agree.

Sarang squeaks, a mortified look on her face that mirrors River's.

MS. KAPULE

My god, that's precious. Sarang, you're clearly passionate about the work you do here. How'd it feel when your boyfriend helped turn the cafe into a viral sensation?

Sarang and River look at each other. Mixed emotions muddle behind Sarang's eyes. She blinks a few times, mouth parted dumbly. River gives an almost imperceptible shrug, as if to say, This is what you get for springing an interview on us—now fix it.

But then understanding zips across her face, and she sets her jaw in rigid determination.

SARANG

(hesitantly)

I . . . really appreciate it. What River's done for the
cafe. He's a—a great boyfriend in that way.

River looks like he might choke on his own tongue and pass out. Sarang turns to him and doesn't break eye contact when she speaks again.

SARANG

It's taken me a while to embrace, but I'm grateful
for the online supporters and what they've done for
our store. If they're interested in my and River's
relationship, I'm glad.

(pointedly)

Because it means my dad's cafe won't go out of business
if we're entertaining them, *yeah*?

Realization dawns on River slowly at first, then all at once, his face turning ashen. He bites his lip, considering her words. Then he reluctantly reaches for her hand. The camera zooms in on their fingers lacing together in between them.

RIVER

. . . Right.

13. ABUSING MY OLDER SIBLING PRIVILEGE

Ignoring Dad's nagging over breakfast has never been easier when I'm hyperfocused on the mind-dulling news segment of cracks in the city sidewalk playing on the television. I have no idea when the interview from yesterday will air, which means I'm suddenly more interested than ever in revamping Seattle's streets, waiting for what may or may not play next.

"Cece's struggling without a co-manager," Dad says pointedly, shoving a spoonful of cheonggukjang into his mouth.

I mindlessly pick through the banchan, facing the TV. "Why don't you hire somebody?"

"No, a stranger won't care about the family business like you do. Besides, the new location's sales have dipped lately, so we can't afford it. If this keeps up, I don't know how we can start franchising nationally. We need you, River. Why don't you do your tutoring on the weekends instead?"

"Uh, the tutoring center isn't open on weekends."

Umma leans forward in her chair. "Jace, can you turn the volume up on the TV? I can't hear the news."

"Muh-huh," he says around a mouthful of food. Jace reaches

over to my side for the remote and aims it at the television before I can snatch it away. A familiar voice fills the dining room.

"Good morning, Seattle, this is Lani Kapule with KING 5 News. Up next, a wholesome segment on a local family-owned Korean cafe, Bingsu for Two, that has captivated the hearts of coffee drinkers and online fans alike."

"Oh, isn't that near Cafe Gong?" Umma asks, turning around in her chair to face the TV.

My heart drops. "Actually, it's kind of loud, can we turn it off? I have a headache," I say, voice tight.

"Do you want some ibuprofen?" Dad asks.

"No, I think it's just the noise. *Jace*, can I see the remote?"

He turns to me, confused at my strained expression. I can see when the lightbulb flashes above his head. "Oh shit, yeah, here you go."

But when he holds it out, Umma grabs it. She volumes it down but keeps it on.

"Is this better? I want to see this; I'm surprised they're on the news. They're a small business, aren't they, 여보?"[3]

"Yeah, I can't believe we haven't run them out of business yet." Dad leans forward, thoroughly engrossed in the television. Oh my god. There's no way I can just turn it off now.

Ms. Kapule's voice chimes in. "Stay tuned till the end for a special announcement from two of the baristas about their relationship status. But first, an interview with the owner and his daughter."

---

3.   honey

I wheeze. "I'm going to use the toilet."

I practically sprint out of there. The sound of Sarang and her father talking on the television follows me even as I lock myself inside the bathroom. I pull my phone out and call Jace. *Pick up, pick up, I know you have your phone on you, asshole.*

He answers right before I'm sent to voicemail.

"What?" Jace asks.

"Pretend I'm your friend Solomon."

"What are you talking about?"

"Just say 'Hi, Solomon.'"

"Hi, Solomon?"

"I need you to do me a favor right now."

"Another one? What's in it for me?"

I shut my eyes. "Fifty bucks."

"Hit me."

I listen to the interview out in the dining area through Jace's end of the line. Mr. Cho is talking about how he and his late wife immigrated from Korea to Seattle and started their cafe. There's not much time before the next segment.

"Jace, I need you to listen very carefully. You have to stop Umma and Dad from watching the news," I say. "I'm featured in the interview coming up."

I hear shuffling on his end of the line, and through the door I can tell he's moving out of the kitchen and into the hallway next to the living room. "How the hell am I supposed to do that? They're really into it, and Umma's holding the remote," he whispers. "Why would you do an interview?"

"Because I'm an *idiot*. Just don't be suspicious, whatever you do."

"Man, this is hard. Fifty bucks isn't enough. You also have to do my chores for the next two weeks."

"Whatever, fine—"

"All right," Ms. Kapule says. "Now for the next segment, featuring all the employees at Bingsu for Two."

I clutch my phone and mash my mouth against the speaker. "Holy shit, Jace, *do something right now!*"

The funny thing about Jace is that he doesn't perform well under pressure.

He performs, sure. But not well.

Jace goes, "UHH." Then, the sound of rushing air, broken by a *WHACK!* that makes me cringe away from my speaker. I hear something else shatter, maybe glass, and a moment later Dad's voice booming through the apartment, "What the fuck was that! Jace? Jace! Why did you throw your phone at the television? Get back here!"

I thump my forehead against the door, letting out a shuddering sigh of relief. I owe Jace big-time.

14. DEATH BY CONDENSED MILK AND SEX JOKES

I call out of my next three shifts.

I think I'm allowed some leeway here, right? Ignoring the fact that I've only been working at the cafe for a few weeks, I mean. And that we've been slammed since the news segment.

Okay, maybe I feel a *little* bad about calling out.

Kai calls me a coward at school; Haneul calls me five times a day to get my lazy ass to the cafe. Surprisingly, it's radio silent on Sarang's end. She once texted me because I was running two minutes late to my shift, but now? Nothing. Not that I'm complaining. I may or may not be calling out to avoid her, and it looks like she's fine with that.

Calling out four days in a row might be pushing it, though, so despite the little voice inside me telling me to put in my two weeks' notice, I head to the cafe on Thursday after school.

Sarang's working the register when I walk in, and she freezes in the middle of taking a customer's order. Her face fixes with anger in an impressively short span of time—good reflexes. I can already hear what she's going to shout: *How kind of you to show up to your job, you bean pole of a dickhead. Do you see this line? What are you still standing in the doorway for?*

But then she snaps her jaw shut, and her mouth twitches.

Wait. That's a smile.

"Hi, River."

Why does she sound like that?

That's when I notice the other customers. The ones in line and in the dining area are all staring. I touch my mouth, wondering if there's anything on my face, but then I remember. We're supposed to be dating, and they all know it.

I'm glad I'm covering my mouth, because my stomach does a flip that makes me worry my lunch is going to make a surprise appearance from the opposite end it usually does.

Everyone's watching, though, so I swallow any bile and instead clumsily blow a kiss at Sarang.

She shuts her eyes and mutters something under her breath.

Ignoring a small "Aw!" in the corner of the dining room, I scurry into the kitchen, where Haneul is making bingsu while Dario takes pictures for the social media accounts.

"Look who decided to come in for once," Haneul says as she struggles to load frozen milk cubes into the ice-shaving machine. Her following string of complaints is drowned out by the angry clanking of the machine, so I mouth, "Sorry, don't fire me," and flee toward the cubbies. Dario joins me.

"You weren't actually sick, were you?" he asks.

"I *was* sick," I say. Lowering my voice, "Sick of waking up every day."

The kitchen curtains rustle. Sarang enters, her face fixed like stone. She walks up to us and locks eyes with Dario.

"I'm taking my thirty. Cover for me."

"Since you asked so nicely," Dario grumbles. Haneul carries the bingsu as she follows him out. It's just us now.

Sarang sighs, her whole body falling with the exhale. She looks exhausted, going by the plum-tinted shadows under her eyes and the stray pieces of hair falling from her short ponytail. My fingers itch to tuck them behind her ear; a habit from when I was dating Cece. I think she's about to berate me for ditching work, but instead she says, "We have a problem."

"I think we have more than one, Sarang," I say.

"I have *several*, and you account for half of them."

"I'm flattered I take up so much of your thoughts."

She looks up with a shake of her head. "You are awful. Are you only like this with me? Because everyone else seems to think you're a sweetheart, some precious nerd who needs protecting, according to our subscribers."

I open my mouth, then close it. I think I *am* only like this with her. I certainly never had the balls to talk like this with Cece—for better or for worse. "Maybe you bring out the worst in me."

"No, I think I bring out the *real* you."

"Do I bring out the real you? No one can *pretend* to be so unbearable."

"You don't know anything about me," Sarang snaps.

I blink, taken aback by the cutting edge of her words. She's right. I don't know anything about her. We're still practically strangers.

Running a hand through my hair, I swallow back my reply. I don't want to make a habit of being mean to Sarang or anybody else. I hate how easy it is to speak without a filter around her. "What's the problem?" I ask.

Sarang ducks her head, and when she lifts it, the lines of anger on her face have smoothed out. "People don't believe we're together."

"Thank God."

"Thank *God*? If they find out we lied, they'll hate us. They could boycott the store."

"The term's *'cancel.'* They could cancel the store."

"Thanks, dweeb, I'll make sure to remember that."

"I know we're in trouble if they find out we're lying. But what are we supposed to do about it?"

Sarang makes a screwed-up face that's reminiscent of twisting up a T-shirt to tie-dye it. "Convince them."

My stomach flops. "Uh. How?"

Her cheeks light up in a blush.

One creeps up on my face too. "I'm not making out with you on camera or anything."

"*What?* What are you talking about?"

"Is that not what you . . ." Of course that's not what she meant. I forgot I'm the only cultured person in this room. "In fan fiction, when a couple is fake-dating, it's a common trope for them to practice kissing so that their chemistry is more believable. I thought you—"

"*No*, Jesus, River! I don't want to kiss you! *God*."

"Then what do you suggest?"

She fidgets again. "I was thinking we record a video of us, I don't know, making bingsu, or something."

"Oh." I straighten. "Sure. That's fine. Could be fun. Why were you making it seem like a big deal?"

"It *is* a big deal!" She shakes her head, rubbing her temples. "Whatever. Okay. We'll film a tutorial of how we make bingsu, and convince everybody we're soulmates."

We stare at each other.

"Wait, now?" I say.

"No," she deadpans. "Let's just wait until they've *already* figured out we're faking it."

We scrabble together the ingredients and prepare our set. The kitchen resembles one in a home more than the industrial kind you'd expect to see in a restaurant. It takes up one corner of the back room, and consists of a meager stove, an oven, fridge, and a large island countertop. I prop my phone up against a bag of flour, but before turning it on, I turn to Sarang.

"What should we do?" I ask. "Like, how far do we need to take this thing to be convincing?"

She shrugs. "How the hell should I know?"

I blink. "Haven't you been in a relationship before?"

Her eyes narrow in a glare. "What's it to you?"

"Nothing. I mean, it's not a bad thing at all. Uh. A lot of people are into that. *Fuck*, wait, not me. I mean, it's not that I'm not *not* into that. Hold on, I'm making this worse. It makes no difference to me, is what I'm trying to say. I don't care about that stuff. I'm not one of those people who like it better when—holy shit. Okay. Uh."

Sarang's eye twitches violently.

"Forget all that," I say, waving my hands. "It doesn't matter that you've never been in a relationship. It just surprises me."

"Why?" she asks suspiciously, like I might say something creepy again.

"Because you're pretty," I blurt.

I only realize how that sounds once it's out of my mouth. Sarang's eyebrows shoot up, disappearing behind her bangs. All the blood in my body rushes to my face, and I'm sure I'll explode with embarrassment. "Objectively, I mean. Maybe the pastel goth thing isn't for everyone, but you've got a neat face and—Jesus Christ."

"You think I'm pretty?"

"I said objectively."

"Wow. How embarrassing for you."

I groan, turning toward the phone. "Your personality cancels out any good looks. Are you ready?"

She doesn't answer right away, so I glance back at her. Sarang is worrying her teeth into her bottom lip. Abruptly, she holds out her pinkie in front of her.

"Before we start this, promise me one thing: we'll lie to everyone else, but not to each other."

My eyes flicker between her outstretched finger and the serious expression on her face. "Like a truth pact?"

She nods. "I *hate* lying, but I know we don't have a choice here. Being truthful to each other is the only way we'll pull this whole scheme off. Honesty is always the best policy. Promise me you won't lie to me, and I'll do the same."

I'm not sure I get it. What would we have to lie about? But Sarang shakes her hand in the air, urging me on, so I reach out and wrap my pinkie around her much smaller one.

"All right, I promise."

"Good. Now let's get this over with. I'm not sure how long I can act like I'm in love with you for the camera."

"I don't even know if I can pretend to find you attractive."

She smirks at me. "You don't have to pretend, you *did* just admit you find me pretty," she says, and presses the record button on my phone as my cheeks light up with a blush.

INT. "Bingsu for Two"/KITCHEN — CONTINUOUS

SARANG and RIVER stand in front of the island counter, an arrangement of bowls and toppings spread across it. The table takes up around 60 percent of the screen, with the rest of the kitchen behind them. River's face is a particularly alarming shade of red.

SARANG

Hello. River and I are going to show you how we make our best-selling item on the menu: patbingsu. River, want to tell them what bingsu is?

RIVER

Um. Yeah. Patbingsu is, like, a shaved ice dessert. From Korea. Kind of like a snow cone? But with a creamier base. It has . . . what does it have . . . red beans, fruit, rice cakes, sweetened condensed milk—why are you looking at me like that? Stop it.

SARANG

(smugly)

You seem flustered. Something distracting you?

River shuts his eyes and composes himself. After a second, his demeanor changes: back straightening, shoulders erect, and a mischievous glint gleaming in his eyes. He takes a step closer to Sarang, their bodies nearly touching, and smiles down at her as he cups her face and runs a thumb across her cheek.

RIVER

Sorry, it's hard to focus with you right next to me.

SARANG

I—that—what—

River grins, and Sarang nervously tucks her hair behind her ears a few times.

SARANG

Let's just start.

River disguises his snort as a cough, but she shoots him a glare anyway. Sarang turns around and opens a cupboard full of dishes. The large glass bowls for bingsu are at the top, out of her reach, and she looks around for the footstool that has conveniently been nowhere to be found ever since River got hired.

RIVER

Do you need help with that?

SARANG

Yes, please . . .

(pause)

Love.

Something catches in River's throat, like he's not used to being called affectionate names and isn't sure how to feel about it now. He comes up beside her and grabs a bowl from the top shelf, handing it to her.

SARANG

Wow, you're so tall.

RIVER

Thanks.

SARANG

What? No short joke?

RIVER

Nah, it'd be low-hanging fruit. Maybe you'd be able to reach it then, though.

Without a muscle twitching on her face, Sarang kicks his shin and turns back toward the camera.

SARANG

To start making the bingsu, you first add a layer of sweet red beans to the bottom of the cup.

She dips a spoon into one of the bowls of toppings to the side, adding an even layer. River steps up behind her and holds her hand over the spoon. She twists up, glaring at his smirk. He guides her into adding another drop.

RIVER

A little more wouldn't hurt.

SARANG

You have too much of a sweet tooth.

RIVER

Maybe that's why I can't get enough of you.

River chuckles to himself, looking proud of the fact that he's gotten a lot funnier since Sarang's pride became the butt end of the joke. She doesn't look as amused.

SARANG

Aw, so cute. I almost threw up.

RIVER

(suggestively)

Need something to clear the taste in your mouth?

SARANG

(perking up for the camera)

Yes, like some of our locally sourced fruit, which is the next ingredient.

RIVER

Corny.

As Sarang scoops strawberries and kiwis over the red beans, then the ice, River watches with his arms crossed over his chest, looking at her hands. Clearly zoning out, he startles when she suddenly turns to him.

SARANG

Did you hear me, love?

RIVER

Huh?

SARANG

I asked if you wanted to add the last ingredient, the condensed milk.

She scoots out of the way, letting River sidle up to the bowl. He picks the can up and carefully pours it over the ice.

RIVER

All right, you drizzle the condensed milk next, like this.

SARANG

I love it when you add a little thick, sticky cream on top.

He drops the can into the bingsu.

Chunks of ice and red beans explode into the air. River's shirt gets a coating of kiwi, while a strawberry hits Sarang in the face. The force of the impact makes the table shudder, and the phone falls over, angled toward the ceiling.

SARANG (O.S.)

River! What is wrong with you! Ow, there's condensed milk in my eye!

RIVER (O.S.)

Me?! What's wrong with *you*? Why would you say that?

SARANG

Say what?

RIVER (O.S.)

Oh my god. Never mind. Fuck. Forget it. Uh . . .

Hands dart across the screen, and the camera shakes as River grabs the phone and films his frantic, red face.

RIVER

Video over. That was patbingsu. Sort of. Thank you, bye.

As soon as I cut the video, Sarang cracks. She doubles over, holding her stomach and clutching onto the counter as bright peals of laughter ring in the kitchenette.

"Your *face*! Holy crap! That was priceless!" she manages between fits.

I can only gawk at her. A blob of ice falls from my bangs and onto the floor. "Wait. So you—"

"What, you think because I haven't been in a relationship I don't know what sex is?"

If possible, I blush hotter than before.

Sarang only laughs again.

"You're an asshole," I mutter, grateful that I already blocked our account from Umma, Dad, and Cece's phones. This would be a particularly embarrassing video for them to find. I grab a handful of paper towels to scoop the puddle of bingsu off the counter. Sarang procures a dish towel and helps through her giggling.

"That's what you get. You started it, trying to trip me up with those stupid attempts at flirting."

Feeling another petty urge to embarrass her instead of myself, I lay my hand on top of hers. With only the corner of the table between us, I lean down until my lips brush the shell of her ear and lower my voice into a rough whisper. "Did it work?"

She flings the wet towel in my face.

"So it did!" I yell under the dirty rag. When I remove it, she's stomping out of the kitchen.

"Just clean this up!" she shouts on her way.

I laugh so hard I practically forget that I hated this situation in the first place. I'm still not happy about having to lie to everyone, but I'm beginning to see there may be a silver lining to this whole fake dating thing. Like making Sarang miserable.

The memory of how she whispered "Love" makes my laughter die down. Cecelia and I never used pet names—she thought they were cringey—and hearing Sarang call me that . . . I don't know how to feel about it.

Maybe two can play at this game, but I'll have to play it better.

15. THE TASTE OF LIPSTICK IS BITTERSWEET

"Even I'm starting to ship you two."

I push Kai out of my face, and he plops back in his spot on the other side of the lunch table. Around us, the school cafeteria bustles with conversation, laughter, and the clanking of utensils. I take an angry bite out of my apple.

"Gross. Don't say that, I'm trying to eat," I reply.

Kai snorts. "Seriously, though. All our followers *loved* that bingsu video you and Sarang made. To be honest, I didn't think you guys could pull it off. I figured you'd end up murdering each other and Vanna and I'd have to destroy the evidence."

Saying people loved our video might be an understatement. It's safe to conclude that no one's doubting that Sarang and I are dating anymore—the LoveLee ship has officially set sail. A hint of embarrassment tries to burrow between my ribs, but I swat it away. I'm glad she doesn't go to the same school, so we don't have to keep up the act outside the cafe.

"It was just for show," I say.

"A really great show." Kai crosses his arms and leans toward me. "Almost *too* good."

"Seriously? You're going there?"

"I'm just saying, man. You guys have chemistry."

"Chemistry isn't always good. Chemistry kills people. Didn't you watch *Breaking Bad*?"

Kai starts to say something, but then trails off, eyes caught on something behind me. The smile drops from his face.

"So," says a familiar honeyed voice. My stomach sinks. "Not only did you get a new job, but a new girlfriend, too?"

I whip around. Cecelia's standing there with her arms crossed over her chest. She's smiling. No—her lip wobbles. It's a twisted grimace. My heart is a cold, dark lump of coal in my chest at the sight. Before I can speak, she beats me to it.

"Do your parents know about her? Or did you lie to them about *that*, too?"

Cotton dries my mouth. "How do you—"

"Somebody sent it to me."

She slips her phone from her pocket and shows me. It's Bingsu for Two's YouTube account: 312K subscribers, and our most recent upload: "Barista BF + GF Flirt for 17 Minutes (and Show You How to Make Bingsu)"

I think it's an appropriate time to declare myself officially fucked.

Cecelia is halfway across the cafeteria before I can blink.

"Wait, Cecelia! Hold on a second!"

Ignoring everybody's stares, I spring from my seat and chase after her, running between the lunch tables and jumping over stray backpacks. She ducks out of the room and into the hallway.

It's deserted out here since everyone is either in the cafeteria or in class. In the quiet emptiness of the hall, she finally turns around.

I'm terrified that she'll cry. But it's worse. She's angry. The shock of seeing that expression on her steals my breath.

"You were telling the truth," she mutters. "You said you dumped me because you were in love with someone else. I can't believe it. You're a fucking cheater after all."

My throat closes as the situation dawns on me. "I never cheated on you, Cecelia. I swear."

"You expect me to believe anything that comes out of your mouth?"

"Cece, listen to me," I start, hesitant. I've never seen her this way. Upset, sure, but not like this. It unsettles a part of me, the part that thought I understood her. "It wasn't because of Sarang. I didn't even know her before I started working there."

"*Liar!*" she yells. A tear drops from her eye, then another, and soon it's a river cascading down her cheeks. "You did know her before. She came into Cafe Gong the day after you dumped me. The others told me what happened. They said you and some girl with green hair got into a fight."

My jaw drops. I forgot. Of course I should've known that Jorge and Rosalind would happily fill her in. Now it looks like I *am* a liar.

"I'm telling the truth! I mean, yes, that happened. We met once before, I forgot. But I didn't leave you because of her. Holy shit, wait, let me backtrack. I lied. Okay? You were right. I lied about being in love with someone else when I dumped you. I thought it'd be easier for us both if you hated me. Then we could move on."

A realization strikes me then, lagging from the shock of our fight. Strangely enough, its harbinger is what Sarang said to me the other day.

Honesty is always the best policy.

I step forward and hold Cecelia's shoulders, locking eyes with her. "Cece, I'm not really *dating* Sarang. None of the stuff online is real; we're acting. It's for views."

She shakes her head, mouth twitching with contained rage. "You think I'm an idiot."

I realize with bitter finality: nothing I say will make Cecelia believe me. I lied, plain and simple. I set myself up for this.

Desperately, I grab her hands. "Please don't tell my parents that I work there now. It would break their hearts to find out I left the store to go work for a different family's cafe. It'd kill them. I already disappoint them enough, I—maybe it's selfish, but I can't handle letting them down even more. Please, Cece. Think about how they'd feel."

"What about how *I* feel?" she snaps. "You broke *my* heart, too. I also put stake into that store, doesn't that matter? What about all the work I did to prepare Cafe Gong for success? The late nights, the extra shifts, dozens of hours' worth of management training I went through. Or what about how *you* scoped out the location, marked Bingsu for Two as a nobody on the map, and made the final call to wipe them off it? We both expected them to be bankrupt by now, but because of *you*, they have all our customers. Have you thought about that?"

My lips part in a silent defense. I don't know what to say. Because she's right.

Her red-tinged eyes flicker to our clasped hands. Several leaden seconds pass as she recenters herself and her breathing. I squeeze her fingers, and she looks at me.

"I won't tell them," she finally says. "On one condition." Her face, usually so soft, shining with warmth and affection, is now hard like a marble bust. "Come back to Cafe Gong."

Her words run into some sort of barrier within my mind. I chew on each syllable, repeat them in my head to see if I can make sense of them, absorb their meaning. But I can't.

Cecelia continues. "I want you to do for our cafe what you did for Bingsu for Two. Use social media to boost our store. It's the greatest success story: with your marketing skills and my business knowledge, we saved your family's independent coffee shop from a rocky start and turned it into its most successful location all on our own. It'll be perfect for my college applications, and you'll get to prove yourself to your parents."

I wring my hands, wincing. "That's not how it works, Cece. You can't just replicate going viral. There's no guarantee the algorithm would pick Cafe Gong up the same way it did for—"

"It's worth a shot. I need this, River, and so do you. Do you think your parents will ever give you another opportunity like this if you don't show them you're capable of handling the responsibilities it comes with? What are you going to do in the future without Cafe Gong?"

She steps closer—so close—and tilts her head up. Her breath ghosts against my lips. "Everything can go back to the way it was," Cecelia promises. "All of it."

Back to the way it was.

I was happy, wasn't I? Well, I was content. Was I selfish for not being satisfied? What if leaving it all behind really was a mistake? She's right; in ten years, Cafe Gong may be my only future.

Why don't I know what I want?

Don't you, though? a small voice in my mind pipes up. It almost sounds like Sarang. *You don't want* this. *You left for a reason, trust yourself.*

I've never had a good reason to trust myself before.

Cecelia inhales, stealing my breath, and then seals her lipstick-coated lips to mine. She presses against me. My back hits the lockers with a muffled *clang*. Or maybe that's the sound of my heart beating in my skull. Like bells. Alarms. A sheet of cold air falls over me, dressing me in grief. I'm in mourning. What am I mourning? I'm not giving anything up, I'm taking it back, right? I'm getting my life back. My future. My heart.

Cecelia pulls away. My lips tingle. It's my chance to say something. To put my foot down and say I'm not coming back.

I can't. Because she's right.

"Okay," I whisper. "I'll go back tomorrow."

The bell rings.

All at once, the world breaks into movement. The classroom doors swing open, and a flood of students fills up the hallway, splintering us from our private moment.

I look at Cecelia. She smiles like she's asking me to return it.

Instead, I let myself get swept away by the current of people squeezing into the space between us.

16. THE FIRST TIME ANYONE'S EVER WILLINGLY GONE TO THEIR JOB ON THEIR DAY OFF

It doesn't cross my mind to return to the cafeteria and grab my backpack, or to show up to my next class. The only thought running through my head is to get out of this place, with its suffocating crowds and cramped walls and Cecelia. I walk out of the school, down the street, into the city. I don't know where I'm going until I'm there. Bingsu for Two's half-lit sign shines down on me like a beacon. Haneul is drawing on a tablet behind the register when I enter.

"I'll be right with you," she drawls without looking up.

I walk up to her at the counter. "I forgot my uniform."

Haneul does a double take. She stands up straight, eyes widening.

"River? What are you doing here?" She glances at the clock on the wall. "Aren't you supposed to be in school?"

"Can I borrow an apron?" I say, voice dry and quiet.

Haneul studies me, concern growing apparent on her face. "What happened?" she asks.

"I forgot my uniform," I repeat.

"I got that. That's not what I'm talking about. Are you okay?"

I nod silently.

She gives me a once-over, gaze catching on my mouth before rising. The worry doesn't disappear.

"I don't usually condone skipping."

"Not usually?"

"No." Haneul chews on her lip, then points at the back room. In a gentle tone: "There are extra aprons in the storage closet."

The tension in my muscles ease. I nod, grateful, and turn to head to the back, but Haneul stops me. She hands me a napkin.

"You might want to wash up first," she says, eyes flickering to my chin.

Confused, I wipe my mouth. Red smears across the white fabric. Lipstick. My heart stills.

I take my time in the bathroom. Splashing cold water on my face helps cool me down, but it doesn't do anything to ease the bright ache between my eyes or the churning in my gut. When I leave the bathroom, I feel more like a real person. Grounded. The dingy back of the cafe is such a sobering sight it makes me wonder if anything that happened outside of this room was real.

On the table, a folded apron sits beside a steaming bungeoppang and a sweet potato latte.

My eyes sting.

I walk out and falter at the sight of Mr. Cho sitting at the counter. Haneul is on the other side, showing him something on her tablet. They both look up. Mr. Cho smiles and gestures for me to join.

I'm wary he's going to try to "dad" me into talking about my feelings or ask what's wrong, but he doesn't; he just tilts Haneul's tablet toward me so I can see. My jaw falls.

"You drew this?"

She grumbles in reply. On the screen is a looping, animated drawing of the cafe in a dreamy cartoon style, like it's straight from a Studio Ghibli film. Sun rays glitter across the scene, softening the wood of the tables and floor. Steam rises in creamy clouds from several coffee cups. The fairy lights lining the walls twinkle like falling stars. Then I notice the faces of the people inside: it's us. Kai's animated smile as he sweeps the floor, Dario glancing over at him as he wipes down a table, Vanna winking from her spot on the sofa, and Sarang and I behind the bar. Her tongue sticks out as she pours a cascading stream of milk into a cup, and my eyes flit from her to the espresso I'm tamping. The warmth emanating from the drawing seeps into me, ebbing out the coldness lingering in my chest.

"This is incredible, Haneul. I knew you were good, but this is the *best* thing I've ever seen."

Her cheeks turn pink. She blushes like Sarang. "Thanks. I'm trying to build out my portfolio. I'm submitting it to a few animation studios for the hell of it."

Mr. Cho pats my shoulder. "The video you put together styling the cafe was a big boost for Haneul. She's received lots of interest from companies after they saw her paint that mural."

"It wasn't just me who made that video, it was all of us. And any interest Haneul is getting is because of her own talent. It seems like it's long overdue."

Haneul tinkers with her tablet pen instead of meeting my eyes when she says, "Still, I wouldn't have these opportunities if you hadn't started our social media accounts."

Mr. Cho's smile deepens. "Same with KING 5 coming to interview us. A few weeks ago, no one knew of our cafe, let alone the biggest news station in Seattle. It's because of you and your idea to promote us online that they do now. Not everyone has the passion *and* skills to accomplish what you have in such a short amount of time, River. Thank you."

I swallow, blinking hard. Haneul and Mr. Cho exchange a quick, knowing smile. No adults have ever considered what I do a skill set before.

But then Cece comes to mind and the tendril of warmth inside me is quickly extinguished. Pretty soon, I won't be able to do this for Bingsu for Two anymore. Not if I don't want my parents finding out about my working here.

Afterward, Mr. Cho heads upstairs and Haneul and I work in companionable silence for the next couple hours. It's not awkward, which is nice. She shoots me occasional glances over the espresso machine, but she must be able to tell I don't want to talk, so she doesn't push it.

When I next check the clock, it's two-thirty. School is out. This time tomorrow, I'll be back at Cafe Gong. The shot glass I'm holding in my hands feels so much heavier than it did a moment ago.

The door jingles.

Kai and Sarang are the only ones who are supposed to come in—I checked the schedule earlier. But Dario and Vanna are right behind them, all four crowding through the doorway. I turn to Haneul, confused.

"Did you overschedule us?"

She looks at me out of her periphery, then away. "Thought you might benefit from some company." She pats me on the back as she passes.

"Thanks for coming in, you two," Haneul addresses Vanna and Dario.

"I'm not going to complain about hours." Vanna rubs her thumb against her fingers, dollar signs practically flashing in her eyes.

"It's not that busy. Why'd you call us in?" Dario asks.

"It *is* busy," Haneul deadpans, gesturing to the dining area, not even at full capacity.

Kai squeezes past them and tosses me my backpack, his skateboard under one arm.

"Thank you," I say.

He glances around to make sure no one's paying attention. "What happened with Cecelia?" he whispers.

Inexplicably, a single sound comes to me. The metallic clanging of the lockers echoing down the empty hallway as she pressed me against them. Then a sight: tears spilling from her eyes. Her fist quivering at her side as she gave me her ultimatum. Finally, a taste: her lips on mine, her tongue in my mouth.

"River." The distress in Kai's voice snaps me from my memory. "What is it?"

I can't tell him.

I can't tell him any of it. Not that we kissed. Not that I have to return to Cafe Gong—that I might even end up back together with the ex-girlfriend who's blackmailing me. Because that's what going back means, right? I'm not sure why I can't tell him, but something stops me, a physical blockage in my throat. It sits hot and heavy on my tongue, and I'm afraid that if I speak past it, I'll vomit. They'll all look at me differently. They'll think I'm stupid. Weak. An idiot who can't stand up for himself.

They'll realize what I've always known.

Heat prickles at the back of my neck, coming up over my scalp like a cloak. I duck my head and hold my breath so I won't do something stupid. Fuck. I *am* stupid. I am weak. Cecelia was right about that. She's always been right.

A hand squeezes my shoulder hard enough to shake me out of it. "You're going to be fine," Kai says with the kind of unwavering confidence I've only ever known him to have.

"I'll take your word for it," I reply, managing to smile. He returns it despite the worried crease in his forehead.

To the others he says, "Hey, me and River are going to head out. Is that cool?"

"What?" Sarang says. "You just got here, you lazy shit."

Kai pats his stomach. "Ooh, ouch, stomach problems. I gotta go home. River's house, actually." He turns to me then. "The only thing that can cure me is a night full of pizza, energy drinks, binge-watching the *Son of Sin* movies, then passing out around three in the morning. Right?"

I'm not sure what I did to deserve a friend like Kai. Maybe nothing, and I'll have to pay for it with a bunch of bad karma to balance things out. Whatever. It'll be worth it.

Nevertheless . . . "That sounds nice," I say, "but I don't want to leave my shift early."

"Why not?"

Lifting a shoulder, I say as nonchalantly as possible, "No reason."

No reason except after I get off, I'll probably never be able to show my face here again. This is my last day at Bingsu for Two.

Kai narrows his eyes, scanning me up and down like he can crack through the wall I've erected around myself. After a moment, a grin bursts onto his face.

"I just got the best idea ever," he declares, wheeling around. "Sleepover. Tonight. All of us, here in the cafe."

Dario raises an eyebrow. "Isn't today your weekly call with your grandma, though?"

"Why do you still remember that? It is, but I can call her from here."

"That might be kind of fun, actually."

All five of them turn the full force of their incredulous stares on me, but I don't flinch. "We could make a video out of it," I continue, getting hopeful. "It'd be a hit. We'll answer some subscriber questions, play a few games, and show off the place." Something warm hesitantly buds in the spot over my heart. "One last video for the cafe."

Sarang crosses her arms, narrowing her eyes at me. "What do you mean one last video?"

"I—I meant a video to top the last one."

Dario purses his lips. "I'm not sure, I was planning on hitting the gym later."

"Yeah. Not really my thing, plus I was going to pick up a second shift at my other job tonight," Vanna says.

Kai presses against the counter, leaning closer to the two. "Come on, guys. Please? Dario?"

To my surprise, Dario folds like a deck of cards.

"God, fine. Get those bug eyes out of my face."

"These are *puppy dog* eyes."

Vanna's still unmoved until Haneul, leaning against the kitchen doorway, pipes up with, "You'll get paid."

"Say less."

Sarang twists her head back and forth, looking between me, the others, and Haneul. "What? Unnie, seriously?"

"It'd make for a good YouTube video."

"Since when do you care about our YouTube?"

She glances over, briefly meeting my gaze. Then she ducks behind the curtains. Out of sight, she calls back, "You're joining in on the sleepover too, Sarang, whether you like it or not. Don't be antisocial."

"But *why*?" she moans.

I grin, but when Sarang turns to look at me, she shakes her head, mumbling something to herself.

She won't have to stress over me for long. I'll be out of her hair soon.

But tonight, I'm going to make sure we create a video that blows up. My last-ever contribution to the cafe, and to her. Whatever happens to our social media presence when I leave is in their hands.

I'm also going to make sure I give Sarang *hell* tonight. For old times' sake.

This will be fun.

17. THERE'S ONLY ONE BED . . . JUST KIDDING. THERE ARE ACTUALLY NO BEDS. WE'LL PROBABLY SLEEP ON THE FLOOR.

Kai, Dario, and Vanna head out to pick up food, and Sarang locks the door behind them, flipping the Closed sign outward. I send a quick text to Umma and Dad letting them know I'm spending the night at Kai's, then put my phone away to find Sarang scrutinizing me.

"Why are you looking at me like that?" I ask.

Sarang breaks from her stupor. "I'm not looking at you," she hurries to say, then brushes past me. "I'll close down the bar, you do the dining room."

We close the cafe in silence. If Sarang and I are working together, it's usually accompanied by bickering. Never silence. The quiet looms over my shoulders as I wipe down the tables. I don't think I did anything to piss her off enough to warrant the silent treatment. It's so unnerving it grates at me, until finally, when I stack the last of the chairs onto the tables and look over to catch her watching me, I snap.

"What?" I say, harsher than I mean to. "Why are you being so quiet? What's the matter?"

I cross the room to stand opposite her at the counter. She busies herself with rearranging the sugar packets so she doesn't have to meet my eye.

"I thought you *wanted* me to shut up," she says.

"See? Like that. How come you're not getting snappy and saying something like 'Why would I want to talk to a dumbfuck dork like you'?"

"That's true. Why would I?"

I push the sugar packets out of the way. "Tell me what your problem is."

That does it. "No, you tell me what's *your* problem." Sarang pokes me in the chest. I glance down at her small finger, then at her in bewilderment.

"I don't have one. If you have something to say, then spit it out."

"I saw you earlier," she says with a glare, but her voice is mild. Almost gentle. "You and Kai. You looked like you were about to cry."

My throat squeezes around my breath.

It takes considerable effort to laugh it off. "You worried about me, love?"

Sarang purses her lips, unimpressed. "You flirt to get out of uncomfortable situations."

No, I don't. Do I? We're not really flirting, anyway. "Tell me how I *really* feel, Doctor."

"And earlier, you said 'one last video.'"

"I meant a video to beat our last one."

She sighs. "We made a promise, remember? Our truth pact. We'd lie to everyone else but not to each other. I hate people who aren't honest."

She'd hate people who can't even stand up for themselves to their exes even more, then. I don't have it in me to deal with Sarang's goading tonight. I already know I don't have a backbone.

"You don't have to like me," I snap. "We're only pretending to tolerate each other, remember?"

"Unbelievable."

Sarang turns her back on me to wipe down the fridge, even though I already saw her clean it. I grab the broom and sweep the floors with more force than necessary. For an uncomfortably long time, the only sound in the room is the angry scratching of the straw bristles against the floors.

A knock against the glass doors breaks the silence. I let the others in. They're carrying backpacks and take-out bags. Dario and Kai immediately head to the back room to set up, while Vanna comes to my side.

"There's more tension in here than at a Mormon prom," she murmurs, glancing over at Sarang scowling at the stack of dishes she's carrying into the kitchen. "Did you two kiss?"

"Yeah, we were going real hot and heavy over the handoff counter." I roll my eyes. "She was being nosy. It got on my nerves."

Vanna hums. "I'm not surprised she picked up on you acting off earlier."

I stiffen, shocked that Vanna noticed. She smiles and pats my shoulder.

"Don't worry. I'm nowhere near as kind as Sarang and twice as bad with words as she is, so I won't try and pry anything out of you."

"Thanks," I croak, then clear my throat.

"If you ever want someone to sit in moody silence with, though, I'm your gal."

"I'll keep you in mind."

Vanna heads toward the breakroom and I trail after her, still trying to process the possibility that Sarang might have been trying to act nice earlier. But that doesn't make sense. She was so rude about it . . .

Or was I rude first? I did snap at her, and she hadn't even said anything yet. Oh no. Am I the bad guy here?

Crap. I think so.

Dario and Kai are rearranging the furniture, pushing the tables and chairs out of the way and laying several thick blankets on the ground next to the sofa, which Vanna has claimed a spot on as she records them setting up. In the kitchen, Sarang leans against the island counter, watching them with pursed lips like she's trying to keep herself from saying something. Probably about the way they're putting down the blankets; I bet she has her own particular and unnecessary way of doing that, too. *No, damn it, River, stop thinking asshole thoughts.* She drags the combativeness out of me, but this isn't who I am. Or maybe it is, in which case that should really change. It's my last day here after all. I should spend it mending my relationships, not making them worse.

I lean against the island beside her, crossing my arms. Sarang pointedly doesn't look my way. I nudge her shoe with mine. She snaps her head around to glare at me, but I smile.

"I'm sorry," I say. Her eyebrows fly up. "I shouldn't have been so rude earlier. I was on edge, and I took it out on you."

Sarang steps back and wags her finger at me. "See? *That*. What's that? What's up with you?"

I stamp down the instinctive flare of agitation, and now that I'm listening for it, I hear a trace of genuine curiosity in her voice. Concern. And there's no heat behind her glare; it looks more like she's studying me.

Fuck. Our truth pact. I *did* make her a promise.

I duck my head, trying to collect myself. Sarang waits in silence.

"I . . . ran into my ex today," I confess.

Sarang looks surprised that I told her. "What happened?"

At first, I don't reply, and she continues. "I'm not asking for any details. I don't care what you get up to with your ex. I just thought it was weird since you were acting all emo today."

"Thanks for your concern," I say, low enough so only she can hear. "But it's fine. Or it will be."

"Who says I'm concerned?" she asks. "Stick your head in the oven for all I care."

"If this is how you treat your fake boyfriends, I can't imagine what you'd be like in a real relationship."

She pushes off the counter with a flat smile, eyes crinkling. "You're not a fake boyfriend worth impressing." Sarang walks over to fix the blanket setup the other three have managed.

I roll my eyes. She's so emotionally constipated. Somebody's got to get her some laxatives. Though the mention of our fake relationship makes me think about where we are now versus a few weeks ago, when she poured a cup of coffee over my head, and I dumped espresso beans down her shirt. Working together was miserable at first, but the comedy of it all has turned me numb—or maybe the

horror has. This whole thing reads like a bad fanfic on Archive of
Our Own.

 Frappes and Fake Love

Real Person Fiction

No Archive Warnings Apply, River Langston-Lee/Sarang Cho, River Langston-Lee,
Sarang Cho, Alternate Universe - Coffee Shops & Cafés, YouTuber AU, Fake/Pre-
tend Relationship, Fluff and Angst, Hurt/Comfort, Enemies to Lovers, Slow Burn,
Sarang Cho is Bad at Feelings, River Langston-Lee Deserves a Break, no beta we
die like men

When rumor spreads that social media stars Sarang and River from the uber-
popular Bingsu For Two channel are dating, the enemy baristas must push past
their differences and pretend to be in love for the camera, or risk their internet
fame and the cafe. But is it really all just an act?

—AKA, the one where River and Sarang smooch for the camera, smooch a bit off
camera, and make a lot of coffee.

Language: English   Words: 39,767   Chapters: 17/34

Except this isn't really an 80K slow burn enemies-to-lovers fic.
It's just me—a douchebag—and her—also a douchebag—and our
stupid skit that ends after tonight.

The others have situated themselves on the blankets around a
short, wooden foldout table, so I join them. Sarang opens the take-out
bags, pulling out containers of tteokbokki and Korean fried chicken.
Vanna records the food for our video, then turns her phone off.

"Let's dig in," she says, rubbing her hands together.

"I want to take a picture first," Dario says.

"You and your pics, Jesus. Just let me eat."

"Stop it, Kai, get your spoon out of the shot."

Sitting on the ground between my friends with a steaming
bowl of food in front of me jostles something lost back into place,

replacing the uneasy prickling that had been stuck between my ribs with a soft, homely feeling. I smile dumbly at my chopsticks, hoping nobody notices.

Sarang's elbow knocks against mine as we eat. The silky, spicy aroma of tteokbokki perfumes the air, punctuated by slurping sounds and Kai's rambunctious laughter. Under the table, Dario has some sports game playing on low volume on his phone. The conversation is all over the place: from our latest video to an inside joke of theirs from before my time that takes *way* too long to explain, to Sarang's very peculiar way of using chopsticks. Eventually, my plate empties and my cheeks hurt from laughing.

Kai lets out a huge yawn and reclines onto the floor, splayed out like a snow angel. Sarang kicks his leg. "Don't fall asleep, it's not midnight yet."

"I can't fight the food coma."

Dario stands. "I can make us all some coffee. Get up, Kai. Come help me."

"Pick me up then," Kai retorts, not moving an inch.

"No. You're heavy."

"Sounds like you're weak."

"You want to see weak?"

Dario picks Kai off the ground and tosses him over his shoulder in one smooth motion without straining. I half wonder if maybe we should step in, but then Kai bursts into giggles, banging his fists halfheartedly against Dario's muscled back as he's carried away. I catch a glimpse of Dario's smile before they disappear behind the curtains.

Sarang rolls her eyes fondly at them. "How adorable. They disgust me."

"Same," says Vanna. "I hope they drop dead."

A buzzing disturbs the air. Vanna pulls her phone out of her pocket with lightning quick speed. Something gentle dances through her eyes, and without a word to either of us, she answers the phone and stands, heading for the dining area.

"Hi. What are you doing up so late?"

When Vanna's gone, I whisper to Sarang, "Who is that?"

"I bet that's her younger sister."

"Oh, that's right. I forgot she has one. She hardly brings her up."

"Vanna's super hush-hush about her life. Only reason I know anything about her family is because—"

She cuts herself off, biting her lip.

"Because?" I encourage.

Sarang shifts uncomfortably. "It's not my business to tell. My dad found out about her situation through . . . not so great circumstances. So he hired her immediately."

"It can't be worse than how Haneul hired me," I joke.

She drops her eyes to the dirty dishes. "Vanna was digging through our trash bins looking for scraps for her and her sister's dinner."

I'm just the World's Most Insensitive Bastard, aren't I? "Oh."

Apparently also the World's Most Ineloquent Bastard.

I glance at the kitchen curtains, but Kai and Dario's chatter and the sound of steaming milk drown out Vanna's conversation. Without looking away, I murmur, "So her sister . . ."

"Vanna takes care of her," Sarang finishes. "Wants to, at least. I heard they're both temporarily living with a cousin at the moment, or something. Vanna's saving up for a place so she can gain custody of her."

"I . . . wow. I didn't expect that from her."

"Did you think she's just lazy?"

My cheeks heat at the accusation. "Of course not. But the way she acts made me think she didn't really, well, care about this place, or *anything*."

I expect Sarang to call me a judgmental prick, but she shrugs in agreement. "I'm sure working three jobs would drain anyone of their energy. But I used to think like you too, until I found out what she *really* cares about. Her sister will always be her number one priority."

I can't imagine being in her shoes, how it would feel to take sole responsibility for Jace. I just hum in reply, partly because I don't know what else to say, but mostly because I'm hesitant to damage the fragile air between us. It sits suspended on a string that could snap at any second, catapulting us back into our usual brick-wall tension.

Sarang snips the string herself. She heaves a sigh and gathers a few plates. "Grab the rest, would you?"

I don't argue.

We're working on the dishes, elbow to elbow in silence as I wash and she dries, when Dario and Kai return. They place six hot cups of coffee on the table before hunching over a laptop, scrolling on Netflix. Kai's perkier than he was before. Either the caffeine or Dario's effect.

"I found something to watch," he calls to us.

"Don't say *Boys Over Flowers*," Sarang groans.

"It's *Boys Over Flowers*."

My lips turn up. I love that show.

After finishing, we turn the lights off and settle around Kai's tiny laptop. Dario, Kai, and Vanna claim spots on the sofa, leaving me and Sarang on the floor beside each other. I settle against the couch next to somebody's leg and try to immerse myself in the show. I've seen it so many times that my thoughts naturally wander, despite the others' lively commentary throughout the episodes.

This is my last day, I think, staring at the glaring light of the screen in the pitch-dark room. *I'm never going to work with my best friend or any of these guys again.*

One episode turns into two. Then three. Then four. Eventually the chatter and laughter die down, which doesn't help distract me from my spiraling thoughts.

I won't be able to show my face around here. Kai will understand, hopefully, but the others will hate me. Sarang might track me down and kill me.

I peek at her out of the corner of my eye. The glow of the computer softens her image. She's stunning. And looks almost tender. The blanket slid down at some point and is pooled around her waist.

I wonder if I need to fake-dump her to end our fake relationship. Or maybe it's implied when I quit? God, I hate breakups. I don't want to do this. But it's not like she'll care about that—it's the cafe she's worried about. Even if we lose some engagement online from the breakup, it'll be fine, right? Wait, who will oversee the social accounts once I'm gone? Kai? He could do it, I guess. He—

Something nudges my side, startling me so bad my stomach shoots into my throat. I whip my head to find Sarang already facing me, close enough that our noses bump. I jerk away, flustered by the proximity.

She pulls her hand back. "Jumpy much?"

"You nearly gave me a heart attack," I hiss, clutching my chest.

"You're too young to have one. And keep it down."

She gestures up. The others are knocked out. Dario's slumped over the arm of the sofa, one of his legs kicked over Kai and Vanna's laps, who've both fallen asleep leaning against each other. I check the time on the computer: 5:24 a.m. Holy crap, I was zoning out hard.

"Can't believe you and I are the only ones who stayed up," I say.

"With half an hour to spare before the cafe opens, too."

My heart plummets, rattling against my rib cage on its descent to the ground. Half an hour. Thirty minutes before I have to give this all up and return to what I left.

"Will you tell me what's wrong now?"

I snap my head to the side. The light must be playing tricks on me, because in the dim halo of the laptop screen, Sarang almost looks concerned. No, she *is*. Her voice is yielding. This is an invitation, not a demand.

Still, I force a dry chuckle. "Nothing's wrong."

Instead of saying anything, she holds out her pinkie. Our truth pact. She's trying, she really is. I never expected her to, especially not for me.

With that realization, I wrap my pinkie around hers.

I stand and offer her my hand to help her up, then we head into the main area.

The warm rays of dawn filter in through the windows, bathing the dining area in a surreal tint of nectarine. It's nearly a replica of the scene Haneul drew. I blink, coming to a stop in the middle of the cafe. The sunlight is sobering. I feel like I've been thrown back into the real world after hiding in a pocket away from reality all night.

Sarang stands in front of me, eyebrows lifted in question. I stare down at her, observing her features. She's so beautiful. Usually it frustrates me, but right now, it's a good distraction.

"I'm sorry," I say. My voice is gravelly. "This is my last day."

She's silent for a while. Then, "Are you going back to your parents' cafe?"

My lips part. "How did you know?"

"I'm sure your family isn't happy that you're working at a coffee shop other than theirs. My dad wouldn't be if it were me. Plus, you quitting doesn't make sense, not unless you have to."

"Yeah. I have to."

"Why'd you leave in the first place?"

My tongue feels heavy in my mouth, hard to speak around. But it *is* probably the last time I'll talk to her. I can give her the truth this once, since it's what she's always wanted from me. I made her a promise.

"It was difficult to watch the place I grew up in turn into something that wasn't my home anymore," I admit aloud for the first time. "Our cafe used to be a lot like yours. Small, comfortable—it felt personal. But then business started to grow, and grow, until it stopped being successful for our *family* and became successful for a company. I felt more like an employee than a son. I knew if I stayed there,

I'd get stuck. When my ex-girlfriend and I got promoted to being co-managers, I realized that was it for my future. I'd clock in and suffocate. I'd go home but I still couldn't breathe. I know my parents thought they were doing me a favor by pulling me into the business— God knows there's nothing else I can do—but that just made it worse somehow, finally *having* this proof that they don't think I'm capable anywhere else. I couldn't—" I cut myself off and breathe out through my nose. "I couldn't see a way out of all of it. Cafe Gong, my relation-ship, my hand-me-down future. So. That's why I left."

Sarang blinks like she's trying to figure out something that's right in front of her. "Do you like working here?"

I nod slowly. Then again, more vigorously. "Yeah. Yeah, I love it here."

She looks at the sunlight filtering in. The redbrick walls outside the store are lit up with the embers of dawn. Nothing else is said, and I think this is it. It has to be. I can't stave off the inevitable forever.

But she speaks again. "You're a pretty indecisive guy, aren't you?"

"What?"

"Am I wrong?"

"Indecisive" is the only term I could confidently use to describe myself. I've never known what I want, or who I am, or what to say, or what comes next. I'm like if self-doubt had disappointing sex with insecurity. Doesn't mean I'm thrilled that Sarang is so accurately slicing me apart at not even six o'clock in the morning. "Yeah, you could say that."

"So," she continues, "how come the one time you know what you want to do, you're not doing it?"

My brain buzzes like a cicada. "Because it's not that simple."

"Isn't it? Maybe some things aren't as complex as you think."

Unable to keep her piercing gaze, I duck my head and take my glasses off, wiping them absently with the sleeve of my sweatshirt. The action reminds me of Cecelia, who would always hand me a napkin to clean them with instead.

"It was a selfish decision," I say. "Leaving impacted a lot of people there."

"Won't it do the same here?"

I open my mouth, then shut it. She has a point. Why was I doing this again? *Because if I don't, Cecelia will tell my parents about me working for Bingsu for Two.* That's right. They'd never forgive me. But how much worse can it get than returning to Cafe Gong? Falling back into a relationship that doesn't click? Forgetting how happy I've been here at Bingsu?

"Whatever choice I make, I'm going to be hurting a lot of people," I say with a dry chuckle.

Sarang shrugs. "Well, if you're going to be letting people down anyway, why not go with what you want? You're the one who has to live with your choice, after all."

When she says it like that, everything sounds simpler. For some reason, Sarang's cool, easy tone of voice strikes a particular chord within me, vibrating at the right frequency to nullify all the other strands of worry and anxiety buzzing inside my skull. I feel like I can *think* now. Think. What do I want? I could either . . .

A. Quit and go back. I'd be miserable at work and who I'm with, but at least I won't disappoint Umma and Dad any more than I already have. Or . . .

B. Stay. Stay and be happy, instead of pretending like I am. Stay and have something to look forward to every day after school. Stay at the place that feels like home now, the only place where I know who I am and what I can do.

My heartbeat booms like gongs in my ear. Adrenaline thrums beneath the surface of my skin. I've never felt so scared. Never so alive. I know how I feel. I know.

Sarang is smiling at me. I think I smile back. I can feel my cheeks dimple, but I'm too focused on her face to control what's happening on mine.

"Maybe you're smarter than I give you credit for," I say quietly, though she's the only one awake to hear.

"You shouldn't underestimate me, unless you like being proven wrong all the time." Sarang turns on her heel and heads toward the back room. She waves over her shoulder. "I'll see you later. Or not."

My heart pangs as she disappears behind the curtain.

"See you."

18. THE INHERENT INTIMACY OF THE HIGH SCHOOL BAND ROOM

As soon as I'm outside, I pull my phone out of my pocket and turn it on, blood roaring in my ears. I open Cecelia's contact and send her a text.

Cecelia

Will you meet me at our spot?

Our spot is—*was*—the concrete steps outside of the band room building. I won't lie: we only went there to make out. Not the most romantic spot, but it's on the far side of campus and hardly anybody is ever there.

The sun crawls up the cerulean sky as I walk toward school. When I arrive at our spot, Cecelia is already perched on the steps, cast in pale light. Morning dew clings to the air. When I let out a shuddering breath, it turns to mist before my face.

Cecelia turns up at the tap of my shoes against the damp pavement. She looks more pristine and put-together than any normal person should at six in the morning, but she's always been like that. Her entire face lights up.

"Hi, River," she greets me.

"Morning." My voice is too loud, too rough in the otherwise blanket of quiet around us. If she notices, she doesn't call it out. She pats the spot next to her for me to sit. I do. Cecelia links her hand in mine.

"I'm glad you wanted to meet up so early," she says, leaning in with a gentle smile. "We can figure out our strategy for you coming back this afternoon."

I wince. I've never known how to start these kinds of conversations with her: the ones she won't like.

She goes on, waving her free hand in the air. "But first, I'm sure you have some ideas about Cafe Gong's new social media campaign. How did you start it for Bingsu for Two? Should we copy that introduction video you guys did? Getting Rosalind to participate will be a hard sell, but if we tell her it's a step toward promotion she might—"

"Cece," I say, squeezing her hand, "I have something to say."

She stops and turns to face me fully. "Sure. What is it?"

My mouth dries. *Come on, beanstalk*, I can almost hear Sarang urging. *You said it to me. You can say it to her.*

I steel myself, feeling emboldened by her words from a few minutes ago. "I'm sorry. I'm not coming back. I'm staying at Bingsu for Two."

Her smile falls an increment at a time, staggered, like her brain is lagging with the new information. "You're what?"

"I don't want to work at Cafe Gong. I don't want to be a co-manager. I left for a reason, and I really like Bingsu for Two.

I'm proud of the work I do there." I can't look at her as I speak, but through my peripheral vision, her expression remains hard like stone. I have to get it all out while I can. "I should've talked to you about everything I was feeling before I quit, you're right. It wasn't fair for me to leave you on your own, especially with how important it is to your college apps and your resume that this store does well. I'm really sorry about that, Cece, and I want to help where I can. Maybe I can show you how to set up socials for Cafe Gong and you guys can run them yourself? It'll be better this way, you can—"

She rips her hand out of mine and stands. Towering over me, with her back to the sun, her face is enveloped nearly in shadow.

"Are you joking right now?"

"No. I mean it, I won't come back."

"You—" She breaks off in a short, curt laugh. "Are you serious? *You* feel sorry for *me*? I don't need your pity. I'll be fine, but you? You're the one who needs this. I can't believe you still don't see that."

My eyes widen into saucers. "Cece . . ."

"Don't get mad at me for being the only person who will tell you what you need to hear. River, if you don't have Cafe Gong, you have nothing. Okay?"

I stand up too, but my knees wobble. "I have Bingsu for Two."

"Which could still run out of business any day now. Just because their one store is gaining some popularity from your dumb videos doesn't mean you have a guaranteed job forever. Cafe Gong is a few years away from being a *national* franchise! Your parents would probably give you a share of the company later. Do you know how many people dream of having that kind of silver spoon to eat off of? And you're throwing that away, for what?" She straightens with a scoff. "It's because of your girlfriend, right?"

"It's not because of Sarang, she wants me to do what is best for—hey, she's not even my girlfriend! We talked about this yesterday."

Cece crosses her arms and turns away. "Unbelievable. A few weeks with some goth chick and you turn into *this*. You're so pathetic. She's going to drop you as soon as you stop being helpful to her, you know that, right? All she wants from you is what you can do for her cafe."

I round on her, something sharp ready to spill off my tongue, but I freeze when I catch her rapidly blinking away tears.

"Don't—stop looking at me," she says.

My hands shake, half out of shock and half out of frustration. The embers of rage, embarrassment, and every sickly feeling she's extracted from me simmer in my gut, but I shut my eyes and take a deep breath to fan them away.

"Why are we doing this?" I ask, running my hands through my hair. "This isn't good for us. Exes need time apart before they can even think about being friends, let alone run a business together. You're smart, Cece, you don't need me back at the store. Like you said, all I have to offer are my dumb videos."

"I don't want to be friends," Cecelia snaps a bit too quickly, her eyes red. "This is about—"

"Cafe Gong. Yes. Our futures, I know." I shake my head. Heat prickles my eyes, and I finally look at her. "I'm sorry. I hurt you more than I probably know, and I hate that I did that. I still have love for you, Cece, but . . . this isn't good for us. You're hurting me, too. I'm not coming back. Maybe you're right, and I'm fucking up any chance I have at a future and Bingsu for Two really *will* go belly-up in months like we thought. But if that happens, I want to be there for it."

She's silent, save for her haggard breathing. We stand face to face, less than a foot apart. I could reach out and pull her into my arms, and muscle memory would guide us through the cycle of hurt, comfort, pretend it never happened, rinse and repeat—but I don't.

I watch a bug skitter across the cement step between us. A moment later I glance up, expecting to see her expression torn in a tear-stricken, dejected frown.

But instead, Cecelia's looking down at me like *I'm* the bug writhing on the ground next to her shoe.

"I know you, River," she says, wiping her nose with a sniff. She collects herself quickly. "Which is why I know you'll come back, one way or another. You don't want your parents to find out about this, right?"

The muscles in my face lock. Before I can find a reply to her threat, she continues.

"I'm not sure where you got this courage from, but I hope it lasts you long enough. Because when it runs out, and when you eventually come crawling back for your job at Cafe Gong, you better have the nerve to look me *and* your parents in the eye and beg me to hire you at my store." She steps down, and at the bottom of the stairs, turns up to me with a look of scorn. "I've never needed your help, but you won't have mine anymore."

She leaves me there, staring after her, with a small, tiny voice that sounds like hers ringing in my ears asking, *What if she's right?*

The rest of the day drags at an excruciating crawl as I float from class to class in a daze. My nervous system is kicked into overdrive. I'm glued to my phone, waiting anxiously for the inevitable text from Umma and Dad after Cece tells them everything. She had one condition: I come back, or they find out.

But school ends, and I don't receive a single text.

It feels like a Band-Aid on a stab wound in terms of relief. My parents don't know—yet. I'm not sure how long Cecelia plans to dangle this threat over my head, or how long I can hold out before giving in to her demands.

After a long, terrible day, I drag my sleep-deprived, crusty, cranky self to Bingsu for Two for my closing shift. Back when I thought yesterday would be my last day and this shift would go to some poor unfortunate soul (hopefully Sarang), I didn't consider the repercussions of working after pulling an all-nighter. I'm feeling them now. But hey, anything after the events of this morning will be an improvement.

I open the cafe's door.

"You're six minutes late, you good-for-nothing dweeb."

Okay. Maybe "improvement" was being optimistic.

Sarang skips around the counter. Before I've barely taken three steps inside, she drops a twenty-pound bag of cold brew beans into my arms.

"Jesus, give me a warning, would you?"

"If you'd arrived on time, you'd have plenty of notice," she replies, fixing her apron as she talks. "Haneul had to leave early since she got a last-minute gig with Uwajimaya in International District; they needed some animation done for an event they're hosting later this week or whatever. Couldn't miss it. Which is *incredible*, but now we're behind on making cold brew, and next week's order hasn't been done, and I still have to make cookies, *and* I have an essay for my English class due at midnight."

I adjust the bag in my arms. "Is it just you and me tonight?"

"Yeah."

"Okay. How about you work on the cookies, and I'll make cold brew and do the order. Sound fine?"

Sarang pauses in retying her flour-dusted apron to look up and lock eyes with me. The moment is fleeting—less than a second—but it's there.

"Fine." She walks away. Over her shoulder, she calls, "Since it looks like you'll be sticking around, you might as well start pulling your weight."

I snort. "You won't be getting rid of me that easily."

Before ducking into the kitchen, she stops, glances back. "Too bad," she says, and for the first time, it sounds like she might not mean it.

I purse my lips so they won't turn up into a smile or something else equally stupid.

19. LESSON #10422: DON'T PUT KAI ON LIVE TELEVISION

If you ask me, decorating for the holidays right before Thanksgiving is tacky.

But "Nobody asked you, River, shut up," so I'm hanging paper snowflakes on the ceiling of the cafe on my day off. I'm not even sure I'm getting paid for this, or for the brainstorming session we're supposed to have later to plan more content for our channel.

"Hey, dipstick," I say, trying not to lose my balance atop the rickety footstool. Sarang sits at one of the dining tables below, diligently cutting out the decorations. "How many more of these do we need to put up?"

"I don't pay you to run your mouth," she mumbles distractedly.

"You don't pay me at all, your dad does. Wait, so *am* I getting paid?"

I climb down and collapse into the chair across from her. She's as focused as she is when she's making macaroons: brows pinched, tongue poking out, with wisps of green hair cascading over her face.

"Do you really like doing this stuff?" I ask. "I didn't think you were the arts and crafts type given—" I gesture at her, in all her goth-girliness. Sarang blinks, as if unaware of her intricate spider-web eyeliner, black lipstick, and five studded piercings on each ear. "That, and the fact that you're going to Johns Hopkins to become a radiologist or something."

"There is so much wrong with what you said. You're lucky my hands are busy so I can't slap some sense into you. Just because I'm in STEM doesn't mean I don't have other interests."

"But aren't you guys all cold, unfeeling robots?"

She doesn't take the bait. "I'm going to be a cardiologist, by the way, not a radiologist."

"A heart doctor? How come?"

The instant the words leave my mouth, I remember our conversation from when we were pillow shopping. Her dad has congestive heart failure. I didn't know what it was at the time, but I looked it up a few days later. It's a condition where the heart doesn't pump blood as well as it should, with a life expectancy that made my stomach flop when I read it.

Sarang's voice and face are completely neutral. "Just because."

I change the subject, hopefully to keep her mind from wandering to the fact that when she completes medical school, her dad may not be around anymore—oh god. "You didn't answer my question. Do you enjoy this stuff?"

"I guess." She cuts a final snip in the center of the folded piece of paper, then unravels it. "I get it from Haneul, though I'm nowhere near as good as her. Plus, she's more interested in drawing and animation, while I like making things with my hands and painting."

You really can't judge a book by its cover. Artist-baker-med student-goth girl, and bane of my existence. Huh. I pluck the snowflake from her to hang it up. "Yeah, Haneul's something else," I agree. "But you're pretty talented, too."

She doesn't reply, and I'm too busy taping up the snowflake to see how she reacts. The silence between us feels weird, although things have been off ever since the sleepover two weeks ago.

After that night, after we had—I'm going to barf—that little heart-to-heart, things have changed. We're not buddies or anything, but there's a shift in our dynamic that we've both noticed yet refuse to acknowledge. I wouldn't call it good or bad. It's just . . . different.

That's not the only thing around here that's changed. Kai and Vanna edited the footage from the sleepover and uploaded it to our account: "Spending the Night at Our Korean Cafe!" Not the flashiest video, but I figured it would still do well. They always do.

But I didn't expect it would do *Trending at #3 on YouTube* well.

Business has been booming since then. It's exciting to hear people gush about how much they enjoy our content, and how happy it's made them. It reminds me of my fandoms. It's hard to feel completely excited, though, knowing Cece's aware of and watching our every move online and can run to my parents with evidence at any time. Our last conversation hangs over my shoulders like a heavy, itchy coat. She sounded *so* certain that I'd come back to Cafe Gong. Back to her. I've never known her to be wrong.

Curiosity got the better of me, and I checked about a week ago to confirm my suspicions: they *did* make an account for Cafe Gong.

It's . . . well, pretty awful. Their Instagram presence gives off the same vibe as an out-of-touch great-aunt's: lots of unedited and lopsided photos with captions so clunky it makes me wonder if they're using auto-suggestions or an AI generator.

Part of me (okay, most of me) delights in seeing Cece suck so spectacularly at something I'm good at for once. After how we left things, I can't get over the petty urge to rub it in her face. I want to do something *big*. Something that'll prove that I really don't need her or Cafe Gong to succeed.

Unfortunately, the smaller, logical part of me knows a flashy statement would only increase the risk of my parents finding out on their own, though, so I taper the urge.

We're doing great in sales as it is, though, so it's fine. The only downside of this recent flush of customers is that Sarang and I have to keep up the fake-dating act all the time. With this weird new tension between us, it's made that whole gag particularly awkward.

My eyes drift down to her. Maybe *I* should be the one to address the change since she clearly won't. What if she pretends she hasn't noticed it? What if there's nothing there and it's all one-sided? I'm overthinking this, aren't I? *Just say something, anything—*

Suddenly, from the kitchen: "What the *hell*, Kai?"

Dario's shout startles me enough that I nearly fall off the stool. A second later, Kai storms out into the dining area, his face pink as a cherry. Dario bursts through the curtains after him, looking equally flustered. It doesn't seem like they're messing around.

"Hold on, stop, I'm sorry." Dario catches up and grabs Kai's elbow. "You surprised me. But why would you try to—"

Kai yanks free. "Don't turn this around on me like that, like I'm the weird one. *You're* the one who's been acting all—all *normal* these past few weeks!"

"Normal?"

"Yeah. Like *before* normal. Like when we were still dating. You've been joking around, texting me again, touching me. What was I supposed to think?"

Dario balks. "I'm not acting like anything. We're broken up, Kai, that's it. You can't try to kiss—"

"Screw this," Kai says. He picks up his skateboard behind the counter and stomps toward the exit. Without glancing at any of us, he throws open the door and leaves, the bell clanging angrily in his wake.

The silence sucks the air out of the room. I feel like I'm not allowed to breathe; Dario looks like he can't.

Sarang is the only one brave enough to pierce the silence. "Dario? Are you two okay?"

"Fine," he says with a forced smile. "Just fine. My ex-boyfriend thinks I'm leading him on, and when I try to set some boundaries, *I'm* the bad guy."

The urge to defend Kai rises like a reflex, but Vanna, who's been silently hanging up lights in the corner this whole time, beats me to it.

"Don't play so innocent, tiger," she says. "You can't blame Kai for getting the wrong impression when he's correctly interpreting all your signals. Nobody *stares* at someone's face for so long unless they want to mash their own against it."

My eyes widen. It can't be true. But a look at Dario's flushed, furrowed expression confirms it: he's not over their breakup either.

With a shake of his head, Dario makes for the front door, too. "I'm going to the gym."

Sarang tries to intercept him, but he sidesteps her and escapes out of the cafe. She huffs, shoulders falling.

I whistle low and long. "I can't believe you and I have the best relationship here, and we're not even together."

"Yuck, don't say that."

"I wonder if they'll be okay."

"Knowing Dario, he'll pretend nothing happened and ignore all the tension."

Vanna hums, standing to join us. "Yeah, and Kai's not going to like that one bit."

"No. He won't." I sigh.

Sarang rubs her face. "What are we going to do now? We were supposed to have a meeting to discuss what to post next on social media. Should we reschedule?"

I suck my teeth, considering it. "No, there's no time. My suggestion is time sensitive."

They gather around me as I explain. "Two words: 'scavenger hunt.'"

"Here's one word," Sarang interrupts. She gives me a thumbs-down. "Boo."

I give her a different finger and explain.

After our KING 5 interview, I had been giving some thought to how we could build an audience of customers in the area at large, not just the people who are subscribed to us. The solution? Free stuff, a challenge, and fifteen minutes of fame. Aka, we put on a citywide scavenger hunt for people to see Bingsu for Two in person, find prizes like gift cards scattered around Seattle, and meet us at the end for the jackpot of getting featured on our channel. We would run a promotion for it, too: spend twenty dollars and receive scavenger-exclusive merchandise, with the proceeds to be donated to a good cause.

"Pretty good, right?" I say once I finish. "We can host it next Saturday since it'll be National Espresso Day. Shut up, Sarang, yes, it's a real holiday. We could pitch this to Ms. Kapule at KING 5, she might be interested in covering it. It'd get us a lot of local attention."

I'm pretty proud of this one. It's a little outside my comfort zone of fandom-exclusive PR and more like a *real* marketing campaign, but that doesn't scare me this time. Maybe I'm getting more confident in my abilities to do this—Cece wanted me to do the same at Cafe Gong for a reason, after all.

Sarang looks thoughtfully surprised. "Wow. That's actually . . . not terrible."

"Really?" I perk up.

"It's a good follow-up to our interview with KING 5, and it'll entice people to come to the store. Logistically, it won't be hard to set up, either. We already have gift cards, the scavenger locations can be in public places, and you just have to do your thing by promoting it on the internet." Sarang catches herself being a little too earnest and quickly dampens her expression, shrugging flippantly as she adds, "I guess we keep you around for a reason."

A pinch of frustration bites at me. Cecelia's words from our fight float into my head.

She's going to drop you as soon as you stop being helpful to her, you know that, right? All she wants from you is what you can do for her cafe.

Vanna slaps my and Sarang's backs, physically snapping me out of it. She loops an arm around our shoulders and drags us all closer. "Nice work, Bean Boy. This could be really fun. But about that promotional offer you mentioned—where would the proceeds be donated to?"

I'm going to talk to Haneul to figure out the logistics of it all, but I want to donate the earnings to Vanna's custody case. A gut feeling tells me Vanna would never agree if she knew that was the plan, though.

"Somewhere local. We can figure it out later."

She steps back with an impressed nod, crossing her arms over her weathered crewneck. Sarang glances over at me, her eyes flicking up and down in a quick assessment, and she nods to herself as well. I beam. This will ensure Bingsu for Two is here to stay for the long run, and that I am, too.

Which increases the likelihood of Dad and Umma finding out—a problem I know I can't ignore much longer.

After getting the green light from Haneul and Mr. Cho, I announce it on our Twitter account that night.

Bingsu for Two
@bingsu4twocafe

Celebrate National Espresso Day with us, Seattle!
On Sat 11/23, join our city-wide scavenger hunt to win
fun prizes and a chance to be featured on our channel!
Stop by on Friday to learn more and earn exclusive
merch with a $20 purchase. All proceeds will be
donated.
See you then!

7:06 PM · Nov 19, 2024

2.3K Retweets   **1.9K** Quote Tweets   **6.6K** Likes

Come Friday afternoon, a brick wall of customers is cemented outside the store. It may be busier than it was when our first video went viral. It takes a lot of gentle nudging for me to make it past the line and inside, where it's just as packed.

Everybody's already here: Sarang and Dario are making drinks at the bar, Kai's working on the desserts, and Vanna's at the register taking orders and handing out merch for the promotion. Isabette, who was kind enough to volunteer her help (and smitten enough to do anything if it meant spending time with Vanna), is busy running food in the dining room. Our guests of honor are already here, too. Ms. Kapule and her entire crew are near the handoff counter, setting up cameras and getting ready to air. Thankfully, she was more than happy to cover the segment when I reached out, and I warned Jace ahead of time to hide the (new) TV remote for a few days.

I head to the front counter and pick one of the dozens of folded cream-colored T-shirts beside Vanna. I gasp. "Is this the finished merch?"

"Yep, Haneul and Kai went all out designing them. We have about a million more of these back in the kitchen, and we've already sold almost two hundred with the promo deal we're doing."

I unfold the shirt. It's better than I could've imagined. Drawn in Haneul's signature vibrant, almost-glowing art style is one of the cafe's specialties, coffee bingsu. The bowl is filled to the brim with milky slush, dusted with cocoa powder, and decorated with wafer cookies and chocolate-covered espresso beans. Above the bowl is a tiny ceramic cup pouring a shot of espresso that cascades over the bingsu. In a handwritten retro font, the shirt reads *Bingsu for Two* curved on top and *Espresso Day Scavenger Hunt 2024* below, with coffee dripping over the letters. I can see Kai's design style in the details, too. The font was definitely his doing, as well as the purposeful cracking in the print to make it look vintage, and some distressing on the hems.

I take my spot behind the counter. Dario groans in relief when I put my apron on. "Thank God. Here, take over, I have to piss."

"Don't say 'piss' in front of the customers!" Sarang chastises above the ruckus of the cafe. She notices me, and fire ignites in her eyes. "You!"

"What? What'd I do?" I ask, reaching past her to work on an iced almond milk caramel macchiato from the overflowing counter of orders.

Sarang snatches the carton of almond milk out of my hands and crowds me against the counter. "Haneul said you want to donate the proceeds to Vanna's custody case. Why didn't you tell me? More importantly, why didn't you tell *Vanna*?"

She's way too close. I feel myself blush as she presses her entire front against mine, and I can't exactly lean back any farther with the espresso machine poking into my back. Would this be a bad time for a dick joke? Well, now I'm thinking about my dick. Uh-oh.

"What's the problem?" I whisper back, careful so Vanna won't hear us, although she's too preoccupied with the influx of customers. "It's for a good cause, and it sounds like she and her sister need it."

"It *is* and they *do*, but you don't—" She sighs. "This is *not* the kind of thing you surprise someone with, and especially not the kind of thing we popularize on the internet! Vanna *hates* feeling like a charity case, and you're making her one to the entire city and our thousands of followers."

"Haneul said she'll find a way to sneak it into her paychecks in increments so she'll never find out."

"Yo!" Kai yells from the other end, plopping a scoop of ice cream on an order of honey toast. "Can you guys save the sexually charged argument for another time? There's like fifteen people waiting for their drinks."

"Shut up! I'm making it!" Sarang snaps. She pushes the almond milk into my hand while she goes to work on two grapefruit ades.

As I cue up the shots on the espresso machine, I say to her, "We never told the internet where we're donating the proceeds, and I don't plan on letting them know it's for Vanna. Come on, you really think I'd use her situation with her sister as a marketing ploy?"

"I think you're enough of an idiot to accidentally do so, yes."

"Oh my god, I came up with the scavenger hunt to drum up some business for the cafe." *And prove to my ex-girlfriend how successful I can be without her or my parents.* "And being able to help Vanna is a lucky side effect. Will nothing satisfy you?"

"Sandpapering your face would."

"You're such a—"

"The *drinks*!" Kai repeats.

"We're working on it!" Sarang and I shout at the same time.

It draws the attention of several people, who eye us suspiciously. I curse.

"We're supposed to be dating, remember?" I whisper. "Pretend like you can stand me, or else you'll blow our cover."

"I couldn't do that even if I was an Oscar-winning actor," she hushes back.

A group of friends who had been watching our interaction start gossiping to each other. "Oh, for the love of—" I mutter, before steeling myself. I snake an arm around Sarang's waist and pull her flush to me. She yelps, grabbing onto my shoulders for support.

"Act like I'm flirting with you," I whisper in her ear, still holding her by the waist. She's warm under her apron. I think of something that'll make her blush. Just so it looks realistic, that's all. "You know, you're very attractive when you yell, even if you're usually yelling at me. *Especially* so."

"What?" Sarang pushes me back, looking thoroughly flustered with a crown of flyaway hairs adorning her pink, sweaty face. I grin.

"Yeah, like that."

Ms. Kapule leans over the handoff counter and waves a hand to catch our attention. "Cameras are good to go. Are you all ready for the interview? It'll be quick, we just need one of you."

I raise my eyebrows at Sarang in question. She shakes her head. "Like hell I'm doing it. You do it, it was your idea."

I'm not making the same mistake twice and risking Umma and Dad seeing my face on broadcast news. "I can't . . . I have stage fright."

I turn around. Vanna's occupied with the register, and frankly not our most charismatic speaker. Kai, making a mess while pouring the oat milk, turns around when he feels me staring.

"Why are you looking at me like that?" he asks.

INT. "Bingsu for Two"/BAR — DAY

Standing in front of the counter, against a chaotic backdrop of moving bodies and drinks flying left and right, is a confused-looking KAI, who keeps glancing at someone out of frame. MS. KAPULE stands in front of him, a quarter of her turned back facing the camera as she holds the microphone between them.

MS. KAPULE

Kai, thank you for letting us join you and your co-workers at Bingsu for Two again. We're excited to be here and see that your guys' popularity has only grown since we last spoke. Can you tell us more about what you have planned for the city and your followers tomorrow?

KAI

(to himself)

I would love to, apparently.

(more eagerly)

Tomorrow is National Espresso Day, so we're celebrating by hosting a scavenger hunt across Seattle. People will start here, search for related clues hidden around the city, and snag gift cards, merchandise, and treats along the way. The grand prize is a feature on our channel. Ta-da!

MS. KAPULE

It's so exciting to see you and your friends use your passion and platform to put on an event like this for the community. Can you give us any hints?

KAI

River said that the clues involve famous coffee landmarks in the city. One barista will be manning each spot, so be on the lookout for each of us.

MS. KAPULE

A meet and greet for all those who have followed your cafe's journey online, that's so fun. Remind those at home who may not know who your co-workers are?

KAI

Well, who you can expect to meet on the scavenger hunt tomorrow will be me, Dario, Vanna, Sarang, and River, in that order.

MS. KAPULE

Sarang and River?

KAI

Sarang, *and* River, yeah.

Ms. Kapule turns to face the camera fully.

MS. KAPULE

How sweet! The internet's favorite barista couple will be waiting together to greet the winners of tomorrow's scavenger hunt.

A male voice offscreen whispers incoherently to Kai, who winces with realization.

KAI

Wait, River and Sarang aren't together.

MS. KAPULE

They aren't?

KAI

Shit, I mean they won't *be* together at tomorrow's event. Of course they're *together* together—

A disembodied arm yanks him out of the frame mid-sentence. Ms. Kapule shoots them a warning look for ruining her news segment, before recomposing herself to continue the outro.

MS. KAPULE

Coffee lovers, Bingsu for Two fans, and all of Seattle can expect a fun outing tomorrow hosted by the internet's most famous baristas. Reminder, the scavenger hunt starts at 9 a.m. here at Bingsu for

Two on 6th Avenue and ends with a chance to meet
River and Sarang, the cafe sweethearts.

With Kai out of frame, the camera auto-adjusts to focus on SARANG behind the counter in the background. In her clenched fist is a crushed plastic cup with the icy remnants of a frappe spilling over her fingers. Her eye twitches in a glitchy glare aimed at somebody off to the side.

20. MY FORMAL APOLOGY FOR SENDING PEOPLE TO THE HELLHOLE THAT IS THE FIRST STARBUCKS AT PIKE PLACE

I shouldn't be surprised anymore when I end up in these sucky situations. And yet, here I am. Surprised that it indeed sucks.

"Quit your grumbling," Sarang pipes up next to me. "It's *your* fault for not correcting Ms. Kapule yesterday."

"Me? It's Kai who got us in this mess."

"Well, now we're stuck together for the next God knows how many hours until the winners find us. Hope you're happy."

We're on the sidewalk leaning against the brick wall of The 5 Point Cafe as dozens of people pass by, concealing us from sight. It's slightly past one, which means we've been loitering here for four hours, which is four hours too long to be alone in Sarang's company, but it's also not long *enough* to go inside and wait for the winners there. It's the final destination of the scavenger hunt.

I pull my phone out of my pocket, ignore Sarang peering over my shoulder and snorting at my Son of Sin lock screen, and check our Instagram for updates from the others.

"Have they posted yet?" she asks.

"Let's see," I say. We're using Instagram to track the progress of the race and repost people's stories tagging us as they search for clues. Haneul was up first this morning, having stayed behind at the cafe for the first stop of the scavenger hunt. I scroll past a few videos and click on hers.

INT. "Bingsu for Two"/
REGISTER — MORNING

A frowning, unkempt HANEUL frowns at the camera, which shakes as she sets it down on the counter beside the espresso machine. Her hair is tied up and her black apron is splattered with syrups and whipped cream. Behind her, a crowd waits in the dining area, talking and laughing as she drizzles caramel onto a drink.

HANEUL

I forgot I was supposed to film after the first person showed up. My bad. Anyway, welcome to Bingsu for Two's National Espresso Day Scavenger Hunt. Our cafe is the first stop. It's been about half an hour since the scavenger hunt started and a ton of people have dropped by already. The clue for the next destination is hidden somewhere in the dining room—but there are also red herrings meant to throw you off and take you in the wrong direction.

The caramel gets jammed in the bottle, and when she squeezes it next it explodes all over her hands. Haneul grips the counter and sighs.

HANEUL

Anyway, don't worry: if you end up at the wrong
location, there are still hidden gift cards and coupons
waiting to be found. Good luck.
(*mumbling*)
Wish me luck, too.

Perfect. Sort of. It's good to see people are participating. I scroll
to the next video, which is Dario's.

EXT. "First Starbucks at Pike Place"/ STOREFRONT EXTERIOR — MORNING

*DARIO holds the camera far enough away that we can see
he's standing in the middle of the cobblestoned street
of Pike Place Market. To his left is the never-ending
line that leads into the tourist trap also known as the
First Starbucks.*

DARIO

Good morning, it's Dario. The first group of people have
found me at our second stop of the National Espresso
Day Scavenger Hunt: The First Starbucks. For those who
aren't locals, it's the first-ever Starbucks store, right
across from Pike Place Market. Convenient.
(*glancing at the store with poorly concealed distaste*)
There's a few groups in the lead. Don't worry, the clue
for the next location is still here, and even if you
can't figure it out, come stop by for free gift cards.
Okay, on to Kai.

Sarang snorts, and I notice she's leaned close enough that her head's practically resting against my shoulder.

"It's hilarious you made him wait at the First Starbucks."

"It's an unfortunately iconic location."

Next video, posted about an hour after Dario's, is Kai's.

INT. "Victrola Roastery"/
INTERIOR — LATE MORNING

KAI sits at a table inside a small but bustling coffee shop, with cozy wooden decor and the whirring of machines punctuating the air. On the table in front of him are a dozen bags of coffee beans.

KAI

Hi, everyone! Thank you for participating in our National Espresso Day Scavenger Hunt.

(leaning in)

And thank you *especially*, River, for putting Dario at the First Starbucks. That's mean, man. I like it.

KAI

Anyway, our first few groups found me at Victrola in Cap Hill, a local roastery where Seattleites *actually* go to get good coffee. Speaking of, since it's National Espresso Day and you should always support your small businesses, we bought a shit ton of Victrola's beans and are giving them away first come, first served to those on the hunt. *And* I'm kinda hungry, so if anyone brings me a breakfast burrito, I'll teach you how to skateboard and give you one of my handmade shirts.

Last but not least, Vanna posted a video update about half an hour ago. They're getting close.

My eyebrows rise when I play the video. Sarang laughs and says, "I should've known."

EXT. "Coffeeholic"/DINING ROOM — AFTERNOON

The camera shakes as the person recording struggles to find a good spot to prop it up against. Giggles sound in the background, and a lower-pitched chuckle as the camera finally rights itself to present VANNA and ISABETTE in frame. They're sitting across from each other at a small table, both leaning forward to be in view. They're maybe closer than necessary.

ISABETTE

(still laughing)

Say your thing.

VANNA

(grinning)

Hi, Seattle. This is Vanna from Bingsu for Two, and I have a good friend with me today.

ISABETTE

Oh, a good friend?

VANNA

A *very* good friend.

ISABETTE

Historians will say they were friends . . .

Vanna snorts and shoves Isabette's elbow, fingers linger-
ing. She's smiling more than she has in any other video
on the channel.

VANNA

We're at the fourth stop of the scavenger hunt,
Coffeeholic in Greenwood. It's a small, Vietnamese
coffee shop with the *best* latte I've ever had.
Can I say that? Will I get fired? I'm going
to say it anyway.

Isabette snags the coffee cup next to Vanna's elbow and
takes a slow, deliberate sip, staring at the camera.
Vanna's soft gaze is focused on her only.

ISABETTE

Can confirm—that's the best latte I've ever had, too.

Vanna picks up the camera and brings it close to her face.

VANNA

River and Sarang, the groups are coming your way. We
have more gift cards for those who come by, or don't.
Either way, we'll be here. Bye.

She films her tongue sticking out of her mouth, and the
video ends with Isabette's bell-like laughter tinkling in
the background.

"Of course Vanna would find a way to turn this into an excuse
to take Isabette out," I say, but my lips are turned in a smile, too. I'm
glad it's going well and everyone's having fun.

Well, except me and Sarang.

"It's probably time we head in," she says. "I bet it's less than an hour until the first group finds us."

"Lead the way, sweetheart." I hold my hand out, and when she sticks her nose up at it, I raise my eyebrows and gesture to the crowds of people around us. She sighs, but slips her small, soft palm into mine.

"Right," she says with an eye roll. "How could I forget, *darling*?"

Stepping inside The 5 Point Cafe is like walking into a time capsule, or an alley bar turned disco party. It's as if a bunch of grunge hipsters bought an old '50s-style diner then decorated the place by slapping stickers on every flat surface. The lights are low, barely illuminating the black checkered tiles and the dozens of people lounging in wine-red booths. Arcade games and pinball machines line one side of the restaurant, slot machines fill the other, and a jukebox sits next to the register. If it's playing music, I can't tell, because there are so many people in here that the noise is loud enough to drown out my own breathing.

A host with two lip piercings and a braided beard approaches us. His pearly-white smile is the brightest source of light in this place.

"Morning, guys. Booth or table?"

"Actually," I say, "we're just waiting for some people. Maybe we can grab a coffee at the bar—"

The sound of Sarang's stomach grumbling makes me pause. Her face turns beet red. Cute.

I turn back to the waiter. "A booth would be great, please."

Mr. Crest 3D White leads us to a spot nestled in the corner of the restaurant and largely out of sight, which is good; we don't want to make it too easy for the winners. But then he leaves, and it's just me and Sarang. Getting brunch.

Alone.

She's picking fluff off the black corduroy skirt she wore today. My eyes trace over her outfit as a whole: turquoise velvet turtleneck, a dainty gold necklace layered over it, and knee-high black socks I noticed the second we met up this morning. I swallow, feeling awkward all of a sudden, and I don't think it's because I'm underdressed in comparison with my plain white shirt and denim jacket.

She glances up and catches me staring. "What?" she asks.

Heat blooms across my face, which makes it worse. I panic. "You, uh . . ." I slip the beanie I'm wearing off my head, lean across the table, and tug it over hers. She squawks as I adjust it and tuck her hair behind her ear so it's out of her face. "You stick out like a sore thumb," I rush out. "It'll give us away too quickly if the winners get here and see your highlighter head glowing like a lightbulb in the middle of the room."

Nice, I think, replaced immediately with a second thought: *Damn it, she looks better now.*

"I don't have a *highlighter* head. And don't look at me. Look at your menu," she says.

"*You* look at your menu."

Mr. Crest 3D pops in front of our table. "Have you two looked at the menus?"

Uh.

I order the first thing my eyes land on, potato bacon pancakes. Sarang asks for a vegan omelet. I ask for a pot of coffee for the both of us, which she scrunches her nose at.

When Mr. Crest 3D leaves, I ask, "You suddenly don't want coffee? *You?* The girl who drinks it more than water?"

"I don't trust coffee from other places."

That adds up. "It's good here. Don't worry, princess."

"You've tried it before?"

"Yeah." I grimace at the wash of bitter-stained memories flooding my thoughts. "My ex really liked coming here together."

"Did you?"

I sit back up and look at her. The beanie's crooked, and her hair frames her cheeks. There's an innocent curiosity to her features that makes her appear gentler than I know she is, but the illusion is nice for a moment.

"Food's good, if that's what you mean."

"It's not, but I'm glad to hear it."

Our waiter comes back with a pot of coffee, cream, and sugar. I pour Sarang a cup and slide it over. She takes a sip. Her eyes flutter closed, and the tension drains from her shoulders. Cute.

"Good?" I ask with a grin.

"Walk into the sea," she says, which is answer enough.

I tear my eyes away and scan the dining room area. It's hard to guess when the scavenger hunters will find us. An itch worms down my spine, and I'm feeling oddly exposed at the idea of being caught with Sarang at any moment. What if the winners find us when we're arguing or something, and they discover the truth about our relationship?

Sarang leans over, trying to see what I'm looking at. "What? What is it? Are they here?"

We're so close our hands almost touch. Leaning away would be weird, right? Right. I am nothing more than hormones in a meat sack. "I don't think so."

She sits back in her booth, slouching down in it. "I guess we just . . . wait."

"Yeah."

Oh god.

Reaching for a sugar packet to fiddle with, I say, "So . . . I'm sure this isn't how you usually spend your Saturday mornings. You know, participating in four-hour-long scavenger hunts."

"Are you . . ." Sarang starts. "Making small talk?"

"Maybe."

She snorts. "It was a god-awful attempt."

"At least I didn't ask you about the weather."

"That'd be preferable."

"Pretty nice weather we're having, huh?"

Sarang's lip quirks up. "It's okay, yeah."

I feel myself smile, and I can't wipe it off as my gaze flickers between her and the sugar packet in my hand.

Her expression mellows out. There's a spot of quiet.

"Your ex—"

"Who ordered the pancakes?"

Mr. Crest 3D slides up to our booth, plates of food in both hands. After he sets them down and asks half a dozen times if we'd like any ketchup, he leaves, and silence hangs over our booth. Sarang stares at her omelet, not saying anything but looking like she wants to. I think she's giving me the chance to sidestep this conversation.

I could. I could change the subject and it'd never come up again. It's . . . oddly considerate.

"What were you going to ask?" I say.

"Your ex," Sarang starts gingerly. "What was your relationship like?"

"Why do you ask?"

"I'm curious what happened. You usually avoid talking about her when it comes up."

This is *not* something I thought I'd be discussing over brunch, especially not brunch with Sarang. I chew on the inside of my cheek as I poke at the pancakes. "Our relationship was fine," I say. "We dated for about four years, and then we broke up. Nothing scandalous."

"Why'd you guys break up?"

"It's difficult to explain."

"You didn't love her?"

The pancakes are good, but dry. Or maybe that's my mouth. "Of course I loved her. But not enough, I guess. Or not in the right way."

Ambient noise of the restaurant mingles with the gentle clinking of my fork scraping the plate. I look up. Sarang hasn't touched her omelet.

"I didn't know there was a right way to love someone," she says thoughtfully.

I swallow. "Your food's going to get cold."

She finally takes a bite, quiet.

"How come you've never dated anyone?" I ask.

She chews, eyes on her silverware. Her voice grows more uncertain than I've heard it before. "I don't know. It's hard for me to feel that way for someone. I've had crushes on a few guys and girls before, but it wasn't anything more than attraction."

"That's normal, too. There's no rush to find the right person—*a* right person. I think it's true, what people say about good things coming in time." Glancing up, I find that Sarang's watching me. I give her a small smile. "You're cool, despite your attitude. You care a lot, and that kind of passion draws people in. You'll attract someone who makes you feel something eventually."

As my words hang between us, what I've just said sinks in. Heat warms my ears, but I don't look away. I mean it; despite her flaws—of which there are many, and I'd love to write a dissertation about it—she's a good person. Outrageously smart. Cares about her family and friends more than anything. Has a million hobbies and is unfairly good at all of them. Confident in her abilities. Annoyingly beautiful.

Not that I'd ever tell her any of that, though.

Sarang looks like she's malfunctioning.

"Uh. Um," she stutters. Her cheeks turn pink and spotty. She looks anywhere but at me. "That's—you—" Her eyes widen, then fix on something behind me. Her eyebrows crinkle. "Oh. Hi."

That was quick, but I'm not complaining. Saved from what was sure to be an unbearably painful moment of vulnerability, I twist around in my seat, ready to congratulate the winners of the scavenger hunt.

When my words die on my tongue.

Cecelia stands in the middle of the restaurant, a cold, hard smile carved into her face. To make matters worse, Jorge and Rosalind flank her sides.

"You've got to be shitting me," I mutter.

21. I'VE HAD DREAMS ABOUT THESE TWO MEETING. NIGHTMARES, I MEAN. NOT LIKE—NEVER MIND.

"I mean, *hey*, Cecelia. What are you doing here?"

"What do you mean, what are we doing here? We just won your scavenger hunt," she says. It's impressive, the way she can fake sincerity in her tone but convey her real feelings in those cool, blue eyes alone. Maybe I know them too well.

"I'm just surprised none of the others told me they saw you. Especially Kai."

Rosalind speaks up. "You guys attracted quite a crowd to this thing. It was packed at every stop. We didn't get a chance to speak to any of your nice co-workers, unfortunately."

Cecelia turns the full force of her saccharine smile on Sarang. "It was a lot of fun, and really well organized. Great job."

"It was River's idea," Sarang says distractedly. She scrutinizes Jorge and Rosalind, who looks punchably smug. "You guys seem familiar . . ." It clicks. She sits up. "You were at Cafe Gong that day.

You're River's old co-workers. That makes you—" Sarang turns to Cecelia, and this time there's understanding behind her sharp gaze.

Cecelia's nose turns up. "His ex. But River and I also used to be co-managers. He told you that, right?"

I stand up, fishing out my wallet and dropping a few bills on the table. "Let's go," I tell Sarang. She complies without a smart response, to my surprise.

Jorge puts a hand on my chest. "Hey, what about our prize? We won fair and square."

I pull the gift cards out of my pocket and slap them into his hand, but he laughs. "The grand prize was supposed to be a feature on your channel, wasn't it? You guys have been posting videos all day."

Grimacing, I glance at Sarang, but she looks as lost as I feel. Cecelia and Rosalind watch me expectantly. Their gazes carry the weight of two hands on my shoulders that shove me back down in my seat.

"A quick one," I say aloud, but it's directed at Sarang, who looks concerned.

INT. "The 5 Point Cafe"/BOOTH — AFTERNOON

Stiff as a board is RIVER, with ROSALIND and JORGE leaning across the booth behind him to tower over his shoulders. CECELIA slides into the spot next to River, close. Their arms touch and he stiffens.

RIVER

(uncomfortably)

Hi, everyone. Thank you all for participating in our National Espresso Day Scavenger Hunt. Congrats to all who found prizes and, uh . . . participated. Um, Sarang and I are at The 5 Point Cafe with the winners. Here they are.

Jorge leans over and grabs the camera, angling it higher to focus on his face.

JORGE

What's up, River's devoted fans? It's crazy how much you guys love him and his co-workers, but did you know he used to work with us? At a coffee shop just down the street, too. What are the odds, huh?

The camera jostles as somebody else grabs it. Cecelia holds it, aiming it at just her and River. She leans into his side, smiling sweetly while River grows paler by the second.

CECELIA

We just want to thank Bingsu for Two for hosting this incredible event and bringing the community together. It's amazing to see River do such cool things at his new job, he's always been a go-getter. I would know, we used to co-manage Cafe Gong together.

(turning toward River)

I'm really proud of what you're doing here. It's hard not to miss your presence, though. You did a *lot* for Cafe Gong as co-manager. Do you remember?

River's hand darts out and he shuts the camera off.

I am *not* posting that video.

"Sorry, time limit," I say, squeezing out a smile. I'm sure I look like I'm about to shit my pants. "Videos longer than a minute do terribly with the algorithm."

"Are you leaving already?" Cecelia asks. "I was hoping to catch up. It's been a while. I'm sure your girlfriend won't mind?"

Everyone's heads turn to Sarang, who's been silent at the opposite end of the table. Her eyebrows are furrowed, and she looks between Cecelia and me, then back at me.

She's waiting for my move.

Every fiber of my being wants to stand up, push past Cecelia and the others, and leave. I want to go to Bingsu for Two. It must show on my face, with the way Sarang's waiting. She's never been one to hold her tongue, but she is, for me. But I can't just run from this.

I muster up what I hope is a convincing enough smile. "You can go ahead without me, Sarang."

"Are you sure?"

"Yeah. Tell the others the scavenger hunt is over. I'll see you tomorrow."

It takes another long, stretched-out moment before Sarang finally moves. She inches out of the booth, looks us all over once more, and tries to catch my eye. I nod, and then finally, she leaves.

Jorge slaps my shoulder, fingers digging into the muscle. "Thanks for the gift cards," he says. He and Rosalind leave next, and I watch as he tosses the cards into the trash can on their way out.

It's just Cecelia and me.

I brace myself. I grip my knee so hard under the table my nails dig through my jeans. The expression Cecelia gave me the last time we talked flashes behind my closed eyes: the scorn, the disgust, like I was nothing but the bug under her shoe. I open my eyes and tell myself seeing it a second time won't be as bad. But she's not looking at me like she wants to step on me this time. Her face is a canvas carefully washed blank. She must be savoring the moment, I know it, rubbing it in before she finally goes to my parents and tells them every—

"I'm so sorry," she says.

The restaurant chatter substitutes for a record scratch in my head.

Cecelia continues, running a hand through her blond hair with an exhausted sigh. "Bombarding you here was wrong, I know that, but it seemed like the only place we could talk. Bringing Jorge and Rosalind along was supposed to make it feel *less* like a confrontation than if it was just me showing up, but that was clearly a mistake. I'm sorry."

I blink dumbly at her. "What?"

She shifts in the booth to face me completely. "I feel terrible for what I said to you last time. I don't know where that came from. I didn't mean any of it."

"What part?" I blurt. I think of Sarang. What would she do? "The part where you said I have nothing without Cafe Gong? Or the part where you told me my girlfriend's only using me and will dump me the second I stop being helpful to her?"

Cecelia casts her eyes down. "All of it. And for what I said about if you came back to Cafe Gong." Her voice lowers. "How I wouldn't help you if you did."

"You said *crawl* back. How when I came *crawling* back, you wouldn't help me."

She keeps her head down. I wonder if she's crying. Or maybe she's not showing me her face because there aren't any tears there.

I certainly don't have any left.

"I know you might not be able to forgive me, but I just wanted a chance to say I regret saying those things, and that I really *am* proud of you for what you're doing at Bingsu for Two." Her voice is barely loud enough for me to hear, but the words rattle in my skull nonetheless. "I saw so many people out and about today because of what you're doing. They *aren't* dumb videos. I know that, I know how capable you are. I just wanted to clear the air and let you know I'll always have your back, no matter where you decide to work."

I stand up. Cecelia steps out of the booth and I follow. I was right, there weren't any tears in her eyes.

There's a ringing in my ears, and an emotion so tightly wound inside me I clench my jaw to contain it. It rattles my teeth, yet my voice doesn't shake. "I saw you guys started up socials for Cafe Gong. Instagram didn't look like it was doing so well. Neither were any of your other platforms, or the post you made copying our introduction video. Good job for trying. You never give up, that's for sure."

Her ears start to glow red, stark against her blond hair. "We—"

"You blackmailed me, Cecelia, and now you're saying you didn't mean any of it? If I don't return to Cafe Gong, you'll go straight to my parents. One way or another, that's what you told me."

She winces. "I know what I said."

"You *said* you *knew* me, which is why you *knew* one way or another I'd come *crawling* back to Cafe Gong. You told me you didn't need my help, that you *never* needed my help." I take a deep breath, and the knot inside me unfurls. "Stop trying to convince me and prove it to yourself."

I leave her there, fists clenched and face ablaze with the same heat and shame she fanned me with last time. Mr. Crest 3D nods at me when I exit the restaurant. The air is cool out here, tinged with autumn in a way that eases the suffocating hand around my throat.

"Hey."

To the left, leaning against the wall of the building, is Sarang. My lips part.

"You waited?"

"Of course." She steps closer. When she's right in front of me, she pulls the beanie off her head and grabs the lapel of my jean jacket to drag me down to her height. She pushes my hair back and slides the beanie on. Our eyes catch. Her gaze pierces me completely open. I can't look away from the warm, endless depth of her irises.

For a second, I wonder if brunch is giving me heartburn. A rush of something warm balloons in my chest, breaking the iron rings of anxiety that were constricting it. Sarang watches me expectantly.

"Is everything okay?" she asks.

I nod. "I think it will be. I think she understands."

Then she raises her pinkie. "Are *you* okay?"

My finger lifts to link with hers before I even think about it. "Now I am."

She smiles, and it's compelling in the same way the sun is to a planet in orbit, all-encompassing. I couldn't turn away from her even if I wanted to. She waited for me.

We head for the bus that'll take us to Bingsu for Two. I don't realize my hand is fidgeting at my side until Sarang grabs it. My pulse spikes. Her fingers are practically half the size of mine, but they interlock perfectly. She looks ahead when she speaks.

"Just in case anyone from the scavenger hunt spots us. We can't turn the act off yet, you know."

I rub my thumb across her knuckles. They're so soft. Without letting myself think about it too long, I bend down to kiss her fingers. After all, I can't let her be the more romantic fake partner. "I think you just want to hold my hand, Sarang."

"Shut—*shut* the fuck up. If I didn't, you'd probably trip over your spider legs and crack your big, hollow skull open, and *I'd* have to be the one to clean your brain goo off the sidewalk."

"That'd be awful," I hum, not pointing out that if my skull was hollow, there'd be no brain goo to clean, because she's still holding on to me.

"Yeah. You're welcome."

I walk a little closer to her after that, and if she notices, she doesn't move away.

22. I'M LIKE KING MIDAS, EXCEPT EVERYTHING I TOUCH TURNS TO SHIT INSTEAD OF GOLD

Mr. Cho ordered us all to get some rest after the scavenger hunt and gave us a few days off, including Thanksgiving.

It was a tense, uncomfortable dinner, and not just because Dad and Umma were so preoccupied with Cafe Gong's dip in sales that they both forgot about the holiday until the morning of. It didn't help that Dad burned the ham he bought last-minute, and his ensuing temper tantrum sparked another long, loud argument between him and Umma.

That certainly put a damper on the holiday, but so did the anxiety wracking my brain as I spent every waking moment monitoring the publicity from our event, waiting for it or Cece to catch up with me. It hasn't yet, unbelievably. Which is either a miracle or the universe playing a cruel trick on me, dangling hope like a carrot that I keep chasing after. I guess I also have Umma and Dad's general social isolation to thank—they lost a good bit of their friends in the coffee community once Cafe Gong began putting the smaller stores out of business.

It's not until the following Saturday that I have my first shift after everything. Vanna and I spend the afternoon catching up as we work the front.

"So," she starts, pouring coffee beans into the grinder as I catch them in a bag. "How was your date?"

My hand slips and some of the coffee grinds miss the bag and spew out all over the counter. "How was *yours?*" I shoot back.

"I asked first."

"Sarang was Sarang," I say, repositioning the bag. That's not true, though. How she acted at our brunch . . . *date* was so out of character. Or maybe I'm still finding out what else there is to her. "It was nice. Fine. Not a date—not in the same way."

Vanna makes a crude gesture with her tongue and fingers that I groan and turn away from, which is how I see the figure darting outside our window and running into the store. The bell chimes in their wake.

"Haneul?" I say.

"Is Sarang here?" she says curtly.

"She's in the back," Vanna replies, stunned. "Are you—"

She dashes into the back. Out of sight, Sarang makes a sur-, prised noise from the kitchen.

"Unnie? What are you doing here? Don't you have a commission—are you crying?"

My stomach plummets at the panic in Sarang's voice, then rockets back up. Vanna and I freeze, exchanging a quick, confused look. Before I can even think about moving, Vanna starts inching toward the kitchen.

"We shouldn't," I whisper.

"I just want to make sure everything's okay," she replies. Hesitantly, I join her at the curtain entryway, peeking in through the space between the doorframe to catch the rest of their conversation.

"Why are you upset?" Sarang says in bewilderment, the smile on her face contradicting the confusion in her eyes. "Illumination Entertainment! They're *huge*. I knew all your commission work would pay off."

"Sarang, I can't accept it," Haneul says. Her voice cracks on Sarang's name.

"What? Why not?"

She laughs. Or sort of; it sounds like a wet hiccup. She wipes her eyes. "You serious? The *cafe*. I can't move to California. I can't leave the family business, not after all Umma and Appa put into it."

Sarang scoffs, a disbelieving smile on her face. "Appa knows how much your art means to you. Just get your ass down to California and live your dream. Why are we having this conversation?"

"Who would be the manager?" Haneul asks with a bitter smile. Without hesitation: "Me."

"You're going to Johns Hopkins next year, remember?"

"Yeah, but not for a few months. Dario can take over."

"Dario also has a full-ride scholarship. Basketball in Florida?"

For a few seconds Sarang's still and quiet. "Fine. Then Kai or Vanna."

I glance at Vanna, whose eyes widen with hope. *She could be manager*, I think.

"Kai's too young, managers have to be eighteen by law, and you know Vanna's situation; I don't think she can handle the manager role, especially with her time split between two other jobs and fighting the courts."

Vanna's face falls, then tightens. The quiet, simmering rage there stuns me, but I put it aside for now and focus back on the sisters.

Sarang's shoulders quiver. Her voice is thick like she's trying not to cry, and Haneul doesn't sound much better. I grip the edge of the doorframe, not daring to look away.

"Then River," Sarang says.

Haneul shakes her head. "This conversation is pointless. You know Appa will only let family run the place. He's not there yet."

They're both quiet. Haneul tilts her head up to the ceiling and blinks rapidly, face red. The veins on her neck jump as she swallows.

"It's okay, Sarang," Haneul says so quietly I strain to hear. "It's just a job. I'll turn it down and stay here."

"It's not just a job, it's your *life*," Sarang cries. "You already gave up art school after Umma died. You—that's already too much. You can't give this up, too. What if this is your last chance to do what you love?"

At that, Haneul buries her face in her hands, and silent sobs wrack her body.

I can't look any longer. Ears burning, I drop my eyes to the ground.

Silence.

Then Sarang speaks.

"I'll do it."

"You can't," Haneul hiccups. "You're leaving in—"

"No. I mean I'll stay."

My neck cracks as I whip my head up.

Haneul drops her hands. She gapes at Sarang, whose stiff expression threatens to waver.

"Shut up."

"I'm staying."

"You have a full-ride scholarship to *Johns Hopkins University*. You're not giving that up."

"But it's okay for you to give up *your* dreams?"

"Yes!" Haneul shouts. "Because I'm the oldest! That responsibility falls on *me*, not you."

"But you made the sacrifice last time. It's my turn."

"That's now how it's supposed to work," Haneul sobs.

Sarang takes a deep breath, standing up straighter. Tears glisten in her eyes but she refuses to let any of them fall. She manages a wobbly smile. "It's okay. I can still go to college. U-Dub has a good pre-med program, too."

"I'm not letting you ruin your future, Sarang. I can't. It's my job to look out for you."

"I can't let you ruin *yours* either," Sarang snaps. "It doesn't matter who's older, or who's younger, or any of those stupid family burdens. What matters is I love you, and it'd kill me to see you give up on your dream again."

I've inched forward without noticing it. I'm standing right at the edge of the doorway, clutching the curtain in my white-knuckled grip. My face is cold. The slow thumping of my blood is like a drum battering the side of my head.

She can't be serious. She can't be.

Haneul's lip wobbles. Her entire face creases. She chokes through another sob, then throws her arms around Sarang, squeezing her in a hug and burying her face in the crook of her neck. From the angle I stand at, I have a perfect view of Sarang's face as she wraps her arms around Haneul's waist and hooks her chin over her shoulder. She's crying, too. The tears she fought so hard to keep at bay spill freely now, down her cheeks and across her tightly pursed lips.

Heat prickles at the back of my eyes, and I close the curtain.

Pain doesn't suit her.

I glance at Vanna and do a double take. She's *fuming*.

"Are you fucking kidding me?" she hisses. Her lax, sleepy expression is molded hard with fury. "I have no *time* to be the manager because of my other jobs? If she made me manager, I could make enough money to finally *quit* those. I need this, Haneul knows it."

Unsure of what to say, I watch as Vanna stomps over to the espresso bar. She laughs quietly, coldly, shaking her head as she stares glassily at the floor.

"Vanna," I start, hand hovering uncertainly in the air. "Are you—"

She blows me off. "This is bullshit."

Tugging her apron over her head in a violent jerk, she tosses it to the ground and storms past me. "Tell them I went home early, if they even care."

I gape at her tense back as she escapes, leaving only the angry clamoring of the bell in her wake.

The digital clock above the stove flashes 8:15, fifteen minutes past my shift, but I linger in the breakroom anyway, fiddling with my apron until Sarang walks in. She halts upon seeing me.

"You're still here?" she snaps, harder than I know is intended for me. Her eyes are puffy, but I pretend I don't notice.

"Is your dad upstairs? Could I talk to him for a sec?"

"Why?" she asks suspiciously.

"I have a question about my paystub."

"I can help you with that."

I press my hand to my chest in mock indignation. "That is private and *highly* sensitive information, Sarang. How do I know you won't steal my Social Security number and give it out on the dark web?"

"Jesus, paranoid much?" She rolls her eyes. She's in a bad mood, understandably so, and I think she won't help until: "Fine, whatever. Just don't touch anything up there. I don't trust that you wash your hands properly."

Sarang heads toward the stairs in the opening in the wall. My heart races in my chest as I climb behind her. She gives me one last skeptical glance, then unlocks the door to the apartment and steps inside.

It's quaint. The entryway is small and cramped, and the hallway wall blocks sight of the kitchen and living room. I press against the door so I'm not bumping into Sarang.

"Appa?" she calls out.

"여기에,"[4] her dad replies from somewhere.

---

4.   Here

The narrow corridor of the entrance feeds into the living room, which has wooden floors and a thick carpet laid on top. Her father is sitting on the ground in front of a short round table, tapping away at his computer. His eyebrows rise, but then he smiles, and it lights up his whole face.

"River! So nice to see you."

Sarang says something in Korean. I understand 질문: question. Mr. Cho nods and pats the ground next to him.

"I'm happy to help. Come sit, River."

I look at Sarang pointedly. She scoffs, but leaves. I awkwardly sit on my knees next to the table.

"You're confused about your paycheck?" Mr. Cho says, slipping his glasses on and tapping on his computer. "No problem, I can help. What do—"

"Sorry," I interrupt. "Actually, I wanted to talk about something else."

He looks at me over the computer. "Sure."

I fidget, shifting my weight from side to side. My palms are clammy where I clench them under the table. *Just say it. Say it before you lose your nerve.*

"I'd like a promotion."

Mr. Cho laughs. *Ouch.* He collects himself quickly.

"I'm sorry, you caught me off guard. What position are you interested in? Trainer?"

"Manager," I say.

He doesn't laugh this time.

I can feel my courage slipping like dry sand between my fingers. I'm not confident in this decision—I only made it a few hours ago. That was plenty of time to agonize over every single reason *why* this is a bad idea, but the sight of tears rolling down Sarang's cheeks flashes across my mind's eye, and I strengthen my resolve. There's no one else. Although, my heart pangs when I think of Vanna. I agree that she *needs* this position more than anyone, certainly more than me, but after hearing Haneul today, I know I'm the more realistic sell; I have management experience and helped grow the cafe. *I* have to do this.

No. I want to.

"Please, Mr. Cho," I beg. "I know Haneul got a job offer at an animation studio, and you'll need someone to take over in her place. I'm qualified, I was a manager before, and most importantly, I have no plans for the future, so I'm not going anywhere."

Mr. Cho blinks. He slowly closes his laptop.

"You want to take over the shop?"

My chest aches like it's been hollowed out. I nod, bangs flopping into my eyes.

He takes his glasses off and rubs his eyes with his index finger and thumb. My crossed legs tingle as I wait for him to reply.

"You're a smart kid," Mr. Cho says. "I'm glad to have you here, and I know my daughters and the others feel the same. I can't ever thank you for all you've done for us." He looks up. "But you can't be manager."

"Why not?" I ask.

"This cafe is not a business—it's a home. It's all I have left of my wife. And no amount of work ethic can make up for the love that's needed to take care of this place, which I'm not sure you have, yet. I'd rather close our shop than let someone who's only in it for a job manage it." Mr. Cho reaches over and rests his hand atop mine. He smiles apologetically. "I'm sorry, River."

A seed of remorse blocks my throat. I swallow it, and it blooms in my chest as grief.

I rise to my feet. Unable to meet Mr. Cho's eyes, I bow my head and mumble half a thank-you and half an apology. I show myself out, hurrying down the narrow hallway decked with family photographs.

Sarang is blocking the entryway. Her face is red, and not with a blush.

She beckons me to follow, and stunned to see her still here, I comply wordlessly. Once outside, Sarang backs me against the wall of the unlit upper landing of the stairwell. She immediately turns on me, her features hardened.

"What was that back there?" she asks.

"You were listening?"

"You want to be *manager*?"

"Somebody has to. Haneul's leaving—"

"I know that!" she snaps, and I can see the last tether of calm she'd been clinging to all day splinter with it. Her dark eyes pop open, and the tear streaks on her face are enunciated against the red flush of her skin. Everything she was bottling up for her sister comes spewing out now, and I'm not sure how to handle the mess. "You don't think I know that? That's the whole fucking problem, *genius*. It's why I have to give up *everything* so Haneul doesn't have to this time."

"It should be me," I say.

"This is a family matter, River, not your business. Who do you think you are to go over my head like that, anyway? Like I'm too fragile to even discuss it with? Is this what you consider being help-ful, stepping in to solve my problems like I couldn't possibly know what's best for me? That's so condescending."

I stare at her dumbly, an empty expression on my face. "I didn't think of it that way. But I didn't do it because I don't think you can solve your own problems. It's just . . . this is a way for both you and Haneul to follow your dreams. I promise I just want to help." For once, I'm not trying to provoke her, but she mistakes my tone for patronizing.

"Yeah, right," she hisses. "I don't know what you're up to, but I know you're not *this* selfless. You didn't even want to be a manager for your own folks, why the hell should you be one for mine? I don't trust it."

I know she's just angry, just frustrated at how unforgiving the whole situation is, but it's hard not to let that one sting. Desperately, I hold my pinkie out to her. "Our pact. We'll lie to everyone else but not each other, right?"

She smacks my pinkie out of her face.

Hurt sinks its claws into my chest and drags. Then fire scorches in its trails.

"Are you serious?" I say. "You're mad at me for trying to help you out?"

Her lips pull back in a sneer. "Yes, thank you so much, my knight in shining armor. Thank you for *swooping* in to save us for *totally* not selfish reasons. Is this just another publicity stunt for your video, huh? How are you going to spin it for your fans this time? I can't wait to see."

Like a furnace being ignited, anger sparks through my body and evaporates all traces of shock. I bark out a laugh. "Only you could manage to twist this. You're a control freak, Sarang. You can't stomach the idea that you might *need* help, especially from me. You'd rather sabotage your future than admit you can't do everything yourself?"

Her face darkens. "Don't act so noble. What you're doing is looking for a purpose in your life since you don't have one—you've never had one and you never will. You're going *nowhere*."

Red fogs up my vision. Her voice echoes Cecelia's in my ears, repeating the same words that I know Umma and Dad say to each other behind my back, too. I bite my lip so hard the taste of copper seeps across my tongue.

"Looks like *neither* of us will be going anywhere, actually," I spit.

I thump down the stairs, grab my shit, and leave.

23. IS THIS A HEART ATTACK OR HEARTBREAK? I HOPE THE FORMER. THE LATTER IS TOO EMBARRASSING.

Of course it's raining.

I didn't bring an umbrella with me, but home is about the last place I want to go, so I hike my hood up and deal with it.

The Waterfront Pier Boardwalk is next to Pike Place Market, and about a twenty-minute walk from the cafe. I figure the air will do me good, help unwind this coil of anger slithering around in my gut like a disgusting parasite.

I pass the outdoor market/tourist hell spot, and the boardwalk comes into view. Pier 62 is far enough away from the Ferris wheel that not a lot of people bother with it, which is why it's my favorite place. Hidden from view is a metal ramp that leads down to the Floating Dock, a small wooden platform beneath the pier floating right atop the Pacific Ocean. The ramp clangs under my feet as I walk down it. There are no barriers or lifeguards of any kind on the dock, and you're below sight of the streets, so I'm cautious.

Almost immediately, the tightness in my chest eases. I'm careful not to let it unravel too quickly, or like an anchor slipping free from a boat's windlass, I'll lose complete control over it. I take a seat on the dock, staring out at the dark sea and the dim, cobalt blue sky above it. The waves slosh gently, rocking the platform side to side. Shutting my eyes, I focus on the smell of sea salt, the wet splashes of rain on my skin, the evening chill biting my cheeks, and don't think about Sarang. Shit, now I'm thinking about her. My anger is fresh all over again, and so is the aching pit in my chest.

My phone pings. My stomach does a weird flop but settles once I see it's Jace.

Jace

R u going to be back for dinner?

Pls say yes

Umma and Dad r going to make me bash my head against the wall

Dad won't shut up about how Bingsu for Two is taking all of Cafe Gong's business, I think they're cutting the new location's hours by like 3 days a week

Ok maybe ur dodging a bullet by not being here

Lmk when ur on the way

I don't have the energy to reply, so instead I halfheartedly scroll through the Son of Sin fanfics I bookmarked but never read to pass the time until . . . I don't know, I start feeling like a person again. The chill has settled into my bones when the clanging of footsteps on the metal ramp behind me nearly makes me fumble my phone into the sea.

I can't tell who it is in the dark. The figure's steps are slow, faltering. Maybe they can't see me, either. When they step onto the boardwalk a few feet away, the reflection of the city lights on the water plays a flickering glow of blue shadows across their features.

Sarang.

She looks hesitant. Or maybe that's the light playing tricks on my eyes.

"Uh," I say eloquently. I try again. "Uh."

"Are you rebooting?" she asks.

"How'd you find me?"

"I texted Kai."

"Kai doesn't know where I am."

"I told him you stormed off, and he said you'd be here. Said this is your spot, or something."

I'm not sure whether it's creepy how well Kai knows me, or sweet.

The rain continues to drizzle over our heads as we look at each other.

Sarang sits beside me. She scoots something over: a carry-out cup.

I stare at the drink. "Is this an apology?"

"It's a sweet potato latte."

"My favorite."

"I know."

I grab it and take a sip. The hot milk warms up my insides, contrasting with the iciness between us chafing my skin. "It's good. Still not an apology. Or are you the type who refuses to apologize?"

"I'm sorry," Sarang says. "For what I said, and for not honoring our truth pact back there. I believe you."

"*Oh.*"

She hugs her knees to her chest and wraps her arms around them. Neither of us says anything else. I hold the latte out to her. She considers the offer for a moment before accepting and taking a sip.

"God, I'm great at making these," she says.

"And you're also super humble."

"That too."

I chuckle.

The rain doesn't let up. When I look over at Sarang, hunched in on herself and gazing blankly at the waves before us, a raindrop falls in my eye. I blink past it so I can see her.

"I'm sorry, too," I say. "Not just because you apologized and now it's my turn, but because I said some shitty things I didn't mean. You're right, it wasn't my place to try to solve your problems without talking to you. I really am sorry."

"So you don't think I'm a control freak?"

"That was a harsh way to put it. I think you *like* being in control because that way you know things get done. But I don't think you're so obsessed with doing everything yourself that you'd purposely sabotage your dream. I shouldn't have said that. You're not stupid."

She snorts humorlessly. "I guess I do take over sometimes."

"No one's saying you're not *bossy*."

"Of course I'm bossy; I'm going to be the next boss."

It's a poor attempt at lightheartedness. The way Sarang's voice cracks at the end betrays her.

"For the record," I say, "I know you'll be a great manager."

"Thanks."

Our argument replays in my head. Something itches inside me, clawing at my esophagus to try to free itself. Whatever it is, I know it can't be good, so I fight to hold it back. Until I can't.

"That's not why I did it," I blurt.

Sarang looks at me. "What?"

"Asking your dad to let me be manager?" I lock eyes with her. It's easier in the darkness. "You said I did it for the channel, or so I'd have a purpose in life. Something to do with myself."

"River, I didn't mean—"

"No, it's okay. It's a fair guess. But . . ." My eyes roam over her face. The rain soaking her hair runs in droplets down her cheeks, following the trails her tears left behind. I swallow thickly. "That's not why I did it."

Her breath hitches. I look away so I can catch mine.

"River," she says softly. "If you're going to do something, do it for you. Not anyone else."

I don't know how to tell her that there's only one person I'd volunteer to be manager for, and it isn't me. Sarang's staring somewhere along the horizon line, which is beginning to blend into the shadows of the cresting waves. The skyscrapers behind us illuminate her side profile. Either a tear or a raindrop gathers at her lash line, smudging her makeup. Before I can think too hard about it, I reach over and wipe it away with my thumb, letting my palm linger on her cheek. She blinks rapidly.

"You'll catch a cold if we stay out here any longer," I say.

She sniffs and scrubs her face. "*You'll* catch a cold."

"Nah. I've got your love to keep me warm."

"Shut up." Sarang laughs. Then hiccups, and dissolves into quiet crying almost muffled by the rain. I scooch over and wrap my arm around her shoulder. To my surprise, she leans into my side. Her hair tickles my chin.

"Do you want to talk about it? You know, Haneul leaving?" I ask.

Her fingers dig into the front of my sweater. "No. I don't know. Not now."

"That's fine, too. We can just sit here."

Waves rocking the platform conceal the motion of me rubbing my hand up and down her arm. Or maybe she notices, but she doesn't move away.

It's not so cold anymore.

24. YOU DON'T HAVE TO BE RIGHT ON THE INTERNET; YOU JUST HAVE TO BE FIRST

"Have you heard? There's supposed to be a huge snowstorm tomorrow night," I tell Kai, scribbling some halfhearted answers on my chemistry homework from my spot at the counter. I'd neglected it yesterday because one of my favorite YouTubers released a two-hour-long analysis of the character de-evolution in Son of Sin.

"Dude?" Kai says while he wipes down the espresso machine. "Shut up about the weather."

"It's so weird, it hardly ever snows in December here."

"I'm going to stuff this dirty rag in your mouth if you say another word about snow."

I put my pencil down and look up. "Who pissed in your cereal this morning?"

"That's so nasty."

"What's the matter? Seriously."

Kai glances around the cafe. Sarang and Dario disappeared to the back a while ago, and Vanna is taking her meal break in the corner of the dining area. She's hardly spoken a word to any of us all night, and she's been cold and distant ever since the whole management thing. I tried asking her if she was okay once, but she just muttered something about her family and walked off.

Despite her and the few customers in the room being out of earshot, Kai still lowers his voice.

"It's Dario," he says.

"Are you guys fighting again?"

"*Again?* Again would imply there was once a point in time where we weren't fighting. Yes, we're *still* fighting. Sort of. He's getting on my nerves."

"I didn't notice him do anything to you today."

"Exactly. He's been ignoring me for a week."

I wince. "Kai—"

"No, don't give me that bullshit about how since we're broken up, he doesn't care about me anymore. You know what, even if that is true, *I* still give a shit about *him*. So . . ."

Kai trails off, scrubbing a spot that's already clean. I chew on my lip in consideration. The day Kai tried to kiss Dario comes to my mind. Dario's reaction when Vanna accused him of still having feelings is branded in my memory. He looked like a deer caught in headlights—or someone caught in a lie.

"You think he still cares?" I ask gingerly.

"I know he does. We had a conversation after our fight the other week. After I—whatever. I asked him if he lost feelings, because yeah, that would sting but at least I could move on." Kai drops his head, glaring at the countertop. His mouth twitches downward.

I push when he doesn't continue, readying myself to console him. "What'd he say?"

"He said he still loves me."

My eyebrows shoot up.

"Holy crap. Kai, that's—" I cut myself off, my smile withering. Kai looks anything *but* happy. "Wait, what's the problem then?"

"The problem is love isn't enough." He looks up, arms crossed over his chest. "He said he dumped me because it would be easier to try to forget his feelings than for us to do a long-distance relationship for the next couple of years. He"—Kai laughs, sharp and bitter—"he said *logically,* this is the best option for both of us. He can focus on his career, and I can focus on saving enough for Ma to go take care of A-má in Taiwan."

My jaw falls. People usually only say that about long-distance relationships when they're trying to look for an out without seeming like an asshole, but that's not Dario. I remember comparing their relationship to mine and Cece's, even unconsciously. I never knew it was possible to love someone as much as Dario loved Kai.

So why does he think taking the easy way out is better?

Kai changes the subject before I can respond. "That's not why I'm on edge, though. I mean, that's not the only reason." He leans closer but keeps his narrowed gaze on the few customers in the store. "Everyone's been *looking* at me weird. The last five customers I rang up all gave me the same look. Like—like I was disgusting or something."

"I'm sure they . . ."

Seeing Isabette dashing outside our window makes me trail off. She hurries into the store, panic seizing her features and lungs.

"River. *Kai.* I'm so—so sorry," she says between breaths. "I didn't know they—have any of you looked at your social media accounts today?"

"No, why?" I say.

Kai whips out his phone and taps madly. "What is it?" he urges, his finger flicking across the screen. "Did someone say something about—"

His eyes widen, hands freezing.

I peer over his shoulder. A dozen people on Instagram have tagged us in new posts, but there's one in particular with nearly two hundred thousand likes. It's from one of those influencer scandal accounts—basically, the enablers of the internet who gossip about current drama floating around. At first, I'm not sure what I'm looking at, or why. It's a screenshot of somebody's Instagram DMs, but whoever's account it is has been blurred out. I squint at the username at the top. They're messaging *Kai*.

The blood drains from my face as I read.

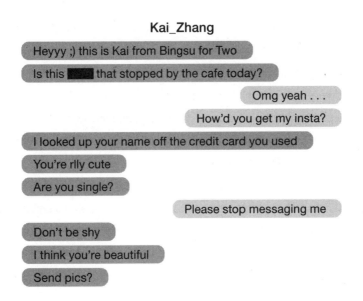

Kai_Zhang

Heyyy ;) this is Kai from Bingsu for Two

Is this ▮▮▮ that stopped by the cafe today?

Omg yeah . . .

How'd you get my insta?

I looked up your name off the credit card you used

You're rlly cute

Are you single?

Please stop messaging me

Don't be shy

I think you're beautiful

Send pics?

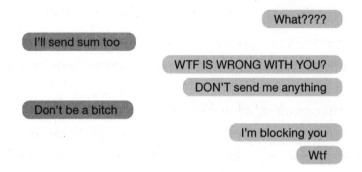

I stare at the screen. I don't blink. Eventually I force my body to move, to step back and look at Kai.

He looks like he's about to throw up.

"Kai," I say slowly. "What is—"

"Holy shit," he mutters. His hands shake so hard he drops his phone. "Holy shit." Kai shakes his head, a slow back and forth. "That's not me. I mean, that's my username, but I never—" Urgently, he snatches his phone off the floor and zooms in on the screenshot. "That's my account. But I never sent that text! I never looked anybody up on Instagram, that's so fucking creepy! Oh my god. All these people think— They tagged me. They tagged my account. All these people think I'm harassing strangers online and—"

"Woah, woah, *woah*." I steady his shoulders when it looks like he'll keel over. "That's not you?"

"No! I would never do anything like this, *ever*!"

I'm an idiot, of course he wouldn't. I didn't stop to consider it could be fake—and I know Kai inside and out. The two hundred thousand people who liked and commented on the picture don't. They know nothing about him except that he harassed some poor person online for nudes.

Isabette wrings her hands together, sending distraught glances between Kai and Vanna, who crosses the cafe to join us and stand by her side with a look of concern. She grabs Isabette's hand.

"What's going on? What happened, Betty?"

Isabette's lip wobbles. Responding to both of us, she says, "It was Cece."

The ground falls out from under me.

I pick up the phone and scroll frantically through the flood of notifications to find the first person who reposted it; a fan account, ironically. My eyes widen as I read through the comments.

HannibalSzn4When: this is crazy. source?

> **LoveLeeLover_316:** *this other Seattle cafe account posted it earlier, I found it under the #BingsuForTwo tag*
>
> **X_Rita_X:** *^^ I saw it too. The account is @UnionStreet_CafeGong*
>
> **Callmecollin:** *they deleted it*

My gut folds like I've been sucker-punched. I click on the username and see the account for Cafe Gong that Cece recently created, the one I checked up on just *days* ago, is slowly but steadily going up in follower count despite the fact that the rest of their posts are still low quality and have almost zero engagement. A swipe to their tagged photos reveals dozens of identical screenshots, confirming them as the source.

Kai's breathing catches my attention. It's fast. Too fast. Shit, he's hyperventilating. A panic attack. He hasn't had one in a while, at least not that I know of. Adrenaline spikes through my veins like a sting of electricity.

"Vanna, stay out here, watch the front," I order.

I steer Kai by the shoulders toward the back room. Isabette hurries to Kai's other side, shielding him from the customers' curious gazes. Sarang and Dario are baking something in the kitchen and look up when we enter.

"What's the matter?" Sarang asks.

Dario drops his whisk and rushes over. He practically pushes me out of the way to grab Kai's arms, bending to look him in the eye.

"Kai? Just breathe."

"I—" Kai stutters through an inhale. "I *am*, asshole."

Dario guides him to the sofa, plopping him down and taking a seat next to him. He cups Kai's face in his hands and pushes his bangs off his forehead. A sheen of sweat coats Kai's ashen face as his entire body trembles. His eyes dart around wildly before settling on Dario.

"They think—everyone thinks—I'm not—I would never. *Never.* That—th—"

"No," Dario interrupts. He rubs his thumb across Kai's cheek. Kai latches onto both of Dario's wrists. "Don't think about whatever it is," Dario says soothingly. "Let's talk about something else."

"Like what?"

"Did you get enough sleep last night? I know you worked the opening shift."

"Of course I didn't get enough sleep."

A smile breaks on Dario's face. "That's your own fault. You were probably up late designing more of your clothes, weren't you?"

Kai shifts on the couch. His legs won't stay still. He taps a foot against the floor before folding it under him, then moves it again. He blinks, swallowing heavily, his Adam's apple bobbing with the motion.

"It's hot in here. I might pass out."

"It's not hot at all. Focus on me. Did you make any new designs last night?"

"No. I went skating."

"Adds up. Hey, did you ever figure out how to do a nollie heelflip? I remember you were going to learn that one next."

Kai's shoulders start to ease up from their bunched position by his ears. "I got that down a few weeks ago, actually."

"Seriously?"

"Uh-huh."

Dario goes back to stroking Kai's hair out of his face. He smirks. "That's kind of cool."

"Kind of cool? It's *sick*."

"You should show me sometime. I miss watching you at the skate park."

I inch away, although I'm pretty sure they wouldn't notice me even if I called out their names. Isabette and Sarang hover near the kitchen island, whispering fervently to each other.

"It was Cecelia, just like you said," I interrupt. "She posted it on Cafe Gong's Instagram and the algorithm picked it up. People are tagging them online."

Isabette nods, curls bouncing around her creased face. "I think Jorge and Rosalind helped, too. They must have photoshopped Kai's account onto some fake message thread they made."

"What a bunch of pathetic lowlifes," Sarang spits. "Is this their attempt to sabotage us because we're stealing their business? By turning our subscribers against us?"

I dig the heel of my palms into my eyes with a long, heavy sigh. Oh god—my sighs are starting to sound like Dad. "Yeah. That new location is suffering because of all our new success, especially after how well the scavenger hunt went. But I think there's more to it." I look up. "Cecelia asked me to come back and be co-manager with her, so that I could make videos for Cafe Gong like I did for Bingsu for Two. I told her no, and she didn't take it so well. This feels personal."

Stunned, Sarang asks, "Is that why you almost quit and went back?"

I nod, pursing my lips. I thought me and Cecelia's conversation at The 5 Point Cafe was the end of things, which was wishful thinking. She never gives up.

"Fuck, why didn't she go after me instead of Kai?" I groan.

At that moment, the kitchen curtain rustles and Vanna slips in. She beelines our way, and for the first time in a while, addresses Sarang directly. "Hey, everyone out there is talking about some shit with Kai online. I looked it up—it's bad. What the hell are we going to do?"

Sarang turns to me, waiting for my move again. Trusting me with our next step.

Think, River. You've been online long enough to see plenty of influencers and celebrities canceled. What would an overpriced PR team do in this situation?

I straighten my shoulders back. "Okay. We need to address this online and set the record straight, but let's take our time to figure out a response. Right now, I'll go talk to Cecelia. Dario can take care of Kai. Who wants to deal with the customers up front, and who wants to monitor our channels and turn off comments temporarily?"

"Me and Betty can handle the channels," Sarang says. "Vanna, how about you watch the cafe?"

"Why?" Vanna replies curtly. "That feels like something the *manager* should oversee. I'm a little too tied up to be able to handle that kind of responsibility. Too *busy*, right?"

The three of us gawk at her, but I'm the only one who understands where she's coming from. Defense tinges the confused crease on Sarang's face. "What are you talking about?"

Vanna glares, but then her eyes catch on Isabette. It softens whatever her response would've been, because instead of replying, she mutters something under her breath and heads out of the kitchen back to the lobby. Fuck, that's not good, but there's no time to explain to Sarang, no matter how much her injured frown stings me. *Later*, I mouth.

Sarang is the first to snap out of it. "We have to focus. Kai needs our help," she says. Her voice is solid, steady. "We can fix this."

Something like awe strikes me in my chest. She's so level-headed, so confident. She's everything I'm not, and the knowledge of it doesn't feel like a burn this time. It's admirable—I admire Sarang. Wow, it's weird to admit that, even in my thoughts.

I don't hate it as much as I would have expected to, though.

She catches me staring. "Are you waiting for an invitation?"

Shaking my head to snap myself out of it, I turn to Isabette. "Is Cece still there?" I ask.

She nods.

My already-racing pulse jumps as I run out of the cafe and down the streets of Seattle. The sound of my heart pumping in my ears increases my anger; each rapid *badump badump badump* is a strike against my rapidly weakening resolve. Cafe Gong's glowing sign burns into my retinas.

I throw the front doors open. The abnormally few customers inside jump, whipping their heads to gawk at me. I don't see them. I only see red.

Until the tall man behind the counter that's not usually there turns around to face me, and my soul leaves my body.

"Dad?" I rasp out, the air and confidence deflating from my lungs.

He squints at me in confusion, a clipboard in one hand and a bag of espresso beans in the other: inventory day. *Of course it is.* One of the few times Dad shows up at the store. Realization flashes through his eyes, and the confusion transforms to wrath in a blink. He puts his clipboard and beans down and walks toward me, where my feet are glued to the floor.

Oh no. Is the jig finally up?

"What are you doing here?" Dad hisses. "You're supposed to be at your tutoring lesson."

Okay, not what I thought it would be, which is good, but I still clam up. My mouth opens and shuts uselessly as my brain whirs like an old computer battery. Dad's eyebrows furrow, and he crosses his arms.

Cecelia steps out from the back then. She makes eye contact with me and smiles. My rage at seeing her reboots the system shutdown happening in my head, and I pull myself together as she sidles up next to me and Dad.

I force my voice steady. "I wanted to see Cecelia."

A raise of the brow and a quick, meaningful glance at her gets the point across to Dad, thankfully. The anger instantly defuses into discomfort. He mouths the word "Oh," nodding. "All right. I'll leave you kids to it. I'll get back to . . ." He looks awkwardly for an exit and takes it before bothering to finish.

Cecelia turns to me, a perfectly pleasant look on her face. "We should go to the back. You're disturbing the customers," she chirps.

My eye twitches. She turns on her heel and I follow her into the back of the store. From the breakroom, Rosalind's obnoxious laugh echoes out, and I make a hard turn to avoid heading that way. I step around Cecelia and point her to the closest door: the walk-in fridge.

"After you," I say with a forced smile, opening the large, heavy metal door.

She steps in and I close the door behind us. A waft of cold air wraps around me, causing my skin to rise in goose bumps. I take slow, deliberate breaths to calm myself, looking at the metal shelves full of milk instead of her. I can't let my emotions get the best of me. Riling Cecelia up might provoke her into ratting me out or doing something worse—and given what she did to Kai, who knows what else she's capable of. I close my eyes, then meet her expecting, smug gaze.

"Tell me what you're up to," I ask.

"Not much, at the moment. Feeling a little cold."

"How could you do that to Kai? Is this revenge? Or are you try-ing to intimidate me into coming back to Cafe Gong again? Because I've gotta say, it's not the best plan. Sure is a great way to get me to hate you, though."

Cecelia recoils. A sick part of me revels in satisfaction at having hurt her, before immediately being washed away by disgust. This isn't who I want to be. But the more time I spend with Cecelia, the more I see myself doing that.

"I don't have time for revenge," she replies after composing herself.

"Clearly you had time for blackmail, though."

"I still do." Cecelia smirks. "Your dad's right outside. There's only a couple of feet between me and the end of your world."

Part of me wants to scream, *Just fucking do it then.* I can't take it anymore, waiting for the other shoe to drop at any given second. It's inevitable.

But Cece doesn't step toward the door. For some reason, she hasn't followed through on her threat yet.

"Why'd you sacrifice Kai to the internet?" I say, turning us back to the reason I'm here.

Cecelia's lips twist into her cheeks, baring her perfect teeth. It's a warped version of a smile. "Consider it a call to action."

"Cut to the fucking point."

"You kiss your girlfriend with that mouth?"

"*Cecelia.*"

"When you barged in, you must've noticed how many customers were out in the lobby. How *few*, actually. Business is slow these days, as I'm sure you've heard from your parents. This store—*our* store—was supposed to be the most successful location, yet we're doing so badly we have to cut hours. All because a certain Korean cafe blew up online, the Korean cafe *you* targeted for us to run out of business within months. Do you remember that? Cafe Gong is failing because of *you*."

I straighten. Of course I remember. It was my decision, one I regret every day. "I offered before to help you try to get customers the same way we did, but you're the one who said you didn't want my help."

Cecelia crosses the space between us in one step. Her hot breath fans my throat, a painful contrast to the icy air of the fridge around us. I cringe backward, my shoulder blade knocking into the shelf behind me.

"I said I don't *need* it, which is true. I'm going to get our customers back—or get them *away* from you, either will work for me. Then I can prove how I ran *and* saved this family business all on my own. It's a much better success story to sell on my college applications, so thank you. I guess you did end up being helpful in that way."

For the first time, I understand what Kai warned me about all those years I was with Cece. Our relationship was never about me and her; it was her, and what I was *to* her. Cafe Gong's success and my lack thereof were just helpful plot points in her narrative essay of self-made success at seventeen. We're stepping-stones to her better, brighter future at UPenn and beyond, but only now is she finally admitting it.

Better late than never.

"What do you mean that this is a 'call to action'?" I ask carefully.

"The call isn't for you."

"Then who?"

She shrugs. "You'll find out. Don't worry."

"I'm not playing these games with you."

"That's your choice. I'll give you another." Cecelia waits until she's sure I'm listening and paying her my full, utmost attention. "You don't have much longer to reclaim your job here. If you wanted to come back, it'd have to be soon. Just so you know."

I don't bother with a response. She knows my answer. We're done here. Stepping past her and toward the door, I glance over my shoulder. Cecelia isn't smiling anymore.

It hits me then. Why she hasn't told my parents everything. She isn't going to—she *likes* getting to hold this over me. This is the closest thing to the control she used to have when we were together.

I shake her off and leave Cafe Gong. The chill lingers in my body everywhere except where her breath fanned my skin.

25. I'VE GOT AN IDEA! LET'S MAKE THIS TERRIBLE SITUATION WORSE.

It's best to get on top of the Kai Disaster quickly. So that night, after we've closed the shop, the five of us and Isabette gather in the dining area to strategize our approach.

Sarang heads the discussion.

"Why are we even *having* a discussion?" she repeats for the third time in the last half hour. I roll my eyes. "No, don't roll your eyes at me, River. I'm asking *you*. What is there to strategize? The answer is simple: be honest. Tell our subscribers that Kai's innocent and never harassed anyone."

"Like I said, no one will believe us if that's what we do. It'll sound like we're lying to cover it up, which will only make Kai look worse. We have to think carefully about what we're going to say."

"I don't want to say *anything*." Kai slinks down in his chair until only the top half of his face is visible above the table. He glares at the surface. "Why bother trying to clear this up? It's too late. No matter what we say, there's always going to be people out there who believe I'm some sexual predator or whatever. All because some *fuckers* lied about me online for—for what reason?"

Everyone turns to me expectantly. I wince. "I wish I knew. Cecelia wasn't very helpful, just said it wasn't revenge. All we can assume is that they're trying to target our fan base to knock some business down."

Kai clicks his tongue and stands up. "I'm sitting this one out. I'll be in the back."

We all watch him leave, silent.

Sarang sighs and massages her temples. "We can't *not* try to fix this."

Isabette squirms. "What if Kai's right? Maybe talking about it will only fan the flames. Should we let it blow over? What do you think, Vanna?"

Slouched in the seat next to her and glued to her phone, Vanna jerks. She tilts her screen down and mumbles a distracted, "I don't know. I agree with Betty," before returning to whatever she was doing. Her forehead is creased with stress lines, and a sinking feeling in my stomach tells me it has something to do with the family situation she mentioned.

"No," Dario says firmly. "Kai's not the person they're saying he is. We have to clear his name."

The five of us look around the table at each other. I speak first. "I agree. So let's figure out the best way to do that. I think we need to approach this casually. If we seem too forceful—or *angry*—it'll only give the internet more fuel for tearing us down. So, no formal videos. No arguing. No pointing fingers."

"What?" Sarang says. "We're not gonna say it was your ex who's behind all this? That's bullshit."

I put my hands up. "It's not because I want to defend Cecelia, but if we accuse them—a bunch of strangers the internet doesn't even know—it becomes a matter of 'he said, she said.'" My lips purse. "It doesn't matter if you're right on the internet; you just have to be first."

"So what do you think we should do?" Isabette asks.

"Something informal, like an Instagram Live. And it can't focus on the Kai issue—it has to come up naturally. If it seems like *we* don't consider it a big deal, our followers won't either. Speaking of, only one of us should be in the live, to make it more casual. So, who wants to do it?"

"Dario should," Sarang says. Dario's head snaps to her.

"Why me?"

She bites her bottom lip. I watch as she considers her words. "Because people know you guys are broken up, so they won't think you have any reason to lie for him."

I scoff, but quickly cover it up with a cough, ducking my head. Our followers aren't idiots; they can see the love Dario and Kai have for each other. It's why so many people ship them and gush in the comments section every time they interact. Sarang nudges my calf with her shoe. I glance sideways at her. She raises her eyebrows microscopically, looking pointedly between Dario and the kitchen where Kai disappeared to.

Oh. I get it. This isn't just for the viewers—it's for Kai and Dario, too.

I do need to stop underestimating her.

"All right." Dario nods. "I'll do it."

Setting up for the live feels more rehearsed than ever. I direct Dario behind the counter and task him with pretending to clean the espresso machine. Sarang, Isabette, and Vanna sit on the barstools out of frame. Kai has yet to come out of the kitchen, but that's okay, it might be better if he doesn't make an appearance.

"Act casual," I tell Dario. "Don't look at the camera too often. Don't sound rehearsed. Focus on cleaning and looking busy, like you don't care that I'm recording."

"Uh," Dario says.

"You're going to freak him out with all the stage directions, Scorsese," Sarang calls out.

I give her a halfhearted middle finger without turning. "We'll start with a few off-topic questions from the comments, and then gradually work our way toward bringing up the Kai situation. You can talk about how that's not the type of person Kai is, and that someone framed him. But make sure to be low-key about it, okay?"

Dario's nod is less than confident. I step back, point the phone's camera at him, and start an Instagram Live.

INT. "Bingsu for Two"/BAR — NIGHT

Standing stiffly in front of the espresso machine is DARIO, wiping down the steam wand with mechanical, jerky movements. His face is blank yet hardened as he stares at the wall.

SARANG (O.S.)

(quietly)

He's horrible. God.

Behind the camera, River clears his throat, drawing Dario's attention.

RIVER (O.S.)

(painfully rehearsed)

Hey, Dario. You got a second? We haven't done an Instagram Live in a while, and the others are all—

DARIO

Yeah.

RIVER(O.S.)

Yeah, you got a second, or?

DARIO

Sorry, uh, yeah. No, go ahead.

RIVER (O.S.)

Cool. The chat is blowing up. Let me see . . . looks like someone is talking about your biceps. Oh, lots of people are. Is there a question here somewhere? Here we go. Somebody asked if you play any sports other than basketball.

DARIO

A little baseball and soccer, but that's it. And some weightlifting in the gym.

RIVER (O.S.)

Another person asked if you're excited for the holidays coming up?

DARIO

Sure.

RIVER (O.S.)

How come?

Dario leans back on the edge of the countertop, wringing a rag in his hands. Tension melts from his bunched shoulders as he remembers something.

DARIO

I like this time of year. The Christmas lights, the cold weather. It's romantic, I don't know.

RIVER (O.S.)

(reading the comments)

Wow, they like *that*. A few viewers want you to elaborate on romantic.

DARIO

No.

Out of frame, Sarang coughs pointedly. Dario glares and looks in that direction, before shifting and crossing his arms.

DARIO

For the last couple of Christmas Eves, me and Kai—my ex, I mean—had this tradition of going downtown to take pictures of the Christmas lights at midnight.

RIVER (O.S.)

Remind our viewers. How long did you and Kai date?

DARIO

Is this a necessary question?

RIVER (O.S.)

They're just curious.

DARIO

Three years.

RIVER (O.S.)

You know him well. Better than I do, probably.

Dario taps his foot against the floor and makes a face
that says get to the point.

RIVER (O.S.)

Since you've known him so long, you might . . . be

able . . .

River trails off, distracted. Dario frowns.

DARIO

What?

RIVER (O.S.)

Uh. Nothing. Just some of the comments.

DARIO

(extends his hand out)

Let me see.

The camera jumps as River takes a step back.

RIVER (O.S.)

(forcefully nonchalant)

No, it's nothing. Let's get back to the conversation. So

you and—

DARIO

Tell me what they're saying, River.

A stifled sigh. The frame drops to film two pairs of shoes
and sticky, checkered tiles as River lowers the phone.

RIVER (O.S.)

(whispering)

They're talking about the Kai thing.

DARIO (O.S.)

Good. Let's talk about it.

A hand shoots across the frame and pulls the phone back up to view. Dario stands back, a firm set to his features as he glares into the camera.

DARIO

I'll cut to the chase. That post is bullshit. Kai was set up. He never messaged anyone, he would *never* message anyone that kind of crap. Don't believe everything you see on the internet.

RIVER (O.S.)

(panic-whispering)

What happened to casual?!

DARIO

I can't be casual when hundreds of thousands of people need to be put in their place.

River is silent. Too silent.

DARIO

What? What is it?

RIVER (O.S.)

Uh.

DARIO

What'd they say?

RIVER (O.S.)

They don't believe you.

Hushed, angry whispering from two distinct voices sounds in the background.

RIVER (O.S.)

This is why we were supposed to address it naturally.

DARIO

Tell me what they're saying. Exactly.

RIVER (O.S.)

(hesitantly)

They, uh, think you're jealous.

Dario's face does a strange contortion where the bottom half of his face is grinning, but the top half is creased in a glare. It creates an unsettling image caught between comic disbelief and rage. A vein on his temple bulges.

DARIO

Jealous?

RIVER (O.S.)

(reading)

"'Man's mad his ex is out here asking for nudes from other people lol.'" "'Someone sounds bitter.'"

"'You wish that were you, huh?'"

DARIO

OKAY. I get it.

RIVER (O.S.)

Sorry.

DARIO

(strained)

No, I am not jealous. I'm trying to clear his name. You ·all need to get that through your thick skulls, *and* the fact that Kai and I are broken up. Done. There's nothing between us anymore. I'm not in love with him.

RIVER (O.S.)

Someone asked you to prove it?

The camera picks up the fury that darts across Dario's eyes like a flash of lightning.

DARIO

Fine.

In a blur of motion, Dario steps away from the counter, fists his hand in the fabric of River's shirt, and tugs him forward.

The phone falls to the floor with a clatter, still recording.

Dario kisses me.

He smashes his mouth against mine, clashing our teeth painfully beneath our closed lips. It feels like getting punched.

Before I can register anything other than shock, Dario jumps away, face ashen and eyes blown in horror at his own actions.

His gaze snaps onto something behind me.

Kai stands in the kitchen doorway, one hand holding the curtains to the side.

My heart thuds once as his jaw drops. Twice as he looks between me and Dario.

Then it stops beating altogether when Kai throws his head back and laughs.

"You know what?" Kai says, words ripping like gunshots through the terrible stillness of the cafe. Lips stretched in a tight smile, he yanks his apron over his head and tosses it on the ground. "You win, Dario: I quit."

And then he walks out of the store.

26. *EVERYTHING SUCKS*: THE TITLE OF MY AUTOBIOGRAPHY

My heart restarts with a jolt when the bell above the front door chimes. The silence that follows strangles the breath from us all like Kai took the oxygen out of the room with him when he left.

Vanna is the first to recover.

"What . . . the fuck?"

My eyes flick to Dario, who's staring at his feet. No, the floor. My phone. I follow his gaze and realize with panic that the Live is still going. I drop and pick up my phone with trembling fingers, stabbing the End Live button so hard my thumb bends back.

The rickety barstool squeaks as Sarang hops off. The red of her face matches the flames in her eyes.

"*Dario!* What the hell is wrong with you?" she screeches.

That frees Dario from his stupefied state. Color fills his previously pallid face. "What? Kai and I are *not* together!"

Vanna shakes her head, expression dark. "Don't play dumb. You know damn well what you did is wrong whether you guys are broken up or not. River's his best friend."

I freeze as everyone's eyes turn on me. Mortification warms me up from the inside out, leaving a sickly taste in my mouth and a sense that bugs are crawling over my skin. Dario's expression falls with shame before he closes his eyes and looks away.

Sarang slaps her hand on the counter and leans forward. "It's not just about Kai, you beef-headed bag of dicks. You kissed River without asking."

"What's it to you?" Dario immediately snipes back. "Do you like him or something?"

My heart launches into my throat as I meet her eyes. Hers are blown. Uncertain. I watch with my breath trapped in my lungs as a blush blooms across her skin, and her lips stutter around incoherence.

"That doesn't matter. What matters is you can't force yourself on people, especially when you're only using them to prove a point."

My gut flops.

I push myself away from the counter. Both Dario and Sarang flinch, but I don't pay them any attention. Now that the shock has worn off, all that's left is dread.

"I have to find Kai," I say, untying my apron. Sarang watches with a worried expression, teeth wearing into her lip. A rush of emotions I don't have the time to dissect right now threatens to swarm through me, so I look away and head out the door.

It's nighttime and freezing—maybe a snowstorm really will come in tomorrow. Kai has to be long gone. Maybe he'd go to a skate park?

I exit the alleyway and pause on the mostly deserted sidewalk, lit only by the streetlights and the store facades. No, he probably went home. I turn to jog down the street—

And immediately trip over something in the way.

Whirling around, I see what I tripped on: a skateboard. Kai sits on the ground in front of the building, his knees tucked against his chest.

For the first time in our eleven years of friendship, I don't know what to say to him.

"Watch where you're going. You'll bust your face open," Kai mutters drily. I step forward so I can make out his expression. It's dull, besides the whites of his eyes gleaming in the light of the orange street lamp overhead.

"Kai—" I start.

"I don't want to talk," he cuts me off.

"Let me explain. It wasn't—*I* didn't kiss him. It was hardly a kiss. Dario only did it because he was trying to prove that he's over you. But he isn't, which is why he panicked and—"

"I said I didn't want to fucking talk to you, River!"

Every muscle in my body locks. Kai's strained voice echoes through the night-guarded streets. The lamp above us flickers, buzzing noisily in the ensuing, painful quiet. Kai's chest heaves up and down, then he sits back and knocks his head against the brick.

"*Fuck!*" he yells at the starless sky. "I'm not mad at *you*. Well, I am. But I know I shouldn't be. And I hate that I am anyway. And I hate Dario. I hate him so much." Kai grinds the heels of his palms against his eyes, groaning. "But I hate myself most for still having feelings for that prick when he could give less of a shit about me. This is so stupid."

"He does care about you," I say. "He told you himself that he still loves you, and that—"

Kai stands up in a flurry. "Ma is waiting for me. I gotta go."

I latch onto his wrist before he can escape. "You're not really quitting, are you?"

He tugs from my hold. Kai doesn't look at me as he throws his skateboard down and rides out of sight.

It's not my fault. I'm sure it's not.

But why doesn't that matter?

When I walk back in, only Sarang, Vanna, and Isabette are inside.

"Dario left," Sarang says. "The coward."

"I gotta leave, too," Vanna says. "Sorry. I'll . . . I'll help deal with this later."

"Let me walk you home, it's dark," Isabette offers.

"No," she replies, too quickly. Vanna catches herself and blinks rapidly, clearing the fog from her eyes. "Sorry, Betty, you know I'd usually love that, but I have to run an errand."

Isabette, Sarang, and I exchange a concerned look, but Vanna pays it no mind as she shrugs on her coat. She has her phone out before she's zipped up, and whatever text she's replying to occupies her so much she doesn't say goodbye as she leaves. Just before closing the door behind her, Vanna catches my eye, but averts her gaze as if guilty.

Isabette sighs. "I should get going too," she says, but her tone lifts in question. She reaches down and squeezes my hand, and I squeeze back to let her know I'm fine. She wishes us a good night and slips out just as quietly.

It's just Sarang and me now.

I focus on a tile in the floor, pretending to be ignorant of her chunky platform boots stopping in front of me. A finger crosses my field of vision and taps me on the sternum.

"You okay?" Sarang asks.

"Kai's mad at me," I tell the ground.

"I think Vanna's mad at me, too."

I look up at her. A stain of rose dusts her cheeks. She looks good when she's not frowning, and pretty when she does.

Fuck. Shit. *Fuck.*

Not now. This is a particularly *bad time for that.* "I think Vanna's just going through personal stuff," I reassure her. Then myself. "Kai will come around, too. I get why he's upset."

"Are you?"

"Upset at Dario? I don't think so. Not for the kiss, at least, but for kissing me when he knows Kai . . ." I trail off, unsure. My upper lip throbs when I prod it with my tongue, bruised from where my teeth clashed against it. Acid burns in my stomach as what happened replays in my head. "Actually, I don't know how I feel."

She lifts and drops a shoulder. "That's okay."

I never thought she'd back me up for my indecisiveness.

"Thank you. For what you said to Dario," I tell her. "It means a lot."

"You don't need to thank me."

"Just accept my appreciation. Unless you want me to show you it in another way?"

Sarang's features furrow in a familiar scowl that contrasts nicely with the pink spreading down her neck and disappearing under her shirt collar. I pull my eyes back up to her face—no, damn it, that's her mouth. God.

"You're doing it again. Flirting when you're uncomfortable."

"Well. I only do it with you."

"River," she scolds.

"I'm telling the truth. Always with you."

An echo of what Dario said earlier plays through my mind unprompted. *Do you like him?*

My mouth dries up, suddenly parched. Sarang's easy annoyance melts away as she scans my face.

"What are you thinking about?" she asks.

You, I shouldn't say.

"You," I say.

Oh goddamn it.

Sarang's eyes widen. I stumble to fix my slip.

"What you said earlier, I mean."

We're standing awfully close. I'm not sure who moved forward, but her black Doc Martens and my beaten-up Converses are an inch away from touching. Suddenly I can't *stop* noticing her. Her fishnet-covered legs showing through her ripped jeans, her fingers drumming the side of her thigh anxiously, the delicate chain necklaces layered over her collarbones, the questioning tilt of her mouth, the black of her eyes so rich I feel like I could wax bad poetry about their depth if I hadn't already given up my author career after a short-lived attempt at writing fan fiction.

I shake my head to clear my thoughts. I take a deep breath. *We promised to be honest with each other.* "When Dario asked why you cared whether he kissed me, you said it's not about that. You said it doesn't matter."

Sarang keeps absolute control over her expression, but I catch the twitch of her hands, and the way she shifts her weight onto her other leg. "It doesn't. What matters is respecting other people's boundaries."

"You didn't deny having feelings."

"I've got feelings for you," she says with snark. "Like irritation."

"Not hatred?"

"No. Not anymore, surprisingly."

Her voice takes on a startlingly raw tone. The honesty of it makes me tense up. Sarang glances at me, straight eyelashes concealing some of the intensity in her gaze. The same feeling that propelled me to reach out and wipe her tears that night on the pier moves me now. All I have to do is bend down and then I'm there, the closest I've ever been to her, our faces only inches apart. Sarang's heart-shaped lips part, then catch on an inhale when I tuck her hair behind her ear and hold her cheek in the same slow, fluid move. Her face is so small in my hand that my finger tips graze the nape of her neck. Her pulse is strong, steady under my touch, quickening when I stroke the spot where her dimple is with my thumb. I'm not sure what I'm doing, but I'm scared to stop and think about it. To find out what this means. Thinking has never been my strong suit, anyway.

"Is *this* irritating?" I ask, trying to sound light, but the words come out rougher and lower than I mean for her to hear.

Sarang's expression is open, inviting me to fall inside it and get lost trying to capture all the details. Her hand reaches up to lay gently atop mine. "No. It's not." When she speaks, her breath ghosts against my lips.

I could kiss her.

I want *t—*

My brain putters out at the thought, then my heart, which works overtime under my ribs, but I can't decipher what it's trying to say. Are these butterflies in my stomach, or is it acid reflux? Do I hate Sarang, or do I . . .

Do I really know yet?

Or am I going to hurt her as I try to figure it out?

Too much has happened in the last twenty-four hours for me to be rational about this, and Sarang is one person I don't want to make a mistake with. I duck my head and step back, snapping whatever was tethering us together for those few moments.

"It's pretty late," I say. "I should let you get some sleep."

Nothing shows on Sarang's face when I look. As I head to leave, my hand on the door, I give her a small, guarded smile: reassurance and a question all in one. Her eyes flicker to my mouth so fast I'm not actually sure it happened.

27. WHY ARE MY ONLY OPTIONS A ROCK AND A HARD PLACE?

The weather report was telling the truth for once: it snowed overnight.

Sitting up groggily in bed, I gaze out the window at the whiteness blanketing the streets and rooftops outside. It must only be three inches or so, but that's enough to shut the city down, which means no school.

A missed notification from twenty minutes ago catches my attention. It's our work group chat. Nothing good can come from that right now, I think, wincing as I pull open the message.

STOP CHANGING THE GROUP CHAT NAME, KAI

Haneul:

> Unfortunately, this morning Vanna let me know that she will no longer be working with us. She will be off the schedule effective immediately to accommodate her new position at Cafe Gong.

Vanna has left the group chat.

I read the text over and over again, my jaw slack.

Cafe Gong.

My first instinct is to call Sarang. She'd know what to think, and more than that, I want to hear her voice right now, to let her steady confidence seep into me. But the question between us last night still lingers, and I don't know if I have the confidence to give her an answer yet; or the resolve to hear a disappointing one from her.

Besides, there's someone else I have to talk to first.

She answers immediately.

"What the fuck?" I say in greeting.

"So you've heard," Cecelia chirps. "Are you calling to congratulate me on my new co-manager?"

"You—" I throw the sheets off and stand up to pace the carpet. "You hired Vanna as your *co-manager*?"

"I told you your position wouldn't be available much longer."

The room spins. I close my eyes and cup my forehead to make it stop. "This doesn't make any sense," I say mostly to myself. "Vanna loves Bingsu for Two. She wouldn't quit in the first place."

"For someone who hated their own job, you overestimate the kind of loyalty a part-time paycheck buys. Why wouldn't she go to the place offering her a much better-paying, higher-ranking position? From what she said, it sounded like she was never going to move up at Bingsu for Two."

"When did you guys talk?"

"I reached out to her a little bit ago, after overhearing from Isabette that she works more than one job. Once you made it clear you had no intention of coming back, I had to start my search for a co-manager somewhere. The timing was perfect—apparently, your boss and girlfriend had just pissed her off. That, plus the hefty pay increase? She said yes the same day I asked."

The cold outside the window settles in my bones. I don't know what to think, but something between my ribs pinches nonetheless.

"You could've hired anybody. Hell, you can manage the store fine on your own. So, why? What do you want?"

Through the phone, I can hear her smile. "I want you to quit and delete all of Bingsu for Two's social media accounts. Permanently."

I blink. A strange sound bounces from my lungs and up my throat, caught between a laugh and a choke. But then a real laugh bursts from my mouth. I double over and lean on my knees from the force of it. A stitch develops in my side. Cecelia waits patiently for me to get it out, and for several long seconds, my hysterical laughter echoes across the line and surrounds us both.

I stand up chuckling, wiping the moisture from my eyes. "I'm not going to do that."

"It's your choice. But if you don't, Vanna's going to go live this afternoon and speak about the wage theft she experienced at Bingsu for Two."

Suddenly it's not funny.

"Cecelia—what—there was no *wage theft*."

"Are you betting on the internet to believe you?"

I swallow. "We'd prove to our followers that it's fake."

"The damage will be done. That's the funny thing about social media: the more you try to fix a problem, the worse you make it. Look at how your followers ate Kai up yesterday. Your little video didn't exactly help. Imagine how they'll react when they hear *this*."

The reality of the situation perches unevenly on my shoulders. "You can't be serious. Even if you are, Vanna wouldn't do that."

"She was a little hesitant, until I offered a sign-on bonus big enough to cover a security deposit for an apartment for her and her sister." At my dumb struck silence, Cecelia chuckles. "Four o'clock today, River. If those accounts are still up and you still have a job, Vanna's going live."

Time moves through molasses. My exhales and the rush of blood in my ears are heavy, slow. Like I'm in a dream. "You know what this will do to Bingsu for Two, right? This is their family's livelihood. It's more than that, this cafe is everything to the Chos. If you want to get back at me, this isn't the way to do it."

"Not everything's about you."

Cecelia hangs up.

I fling my phone at the wall, then flop back on the bed. Jace thumps his fist on the other side of the wall and yells something, but I ignore him.

We're fucked. Whichever choice I make, Bingsu for Two's future is screwed. Sarang's screwed.

A burst of dizzying emotions rushes through me at the thought—and not the sting of one-layer annoyance I used to feel for her. Whatever I feel for Sarang now makes my stomach twist into a pretzel and my face flush hot.

Fuck me. Fuck this. Oh god.

I have to talk to her. I have to let everyone know what's going on. In a mad dash to throw on some clothes, I text the group chat and Isabette and ask everyone to meet at the cafe. I zip up my winter coat and run out into the hallway, passing by Umma hunched over her laptop in the dining room.

"어디 가?"[5] she asks.

I pause mid-step. "Just going out to meet Kai and Isabette."

"In this snow? 조심해,"[6] she warns with a worried frown. "The weather report says the storm is already rolling in. We might lose power."

I hum noncommittally. "Where's Dad?"

Umma lets out a long-suffering sigh and massages her temples. "At the cafe. There's some bad news. He's in a terrible mood today because of it, so be careful if you run into him."

"What's the matter?" I ask, trying to get a look at the smattering of papers and spreadsheets in front of her.

"Finances. You already know how the new location is doing, but Cecelia just hired somebody new without running it by us, and it's causing some budget issues. I know she's the manager and we specifically told her she has full authority on these kinds of decisions, but she should've known better than to do so right now." She sighs. "네가 이직장에 남아 있었으면 좋겠어."[7]

"What does that mean?" I hate to ask.

Instead of translating, she looks at me with a tired smile. The bags under her eyes are more pronounced than ever, and she suddenly looks old. It makes my heart pang—all of it. The missed opportunities to bond in ways that are intrinsically ours, the fact that my face can only spark half-recognition of a family she left behind, and

5.   Where are you going?

6.   Be careful

7.   I wish you stayed at this job.

how every time I fumble being Korean, it widens the gap not just between us, but also the one between her and home.

"Sorry," she says, dropping her gaze back to her spreadsheets. "This isn't your business anymore, I know. I'm trying to respect your decision. We'll be okay, honey."

That makes the hurt spread from my chest out in webs, ebbing through my veins and prickling my hands with needles of guilt guilt guilt.

With a nod, I leave the apartment, locking the door behind me.

The city is a sea of white. Leaving the safety of the lobby and venturing into the storm is like being smacked in the face with a bag full of flour—which Sarang did to me on my third week of working. I rub the snowflakes caught in my lashes and squint at the streets in front of me, virtually unrecognizable. There aren't many people out, besides the brave kids bearing the cold to make snowmen on the sidewalk until their fingers turn numb. I stuff mine into my pockets and head downtown.

Bingsu for Two is one of the few stores with their open sign lit up, which is pointless, given that no one of sound mind would be risking their lives for our bingsu right now. I let myself in, shaking the snow off at the entrance. Standing around the dining room are Sarang, Isabette, and Dario.

"Where's Kai?" I ask.

Dario has trouble meeting my eyes, which is fine by me. "He won't answer any of my messages."

"In case you forgot, he quit," Sarang says with a pointed side glare at Dario.

"Are you seriously still mad at me?"

She doesn't deign him with a response, but the answer is written all over her face.

I did forget about Kai quitting in the chaos of everything, and the wound opens at the reminder that one of my best friends hates me right now. Seeing my other one here, showing up when she doesn't have to, eases that ache a little.

Until I remember the news I have to break to her.

"I've been trying to get ahold of Vanna all morning," Isabette says, staring down at her phone's screen. "I thought maybe she'd talk to me, tell me why she'd quit all of a sudden, but nothing. She's usually so honest with me. I thought she trusted me."

Sarang wraps her arm around Isabette's, who leans down to rest her cheek on Sarang's head. My stomach turns. I don't know how to even begin explaining, because I don't understand it, either.

None of this makes sense.

"Did you talk to your ex?" Dario asks.

"Unfortunately, yes. She, uh . . ."

"Well? Spit it out," says Sarang. "Why'd she steal Vanna from us?" *Why did Vanna go?* the redness under her puffy eyes asks. Isabette looks up expectantly, too. Why am I the one tasked with breaking both their hearts?

I rub my knuckles, staring at where the cold has cracked my skin. "Cecelia was offering more pay, and Vanna took it. Her sign-on bonus came with a price: unless we delete all of Bingsu for Two's socials and I quit, Vanna is going to go public with fake wage theft allegations against us. We have until four today."

It's silent. I chance a glance up, only to be met with three gobsmacked expressions, all of them ashen.

"Wage theft?" Sarang exclaims at the same time Dario says, "That's only a few hours away," and Isabette utters a soft "Vanna wouldn't do that."

Wincing, I say, "She will."

Sarang hops off her seat on the table and storms around, face and neck flushed with heat, and steam practically shooting out of her ears. "Wage theft? Wage theft? Are you fucking—does she think—believe—oh my god. After everything Appa did to help her and her sister. Through all the . . . oh, that piece of—" She turns around and muffles a frustrated scream into her hands. It deflates everything from her, and her shoulders sink. The silhouette of her back looks smaller than it ever has. I approach from her side, hesitant to overbear her, but Sarang doesn't pull away when I touch her shoulder.

Muffled into the hands covering her face, she says sadly, quietly, "I can't believe she'd do that to us."

Family always knows how to hurt you best, I think to myself. And then a second, simpler thought: *family.*

"It was her sister or this job," I say, trying to help. Evidently, I only know how to do the opposite.

Sarang steps away from me with a glare. "It was her sister or *my* family. Fine, I understand leaving. She was just in it for the paycheck, I guess. But to leave and then threaten us, this cafe? It's all my dad has left of my mom. It's all we have." Her eyes water, and she scrubs them angrily before any tears can escape. "It doesn't matter what choice we pick for this stupid fucking ultimatum, both have the same outcome: Bingsu for Two suffers."

She's right. Without the social accounts, the cafe cuts off the very audience that saved the store and continues to bring new faces in. But if we keep the socials it won't matter, as Vanna's claims of wage theft against us will affect business much, much worse.

"Jesus," Dario says. "You think she'll really go through with it?"

"It's not worth risking," I reply.

"Why not? Maybe people won't believe her."

Snorting, I respond, "We should know after the thing with Kai that the internet has no critical thinking skills."

Isabette's taken a seat at one of the tables. She chews absent-mindedly at her stubby nail beds and stares at a spot of nothing with a glassy, empty look in her usually lively eyes.

"I can't believe Vanna would do this," she mutters again. "I would have never expected this. Even if it's for her sister, even so, this is . . . cruel. I didn't know she was that way."

"Yeah, well," Sarang snaps, "maybe you didn't know her after all. I sure as shit didn't. She lied to all of us."

She's right, but I wince. Isabette doesn't look defensive, though. Just defeated.

"She lied to me," Isabette mumbles.

Both girls and Dario fall quiet. I stand between them, caught in a loop of glancing at Isabette's crumpled, broken expression, Dario's uncomfortable grimace, and Sarang straining to hide her own hurt under a layer of rage.

This is my fault. I put us in this situation. If I had gone back to Cafe Gong like Cece wanted, she wouldn't have offered Vanna a job and put us in this mess.

Bingsu for Two wouldn't be nearly as successful if you had *left us early,* I hear Sarang's voice reason in my head, though that's probably just my subconscious trying to make myself feel better. The one in real life paces restlessly, her eyes closed and face screwed tight.

The reality is I was selfish. I didn't want to go back to Cafe Gong. I didn't want to leave my friends. I didn't want to leave Sarang.

There's nothing to go back to, now.

I swivel around to face the menu sign, trying to focus and not let the soft, muffled cries behind me break the barrier I'm keeping my own emotions sealed under. Not now, at least. I got us into this mess, it's only fair that I maintain a level head and get us out of it.

Oh, we're so screwed if everything depends on *me* making the best choice here.

A small, pathetic laugh wrings itself from my throat. I should've known better than to think I was smarter than Cece, *especially* when it comes to business. I'm more savvy with internet culture and what people like, but she's one step ahead in everything else, including how to stomp on the throats of whoever it takes to climb her way to the top.

I turn over my shoulder to check on Sarang. The soft, spoiled point in my chest reserved for her twinges painfully to see her so wrecked. It's funny. Only a month or two ago, the sight would have made me distantly uncomfortable at most. There's no distance between us now.

Cece knows me *exactly*. She knows how much this place means to me, how seeing my friends here turn on each other would impact me. And yeah, maybe I am self-centered, but I know this is to spite *me* just as much as it is to boost her success story with Cafe Gong.

But I also know every square inch of her, which is why I *know* she thinks I'm too much of a coward to do the single thing that could possibly spare Bingsu for Two—spare *Sarang*—from all of this.

She'd be right. Except she doesn't realize there's only one person that brings the courage to do so out of me. I didn't either, until very recently.

Because if it's a matter of me or Sarang, it's not even a question. It's her.

Sarang's nursing a headache, shielding her face with her bangs when I walk up to her. At the sound of my steps, she turns her head. Her sharp, unwavering eyes are half-lidded and closed off now. She huffs out a dry laugh, shoulders cringing with the motion.

"I don't know what to do, River," she admits. Like it's her first time ever saying the words to herself or anyone else.

There are a million things I want to say and do. Not all of them are helpful right now, but they're all true. I step closer and weave my hand between us: pinkie out.

"I have an idea," I respond. "Do you trust me?"

Sarang wraps her pinkie around mine. "I do."

A smile spreads across my lips. "Everything will be okay." I can't help it: I tuck her hair behind her ear as an excuse to reach out.

"Where are you going?" she asks as I walk toward the exit. Isabette and Dario perk up with confusion.

"I have to go tell someone the truth."

28. OH YEAH. THIS IS WHY I LIED.

The walk to my apartment is a lucid dream where time isn't real and I'm both crossing the distance at light speed and not moving at all. The snow clouds are starting to blotch the sky a dark, hazy gray, and snowflakes fall like an assault across the city line. Everything is muffled; even my own ragged breaths are absorbed by the snow piled up to my ankles. I don't want to go home. I have no choice.

When I get to our building, climb the steps, and poise my key inches from the lock, my hand freezes.

I'm scared.

Unprompted, Sarang's face materializes in my thoughts. Her lipstick-covered pout. Her soft hair tucked behind her ears. The tears in her eyes when she gave up her dream for her sister's; the ones I wiped away as we sat on the dock in the rain. How warm her hand felt laced in mine. The sound of her voice whether she's annoying me or encouraging me. Her.

I want to do this.

The second I turn the key and open the door, yelling from the living room halts me in place. Jace steps out from his bedroom upon hearing me and rushes to my sopping wet side.

"What's going on?" I ask.

"Umma and Dad are fighting. She says they have to close down the new Cafe Gong location." He looks like the scared little kid he used to be years ago, when he'd run in my room to hide from the monsters in his.

We have to close down the new location? I think, stunned. More yelling. I pat Jace's cheek and tell him, "Just wait in your room, it'll be okay. I'm going to talk to them."

"I don't think that's a good idea right now."

It wouldn't be a good idea *anytime*, but I don't exactly have a choice. I ruffle his hair with what I hope is a reassuring smile despite the uneasiness greasing up my insides like an oil spill. Then I tiptoe toward the living room.

Umma and Dad are on their feet and in each other's faces. Umma is stiff and still, but Dad's entire frame shakes with poorly restrained fury. A dozen bills and papers lay scattered across the couches. The closest to me reads *Late Payment—Two-Week Notice.*

"We don't have a choice, Matthew!" Umma shouts. She never raises her voice. "We'd have to close down one of our better performing locations to keep this one running. If we keep expanding so recklessly, we're not going to be able to keep *any* stores open, let alone pay our rent!"

"We've put too fucking much into the new store to just shut it down!" Dad yells. "I didn't get this far by giving up, that's for damn sure, and we aren't going to start now. How will closing shop on a location that *just* opened look to future investors when we're trying to expand nationally?"

"My point is we won't be *able* to branch out if we don't slow down."

He shouts in frustration and tugs at his hair, the veins on his neck pulsing. "This is a fucking *disaster*. We're *screwed*. I can't believe this shit." He turns and kicks a small side table over. "*Fuck!*"

"Stop it!" I interrupt. They both whip their heads to face me, finally noticing my presence. I shrink but force my voice steady for my next words. "Don't yell at Umma, it's not her fault. It's mine."

"What are you talking about?" Dad snaps.

"River," Umma says with an exhausted sigh. "*Please.* Not now. Just go to your room."

"It's my fault Cafe Gong's new store doesn't have any business. Because I—I started working with our competitor, Bingsu for Two."

Neither of them says a thing: they're shocked stiff. I take advantage of their silence and let everything I hid and lied about come spilling out now in waves of run-on sentences and pathetic explanations. How the day after I quit, I went down the street to Bingsu for Two and begged for a job there, despite the fact that I intended for Cafe Gong to run them out of business with the new location. I admit with my eyes glued to the carpet that I hadn't been going to SAT tutoring sessions four times a week, but to work. I walk them through everything: coming up with the idea to use social media to build a platform for Bingsu for Two, how I had a huge part in escalating sales to save them from bankruptcy, and that with every passing day, more of Cafe Gong's customers began crossing the block to come to our place. Umma's shoulders bunch next to her neck when I tell them about Cece asking me to come back and do the same for Cafe Gong, but I refused. Dad has to grip the bookcase shelf for stability when I explain that Cece hired Vanna this morning to blackmail me and my co-workers into tanking the business, or else she'd go live with false wage theft claims in an hour. By the time I stop blathering, my hands are shaking so violently I have to clutch them to my chest, where they rattle in time to my racing heart.

Umma speaks first. Surprisingly, she focuses on just one detail. "Cecelia only hired that girl as blackmail? She would make up a lie like that?"

"She would. Please, you guys have to stop her. She's going to upload it to the account she made for Cafe Gong, which she probably made under the business email—you'll have access. If you deactivate the accounts, she won't have anywhere to share the video of Vanna talking about wage theft. Anywhere it will gain traction, at least."

She's still for several moments. Then she reaches hesitantly for her phone in her pocket. Unlocking it, she taps the screen a few times, then says, "You're right. The account was made under the cafe's business email."

Crack!

My head snaps to the sound: Dad, next to the bookcase he was holding onto for support, with one of the wooden shelves snapped off in his rattling grip. When he looks up and catches my eye with his dark ones, I realize too late he wasn't silent from shock, but rage.

He storms toward me. Between fight or flight, I freeze, but he brushes past me, out of the living room. A few moments later, heavy feet thud down the hallway. He rounds the corner.

I've never, *ever* seen him so pissed off. He's an untreated knot of anxiety and frustration, sure, and that obviously manifests in excessive sighing and grumbling and glaring—but this isn't that. His entire face is red, the veins at his temple throb dangerously, and his broad shoulders quiver with the force of wrath that has been building up in him for years. I press myself against the wall, truly fearful of him for the first time in my life.

In his white-knuckled grip is my schoolbag. He chucks it, and I barely catch it, stumbling back. The zipper falls open, revealing clothes, my wallet, and a blanket.

I look up at him, eyebrows pinched together. "Dad—"

"Get out of my house."

The air rushes from my lungs. "*Dad.*"

"*여보!*"[8] Umma snaps. She hisses a string of Korean at him too fast for me to catch, the sibilants violent across her tongue. Then in English, "Calm down. You're just upset about the cafe closing. Don't take it out on River."

"It's his fault!" he replies. "You heard him. We sacrificed thousands of dollars to open a cafe and trusted him to turn it into a success, only for him to decide our family business wasn't good enough and left to help someone else run us into the dirt!"

"You opened that new location for *you*," I say before I can think twice about it. An ugly, rotten concoction of feelings that have been brewing for a while now spills free from where I've carefully bottled it. "You're the one who's so desperate to turn Cafe Gong into a national franchise. How can you call it a family business when the *family* hasn't mattered to you in a long time?"

A terrifying stillness seizes him. "What did you say to me?" he asks slowly, like the calm before a hurricane. He inches closer to where I'm pressed into the wall.

---

8.   Honey!

"We all know you guys didn't give me that manager position because you *trusted* me to help you franchise it." I turn to Umma at this part, too. "You were throwing me a bone. I know you guys are disappointed in me. You think me going into business with you is my only option for a career because there *isn't* anything else I can do, right? Well, everyone at Bingsu for Two believes in me."

"River," Umma says, and she's crying. "That's not what we think at all."

"You didn't have to say it out loud for me to see it. I know I disappoint you both in everything: I can't speak Korean, I can't keep my grades up, I can't be a good son."

Dad's nostrils flare. "You quit your job and start scheming with the competitor to run us into debt and think—what, we'd be *proud* of you? Because you made a few little videos for them?"

"Those videos stole all of your business and ruined your shot at franchising, didn't they?"

A look passes across Dad's face: anger, layered and deep and one I can see revolves around more than just his son fucking up. It's the years of stress that running a business can take on a man who knows no coping mechanisms besides *work more.*

He grabs me by my elbow and drags me toward the front door. "Out. Get *out.* I can't look at you right now."

Umma starts screaming. I shout in alarm and accidentally knock over the entryway table in my struggle to dig my feet in the carpet. Jace bursts out of his room and runs down the hallway at us.

He throws himself at Dad's back and pounds his fists against his shoulder blades. "Stop it! You can't kick River out in the storm over—"

Dad twists around and accidentally knocks his elbow into Jace's chin, sending him flying back. All of us freeze. Jace parts his mouth in shock, revealing teeth painted with blood. Dad's face pales.

"Oh *shit*. Are you okay, Jace? I'm so sorry, I didn't know you were—it was an accident."

I know it was an accident. I saw it. But the crimson dribbling from Jace's split lip wipes any logical reasoning from my brain.

I launch forward and shove Dad so hard he stumbles and crashes into the wall.

"Don't fucking touch him!" I shout.

Silence. No one says a thing. My uneven breaths are as loud as a scream. Umma gapes at me. Jace covers his bleeding mouth, wide eyes flicking between me and Dad. Dad blinks. Processing.

I fucked up. I fucked up so hard. Guilt and lingering rage infuse with whatever's in my stomach and threaten to rush up my esophagus. I pick my forgotten bag up off the floor and sling it over my shoulder, leaving before Dad comes to his senses or I come to mine. The door slams shut behind me so heavily the frame rattles.

Telling the truth doesn't feel as good as I'd hoped it would.

29. THE SNOWBALL EFFECT, EXCEPT IT'S NOT JUST A METAPHOR

If the shame rumbling around my large intestine doesn't kill me, hypothermia will.

The snow's up to my knees now, which is alarming given the fact that it's only been a few hours since the storm rolled in. Charcoal clouds completely blot out the sky, turning everything into a darkened landscape. My jeans are completely soaked. I can't feel my shins, the bones in them turned brittle like glass from the freezing weather.

Why didn't I stay in the apartment lobby? Right, because I'm an idiot. A big dumb idiot who's now wandering through a deserted Seattle in three feet of snow and frozen Converses.

I pull my phone out with fingers I can't feel. 3:43 p.m. There's only a few minutes until Cece and Vanna will go live with their threats. As I trudge through the snowy Seattle streets, I go to pull up Cafe Gong's social channels on YouTube, Twitter, and Instagram.

Account not found.

I have to actually stop when a sway of gratefulness hits me, making me dizzy. Umma deactivated the accounts. She believed me. Sure, Cece can try uploading the video from a personal account, but without the credibility of posting under a Seattle cafe's alias, people will stop to question it, and it's less likely to get boosted by the algorithm.

I huff, and my breath of laughter condenses in front of my face. It was that easy. Sort of.

A tiny part of me does feel lighter for coming clean about everything, though, despite the outcome and my current situation. Sarang was right—honesty *is* the best policy. I don't have to keep any more secrets from anyone now.

I keep moving. Moving is good. Moving will keep the blood circulating longer. The snow makes the city unrecognizable, turning all the streets into the same flat, white desert.

A single blip ahead of me catches my attention through the falling flakes. A person. Some other moron like me stupid enough to be out in this weather. I keep my head down as I trudge, giving them plenty of room to pass.

Then they call my name.

"River?"

My head whips up. The figure runs toward me, the piles of snow slowing them down like quicksand. Under the halo of a streetlight, Kai stops in front of me, bundled in layers and a scarf I watched him sew last year, his cheeks flushed.

"Hey . . . ," he starts awkwardly. "What are you doing here?"

My entire body aches with the urge to tell him everything like I always do, but our conversation from last night is an impenetrable brick wall between us. I swallow past the acidic pang and manage a weak smile.

"It doesn't matter. What are you doing out?"

"I forgot my phone last night since I left so quickly. Came to grab it."

My eyebrows furrow together. "Left it where?"

"At the cafe."

"Then what are you doing here?"

Kai gives me a once-over, confusion on his face. "What do you mean?" he says, then gestures his thumb to the left. I follow, looking over at the alleyway adjacent to us. A familiar alleyway.

My feet brought me to Bingsu for Two without realizing it.

A particularly icy gust of wind cuts past us, blowing a turret of dry snowflakes into my face that stings like needle pricks. I shiver so hard the chattering of my teeth makes my skull throb.

"Fuck, it's *cold*," Kai curses. "We should go in. I'm not sure we can stay out here much longer—or walk back home in this."

"You haven't seen any of our texts, have you?" I interrupt.

"No, I didn't have my phone, why?"

He doesn't know. I shake my head. "I'll explain inside. Just . . . brace yourself."

"Whatever it is, it can't be worse than dying from the elements. Come on."

Kai turns and trudges toward the alley. I follow in his footsteps.

Halfway out of the street, my phone buzzes. I stop and pull it out, hoping it's Umma or Dad begging their eldest son to come home before he turns into a human Popsicle, but it's not them.

Cecelia

> Wow.

> Four years of knowing you, and this is the first time you've surprised me. I never expected you to have the guts to go to your parents yourself.

> Does telling the truth for once feel good?

> You're forgetting one secret you need to confess. Don't worry. I returned the favor.

The snow crunches under Kai as he paces back to my side. "What's wrong?"

I stare bewildered at the message. "I . . . I don't know." I'm not sure what she's talking about.

The cafe doors are still unlocked when we enter. Isabette, Dario, and Sarang are crowded at the counter. They turn around at the jingling of the doorbell. I wince, anticipating an awkward reunion upon seeing Kai back, but no. They hardly notice him. They're all staring at *me*.

Isabette is glaring—I've never seen her angry before. Dario looks more horrified than he did after he kissed me. And Sarang . . . Sarang is crying.

Suddenly I'm hyperaware of everything: my limbs frozen stiff, the ringing in my ears, the dread solidifying like a block of cement in my stomach.

"What?" I ask, voice raspy.

Sarang grabs Isabette's phone and holds it up. There's a long block of text on the screen, and worse, screenshots. At the top of the screen is Cecelia's contact.

"Is it true?" she asks, voice breaking. "You purposefully chose Cafe Gong's new location to try to run Bingsu for Two out of business? You planned on us going bankrupt?"

I think one of my ribs must have punctured my lungs. *I* made Sarang cry. The air rapidly deflates from my chest. I can't speak. I can't move. I can't explain myself, because all I can focus on are the tears gathering at the waterline of her eyes.

Kai slowly turns toward me. He's studying me like I'm a stranger, like we haven't known each other for over half our lives. "What's going on? This is just another one of Cece's tricks . . . right?"

Speak, I urge myself.

Dario's expression is stiff and blank. "Did you work with your ex-girlfriend to post that lie about Kai, too?"

My heart lodges in my throat. I can't speak past it. It threatens to choke me.

Silence suffocates the room. A moment later, with a dull, muted click, the clock strikes four.

Belatedly, everything comes up like vomit.

"I can explain," I blurt breathlessly. "It's not what it looks like. Back when we were co-managers, it *was* up to me to choose the location of our new store and this was the best option because . . . listen, it wasn't *personal*. Bingsu for Two had no customers, it looked like it was going to close any day so yes, I thought it'd be smart for Cafe Gong to open nearby. It killed me after I started working here, it did, that's why I tried so hard with our videos to make up for it. I didn't know—Kai, I didn't know you worked here, I promise. You *never* referred to it by name, remember? And I had nothing to do with what Cece posted about you online, or anything else. I just went and told my parents everything so they could stop Cece from going live with Vanna about the wage theft allegations. I—I admit it, I *did* try to help Bingsu for Two go out of business way back then, but now"—I seek out Sarang's eyes specifically—"my heart is here. Please believe me."

Sarang sniffs. "I understand," she says, her voice broken like a glass cup dropped on the ground. Looking at her shattered expression is like walking barefoot over the shards.

"You do?"

Ignoring me, Sarang unlocks her phone and begins typing. I watch as she pulls up YouTube, signs into the cafe's account, and clicks on the camera emoticon that says *Go Live*.

She scrubs her eyes as she starts streaming to our thousands upon thousands of followers.

"Hello," she starts. "Sorry for telling you guys this way. I know a lot of you will be disappointed, but this must be said."

The sound of her voice nullifies the rest of the noise in my brain. All that matters is her.

"There's been a lot of controversy and lies surrounding our cafe in the last few days, so I just want to clarify something that's one hundred percent true. River lied. To you all, to us, and to me. That's why I'm breaking up with him. You won't be seeing him at the cafe anymore."

She turns to face me instead of the screen. Her wet eyes locking with my wide, unblinking ones, Sarang utters, "He's not who I hoped he was."

30. HYPOTHERMIA BRINGS OUT THE WORST IN US, BUT AT LEAST WE DIDN'T RESORT TO CANNIBALISM OR SOMETHING

So this is what being dumped feels like.

Except not really, since we weren't actually together. We never were—so why does this hurt so much? A splinter of grief pricks my stomach, and I have to remind myself that I didn't have anything to lose in the first place, so I should have nothing to mourn the loss of. This was all fake. It shouldn't mean anything.

But it does. It means a lot. *She* means a lot to me.

Time goes on. It must, because now the clock reads 4:02. It's only been a few minutes, yet everything has changed. Isabette, Kai, and Dario look at me differently. Sarang won't look at me at all. My head feels like a deflating basketball, twisting the world off-kilter. *Do you really want to end this?* I want to say.

A tiny, unsure voice in my head replies, *End what?*

"Sarang—"

"I don't want to hear it. Haven't you done enough? We're—*this* is over."

The weakness threatening to split me right down the middle is so petrifying that my mind flings itself to the opposite end of the emotional spectrum: anger. It flows through the empty cracks of my soul, tethering the fractured pieces together. Anger at Cecelia and Vanna for teaming up to put us in this mess. Anger at Dario for fucking over my best friend and pulling me into their drama. Anger at Sarang for not realizing everything I tried to do to make up for my mistake. Anger at my parents for not understanding why I feel the way I do about Cafe Gong. Anger at myself for *being* angry, and for being at the root of all this.

"I'll go," is all I say.

Which is when the lights flicker once. Twice. Then plunge us into total darkness as the power goes out. The wind howls like an animal, rattling the glass windows.

"Oh, hell no," Kai says, voice thin.

Something sharper taps on the windows, and we all scream when the front door opens.

"It's just me!" somebody replies, equally alarmed. *Vanna.*

"Is that—?"

"Please," she says. I can't see in the dim lighting, but the floor moves under Vanna's hesitant shuffles. She ends up somewhere between me and Isabette when she finally stops. "I was stuck out there. Please let me stay. There's nowhere else I can go."

"Cafe Gong is two blocks that way, though you don't need reminding," Sarang snarks.

"That's where I came from. I got fired."

"What?" I say.

"We both did—me *and* Cecelia."

My jaw falls.

Sarang barks out a short, dry laugh. "Wow. You got let go from the place that hired you for petty revenge? Who would've guessed. You've got some fucking nerve to show up back here after what you planned to do. Get out."

Squinting, I make out Sarang starting to stomp over until Isabette holds her back.

"She'll freeze if you make her leave. Please, let them both stay, it's too dangerous."

Stiff, awkward silence fills the space. Then a long-suffering sigh. "Motherfucking—fine," Sarang says. "I'm going to get some candles."

"I'll come with you," Dario says.

She doesn't answer.

"No way you're still pissed at me."

"Shut your fucking face hole. I'll be pissed at whoever I want, especially if they deserve it. Somebody who's not Dario or River or Vanna, come upstairs with me to grab the candles and blankets. Haneul and my dad are at a doctor's appointment, so we're on our own."

"I'll go," Isabette says.

Footsteps echo away. As my eyes begin to adjust, I can make out the shadowy forms of Kai, Dario, and Vanna a few feet away. The moonlight reflects on the snow in the alley outside the windows, providing the faintest cool glow. Quiet hangs over us.

Kai sighs. "Maybe—"

"I had nothing to do with what Cecelia posted about you," I interrupt. "Just to get that straight."

"But you had everything to do with trying to close this place," Dario says, approaching.

"That was before I ever worked here or knew about you guys."

"Like that makes it better."

"You really intended for Cafe Gong to put us out of business?" Kai asks me quietly.

I pause. "Yes."

"Why?"

"Same reason I did," Vanna speaks up, surprising us all. "Personal interests."

"What you did is *not* the same," I say. Frustration ripples under my skin. "You were willing to lie and bring down Mr. Cho's entire life and what we all worked so hard to save for, what, a pay increase? Do you know how much you hurt Sarang? She thought you were her friend."

She's silent. Then, "She probably thought you were, too."

I groan into my hands. *Fuuuuckk.*

"Lay off her," Dario says. "You're *both* selfish."

"Who are you to talk about being selfish after kissing your ex's best friend to prove a point?" I snap at him.

I brace for a punch in the face. It'd almost be welcome, at this point. But instead, Dario's silhouette cringes away.

"I'm . . ." Dario hesitates. Starts over. "I'm sorry."

Why does that make me feel worse?

I rub my temples. "Whatever, man. It was just a kiss."

"Not just for that," he continues. "That too, though. I forced it on you—Sarang was right, I seriously messed up, and she's right to be pissed at me for it. But I'm also sorry that I ruined your relationship by doing that, instead of just ruining mine."

I hear Kai inhale sharply, letting it out in a single breath. "What relationship? We're broken up, as you've pointed out so many times."

Footsteps thud from the kitchen, saving Dario a response, and two shadows emerge into the living room.

Sarang and Isabette head toward the beaten-up sofa in the corner. The four of us reluctantly migrate over. Sarang draws a match, lighting several candles and placing them on the surrounding tables. It's worse, seeing each other in the flickering glow of the dim light. I want to slink back and hide in the inky shadows, but the chill is already seeping into the cafe, and sticking together is our best bet for not freezing overnight.

There aren't enough blankets. Which means we have to sit on the floor in a huddle, casting three blankets across our six pairs of squished shoulders. I'm stuck between Dario and Vanna, which is about as horrible as it could get in this situation.

Nobody speaks. Time drags on at a slow, painful crawl. Each passing second of uncomfortable squirming and grumbling about the cold pushes me closer to the breaking point. After about an hour, I'm so on edge I'm ready to walk back into the storm. I'd be doing a lot of people a favor.

I realize then that every single person in this circle is pissed at me, for one reason or another. A short chuckle escapes me before I can stop it.

"What are you laughing at?" Sarang snaps. I'm too tired to fight with her.

"This," I say. "This *sucks*. Everything sucks."

"What, having to face the consequences of your own actions?" Vanna says into my ear. Goose bumps raise on my cheek.

"I could ask the same of you."

"I did what I had to."

"You're saying you had to betray the trust of all your friends?" Isabette of all people chimes in. "Is that the kind of person you actually are?"

Vanna stiffens. "Maybe."

"If this is how you treat your friends of *years*, I can only imagine how you'd treat me." She laughs quietly at herself. "Good thing I won't stick around to find out."

The candlelight casts harsh shadows across Vanna's crumpled expression. "Sweetheart—"

"If it's not an apology, can you keep it shut?" Sarang snaps.

"You're the last person I owe an apology to. You *and* your sister," Vanna hisses with such venom that we all jump in response. "I had no choice but to take Blondie's offer at Cafe Gong. You two were the only ones I told about my sister getting turned over to foster care soon; you knew I needed the money. But apparently that doesn't matter 'cause I'm too fucking busy trying to save my family and fight the courts to be the manager, isn't that right? What it takes to run this place is nothing compared to what I'm responsible for at home every day."

I wince, and Sarang's eyes widen, glassy and stunned. Vanna huffs. "Don't look so shocked. I heard you and Haneul talking about it when you were deciding who would be the next boss." She breaks off into a feverish laugh. "Fuck you for thinking a part-time paycheck buys my loyalty when you've never had my back."

Sarang leans forward, her glare watery but still cutting. "We've *never* had your back? How about when my dad gave you a job to save you from the streets? How about the *months* you crashed in my room when you didn't have a place to stay? Were we just buying you with a paycheck then, huh? I thought we were *friends*, but friends don't try to take the roof over your family's head."

"It was *your* family or *mine*, okay?" Vanna practically shouts. I startle so hard I knock into Dario from how close we're sitting. She lowers her volume, voice unsteady. "I didn't want to do that to you guys. Of course not. But my sister hasn't *had* a roof over her head for too fucking long. This was my last opportunity. If she got into the foster system, I could've lost her for good." Turning to meet Isabette's eyes, she says, "*That's* the kind of person I really am. The kind who's never had the luxury of making the easy decision."

The absence of sound sucks the air out of the room. Kai shifts uneasily, shivering on Isabette's other side. "You guys—"

Sarang lets out a small, strangled sound. She buries her face in her hands. We wait. I watch the shadow of her figure for any movement, my own body tense.

"I wish I didn't understand where you're coming from," she finally says. "But I do. And I'm still pissed, and it fucking stings that you could do something like that to us, but . . . I am sorry we passed you up for the management role so easily."

Vanna appraises her a moment longer. Then, "To be honest, it wasn't really a matter of *my* family or *yours*. That's just what I told myself so it'd be easier. You're my family, too. I'm sorry. I wish it hadn't come down to that."

"Me too."

"I didn't know your sister was about to get moved to foster care," Kai says, tone sympathetic. "I can't imagine how you felt."

"Helpless," Vanna answers. "Until a solution plopped itself into my lap."

Dario says morosely, "I probably would've done the same if it were one of my brothers."

I would have too if it was for Jace, I realize.

Vanna turns to meet my eyes, almost knocking our noses together in the process. "If you hadn't stopped Blondie and me, it'd be hard to forgive myself. Thanks."

Something knotted in my gut uncurls slightly. My unjust anger toward her dissipates. "You were looking out for your sister."

Isabette starts sniffling.

Vanna chuckles and throws an arm around her shoulders, pulling her to her side. "We don't have any tissues, Betty. If you cry, they'll freeze on your face."

"S-s-sorry." It carries more weight than just the single word, but Vanna must get it, because she only holds her closer and wipes her cheeks with her sleeves.

Kai hums. "This is a hell of a conversation to be having while sober."

"You don't drink," Dario says.

"Maybe I do now. You don't know me."

"I could never forget you."

He couldn't have sounded fonder if he tried. Even *my* ears heat up. Kai straightens like he's been electrocuted, the blanket slipping down his shoulders.

"Fuck you," Kai bites. "You always do this. I hate it."

"I know," Dario says remorsefully. "I'm sorry. For yesterday, and the last two months. I haven't done a good job of being your ex."

"No one asked you to be my ex in the first place."

"It's better this way. Think about next September. About Florida. I . . . I can't handle you being two thousand and eight hundred and twenty-nine miles away from me for the next four years. It hurts too much. A clean goodbye is better. Breaking up was the easier option."

"Has it?" Kai scoffs. "Has this been easier?"

The wind whistles outside the cafe.

"Not at all," Dario admits. "I was wrong."

Quiet settles around us in the draft of cold air. It stretches for so long I worry it'll wear thin and dissipate, and I'll lose my opportunity. The pressure builds and builds. Until finally, I shatter the silence in what may be my last chance to.

"What about you, Sarang?"

Her head snaps up. "What about me?"

"I know you're thinking something. I want to hear it."

She blinks, silent for so long I'm afraid she won't answer. But she does. "You know what I'm thinking about?" Her voice gains strength as she speaks. "I'm thinking that I hate people who pretend to be something they're not. People who lie and keep secrets and get you to trust them by telling you sob stories about an ex they conspired with the whole time. And then they confuse you by being selfish and stupid one moment, but also—*also* trying to make up for their mistakes, and staying with you when you cry, and doing all they can to save your family's cafe after they wanted to sabotage it. I'm thinking, out of everybody here who's speaking up, the one who needs to most isn't *explaining themselves*, and I hate them for it."

Something in my core rattles. "Do you hate those who will try?"

Sarang crosses her arms. "Hit me."

So I try. And for the first time, I'm completely honest. No secrets. No lies. I tell them everything. From when Cecelia and I were made co-managers, and I picked the location of our new store just to do *something* right for once in her eyes and my parents'. And then even farther back, to the days when my family's shop mirrored the one we're sitting in now, when I was still a son who had potential instead of an employee letting everyone down. How sick I felt when I realized my decision almost devastated Bingsu for Two—the only place that has ever reminded me of the home I used to have—and that everything I did for the cafe afterward was in pursuit of forgiveness. Until it wasn't; it turned into a passion for this place and the family I had been missing for years.

I try to focus on what I'm saying rather than their reactions. I ignore their stunned expressions when I explain how Cecelia's goal was to turn Bingsu for Two's disaster into her own success story. I force myself not to squirm under their intense, sympathetic gazes when I tell them how the only way to stop her was by confessing it all to my parents, every detail of how I single-handedly ruined their dreams and wasted their sacrifice, and paid the price by getting kicked out an hour and a half ago. How it was worth it, and how I'd do it over and over again just to prove how much this place and the people here mean to me.

Throughout it all, Sarang listens with a perfectly blank expression. She doesn't betray a single emotion, and she never drops eye contact.

When I finally finish, trailing off once I get to the part about Cecelia telling them my secret, I'm sweating. Suddenly it doesn't feel like we're stuck in an icebox of a room without heat or electricity. I forget about the storm. I forget about everyone else. I wait for Sarang.

She looks me up and down. Then she holds her pinkie out, and in a calm voice, asks me, "What did you do all that for, River?"

I blink. Then blink again. I have to tell the truth.

I wrap my pinkie around hers. "You," I reply.

It's the wrong answer.

Sarang stands up without a word and walks out of the cafe, into the night.

31. CAN'T BELIEVE I DIDN'T DO THIS A LONG TIME AGO

I'm frozen in place until Vanna claps her hand on my shoulder.

"If you didn't know, this is when you're supposed to run after her," she tells me.

And then I'm running.

The instant I fling open the door, a gust of wind fogs my glasses up and blinds me, but I sprint out into the cold anyway, relying on memory to guide me. Snow blankets the ground, piled high enough that I sink down into the banks up to my thighs. There's no way Sarang got far in this.

Sure enough, when I make it to the mouth of the alleyway, I spot her standing in the middle of the road. The power is out on the entire block, and the storm clouds blot out the night sky and its stars, but the snow has a surreal glow to it that lets me see her, a dim hue that nearly swallows the muted shadow of her back.

I don't call her name as I approach, but she must hear the muffled crunch of my steps. She doesn't turn around or run. I come to her side, peering down at her. Panic zips to my fingertips.

"Are you crying?" I ask in alarm.

She presses the back of her hand to her eyes, surprised at the wetness that gathers there. "It's just the cold."

"I'm so sorry. I never wanted to hurt you."

She turns to face me, the motion shaking loose a few scattered snowflakes from her hair that float away in the breeze. Her cheeks are chafed with a pink glow. She's painfully gorgeous. I wish the streetlamps were on so I could really see her, but this is nice, too. This way, she feels like something out of a dream.

I wonder when I started comparing her to dreams instead of nightmares.

"You've got to stop doing that," she says.

"Doing what?"

"Saying what you think people want to hear. That back there? When I asked you what you did all that for?"

"But what if I really did do it for you?"

"What if," she echoes dully. "It sounds like everything you've ever done has been for others. What they expect, what they think of you. You should make decisions for *you*. It's *your* life." Sarang enunciates her point with a poke at my chest. "Don't worry about me; I got my shit together. I know what I want." She splays her fingers and presses her palm over my heart. It beats rapidly under her touch. "Do you?"

"I—" When she looks at me like that, my brain goes haywire. I try again. "I'm not sure. I haven't been asked that before."

Her expression falls, darkening under the moonless sky. Her fingers curl and pull back. I grab her hand before she can leave me, and I intertwine our pinkies together.

"Do you want the truth?" I ask. "Do you want to know how I actually feel? What I actually want?"

"Yes," Sarang whispers.

I huff a breath of laughter, entwining the rest of my fingers with hers. "The truth is I don't know. I've never known—it's always been decided for me, I never had to think about it. I was stuck on one path for so long I didn't realize it was possible for me to take any other. So I lied, and I pretended I was happy with who I was and where I was going. But it only caused more problems for everyone in the end. It used to be easier to do what everyone wanted me to, but after meeting you, not so much. I'm done lying to myself now."

Sarang's lips twitch, like she's not sure how to react, or where I'm going with this. But she doesn't let my hand go, which is a good sign.

With her in front of me, I finally get it. Something clicks. I reach up and cup her face, rubbing my thumb across her cheek. She leans into my touch.

"And maybe it's okay to still be figuring out who I am, or what I'm supposed to be doing," I say, quieter. The moment seems to tuck in around us, sectioning us off from the rest of the street and the night. "Maybe it's fine not to have answers for everything all the time. I'm fucking seventeen. Who the hell knows anything at seventeen?"

Sarang smirks cheekily, eyes shining. "Speak for yourself."

Her voice turns smooth as honey when she's happy. How have I never noticed? I savor the feel of it now, its sticky sweetness. My other hand comes up to cup her face. Sarang's smirk mellows out, replaced by something open and nervous. Patient. She clasps onto my wrists. I don't want to step away this time.

"It's always been hard to decipher my own feelings. But never around you," I confess. Vulnerability takes the wind from my lungs— or is that her? My knees shake not just from the cold. "I knew exactly how I felt the first time we met, when you dumped coffee on my head."

"Tell me what you were thinking."

"I thought, 'God, I hate this green-haired chick. And I'm glad my coffee isn't hot.'"

"You had it coming. Plus, you poured a bag of *espresso beans* into my bra."

"That's my point exactly. I would have never done that sort of thing before meeting you. You bring out the brashest, most impulsive side of me I never knew existed. But your courage and honesty are infectious, too; it makes me want to be honest. It's because of you I had the guts to finally quit Cafe Gong, and stand up to my ex, and confront my parents tonight. It's because of you . . . *for* you, that I could finally do and say the things I've always wanted to. It was hard at first, trying to find a name for this feeling I have every time I think of you. It's like being swallowed whole in it. Though I probably always knew what it was, I just didn't have the nerve to recognize it then. I know now. I know how I feel."

Sarang's fingers dance over the thin skin of my wrists. I'm sure she can feel my pulse racing against her touch. Quieter and more unsure than she's been before, Sarang repeats, "Tell me."

"I like you, Sarang."

Nothing has ever felt more right coming from my mouth.

"Are you sure?" she still asks. And I'm glad she does, because finally, I can let spill what I've kept a secret from her and myself all this time. For someone who always struggled to find the right words, they come to me in multitudes now.

"I've never been surer about anything in my life. I like you so much I can't believe it's possible for any person to *feel* so much of *anything*. You make me think stupid things like no one has ever experienced this before, or if they did, they were wrong because it wasn't *you* they were feeling this way about. I'm obsessed with the way your cheeks dimple to the point where it's just embarrassing. Every time I see the color green, you're right there in my mind's eye. Coffee used to be my favorite scent until I stood close enough to smell your perfume for the first time. The voice of reason in my head sounds like yours, and you're who I think of when I wish I was somebody better, somebody honest, somebody *good*. And yes, you have a short temper, and you're impatient, and a little too stubborn, but I like those parts of you as much as I like your kindness, and your confidence, and your selflessness, and your face, which is the prettiest one I've ever seen, by the—"

"Okay, stop!" she says, breaking into a laugh. She ducks her head, tapping her fingers against my forearm. I lean down. When she looks up, her lips are split in a toothy, embarrassed grin, and her face is tinted with a blush.

"We're finally on the same page for once."

My chest balloons with joy. "What page?" I tease.

"You're really going to make me say it?"

"Say *what*?"

She grumbles her answer into my palm. "I like you too, jerk."

She glances up. Her eyes fall to my mouth.

"Are you going to wait for the storm to pass to kiss me?" Sarang rushes out breathlessly.

I bend down and hold her waist, tugging her to me as she throws her arms around my neck. I tilt her chin to slot our lips together, and when we meet, Sarang gasps into my mouth. My eyes slip shut. Her lips are soft against mine, and warm despite the frosty air that chills me everywhere except where she's touching. Sarang's movements are slow, timid. Then she starts following my lead, and it's such a quiet, intimate action of trust that it makes my chest squeeze around the soft, aching pit that is my heart.

Fireworks don't pop behind my eyes and cheesy orchestra music doesn't play in my ears—it's better than that. Because I'm finally, *finally* kissing Sarang. It's more than I ever hoped for, because it's her. It's Sarang's hands threading in my hair. Her lips caught between mine. The taste of her when she parts her lips for me. It's always been her, even before I knew it.

The soft tickle of her breath beneath my nose has me smiling, which makes her grin into the kiss, and our teeth tap awkwardly. Sarang turns her face to giggle into the crook of my neck. I cradle the back of her head to keep her there, holding in my own laugh. When she pulls away, she presses her fingers to her lips, concealing the smile creeping behind her hand.

"So," she says cheekily. "You have a crush on me?"

"My tongue was literally *just* in your mouth," I reply.

"Aw, you're embarrassed."

"Are you going to be a little shit the whole night? Or can I kiss you again?"

She fists her hands in the collar of my shirt, already leaning up. "I can multitask."

I roll my eyes, still smiling like an idiot. Then I pull her flush against me and kiss her again. And again. And maybe one more time, for good measure.

32. HOPE THIS DOESN'T COME BACK TO BITE ME IN THE ASS

When Sarang's lips are bitten red and my lungs feel like they might burst, we realize it's snowing again. I pull away and glance up, and a drop falls into my eye. No, it's *raining*.

I'm grateful for the pitch black of the cafe as we enter, so no one can see the blush or stupid grin plastered on my face. Not that they would, anyway, since there's no one inside.

"Guys?" Sarang calls out.

"Hi," Isabette's surprised voice rings from one of the tables in the dining room. She lifts a hand, her shadow waving at us. "We're over here."

We approach, stopping before her and Vanna at one of the corner seats beside the window. They're sitting awfully close, and Vanna's entire body is leaning into Isabette.

"Have a good conversation?" Sarang drawls.

Vanna replies, "Have a good time making out?"

"*Okay*," I derail. "Where are Dario and Kai?"

Something in the kitchen clanks like a dropped pot. A few moments later, two shadowy silhouettes emerge. I think their hands are interlinked, but when they join us in the corner they're not touching, so it could be a trick of the light. By the smile I make out on Dario's face, it probably wasn't.

"Hey, what'd we miss?" Kai asks, voice higher than usual.

"Vanna and I were talking about the cafe's social media pages," says Isabette.

"Among other things."

"Yes, *thank you*. Anyhow, something needs to be done to save face after everything. So we brainstormed some strategies to—"

"Sorry," I interrupt. They all look at me. "I don't mean to cut you off there, but I thought about this, too." I dart my tongue to wet my lips, suddenly nervous. "I think we just need to tell the truth."

"About?" Dario prods.

"Everything. Like—from the beginning, everything. That Sarang and I were only pretending to date, how we used the internet fame to save the store, and also explain the blackmailing situation with Kai."

"What?" Kai squawks. "Why would we do that? We could lose our subscribers!"

I scratch my neck, wincing. "Honestly? I . . . think we should cut the channel."

He makes a sound in the back of his throat like he's choking.

"You want to do the very thing Cecelia blackmailed us with?" Isabette asks.

"That defeats the purpose of . . . well, everything we went through tonight," Dario says. "This is what your ex wanted."

"Why?" Sarang asks, calmer than I would expect. Warmth seeps through my chest at her patience. She trusts me enough to listen, even about something as important to her as this cafe.

Uncaring of the others, I slip my hand into hers and face her.

"I don't mean we delete the channels, just stop making videos. At this point, it's bringing us more harm than good. Internet fame has changed us." I drop my head, rubbing her knuckles with my thumb. "That doesn't mean some of it hasn't been a good change, but you said it yourself: we're performing. And eventually, the internet is going to get sick of the show we're putting on. We should be honest. I say we make one final video explaining everything as a conclusion to the channel. I've seen somebody go through a similar situation, and this is how they made it out."

"Who?" Vanna asks.

Isabette groans. "Don't tell me . . ."

I grin sheepishly. "The main character from Son of Sin."

"Oh god," Kai says.

"He wasn't under attack from the *internet* per se, but all his lying got him in trouble, and the only way he could fix it was by finally confronting the truth. See, this is why you guys should've read the books."

"But what about business?" Vanna asks, steering the conversation back. "This place was running itself into the ground before we went viral. What if that happens again?"

I purse my lips. "It's a genuine risk we'll have to take, but we're not deleting the channels; our following and engagement won't die off immediately. Plus, we've put in the work to build a community with customers in the area, that's got to count for something."

"So that's it? No more pretending for the camera?" Sarang asks.

They all look at me for a final decision, but I don't shrink under their gazes. This time I feel confident about making the best choice for us.

"No more lies," I repeat with a nod of my head. "Do you guys agree?"

The candles flicker across each of their unsure, pursed expressions. Rain continues to pour outside, beating on the windows and melting the frozen tundra into a wet slosh that the city's more familiar with.

Then, "I'm in," Kai says.

"Me too," Dario agrees.

Vanna kicks her feet up on the table. "If River thinks this is what we should do, I trust him."

Feeling weightless, I turn to Sarang at my side. She's already looking at me, an odd expression on her face.

"What?" I ask, self-consciously squeezing her hand still laced in mind.

She shakes her head with a small smile. "I was thinking that you *did* end up becoming a better social media manager than a barista after all." She holds her pinkie up. "I'm in. No more lies."

Beaming, I wrap my pinkie around hers.

"Our final video," I murmur. It feels more like a goodbye than anything else, and one I'm bittersweet to give. But it's for the best.

As we set up the candles near the couch, getting ready to film, the power comes back on. The fluorescent lights are a sobering shock to the system, like being splashed with cold water. A moment later, the heater kicks in with a metallic whirr.

"Thank god," Kai says. "*Wi-Fi.*"

I search for Sarang, wondering if this realization between us will feel different without the cover and secrecy of the darkness. It does—it feels more real, which makes it all the better. She catches me staring and sticks her tongue out. A grin stretches across my lips. Her makeup is ruined from our kisses and the snow, and her hair's a frizzy mess. She looks like an idiot, and I like her so, *so* much. I can't wait to smudge her lipstick some more.

"Are you guys ready?" Isabette calls as she fiddles with her phone.

Kai and Vanna take a seat on each of the couch's arms. Dario sits next to Kai, not so subtly weaving an arm around his waist. Sarang takes the spot beside Vanna, which leaves me in the middle.

Isabette flashes three fingers at us. Two. One. *Go*, she mouths.

INT. "Bingsu for Two"/DINING AREA — NIGHT

Squished on the couch together, KAI, DARIO, RIVER, SARANG, and VANNA all share silent, blank looks with each other. The half-lit TEAT! sign buzzes noisily above their heads, casting them in flickering lights. Sarang jabs her elbow into River's side.

RIVER

Am I starting? Uh. Hi, everyone. Don't mind all the candles lying around. It probably looks like we were doing a seance, but we weren't. We don't do occult stuff here. We do it elsewhere. Ha, just . . . just kidding.

No, it's just that the power was out and—

SARANG

Would you quit stalling?

RIVER

(rushed)

This is our last video. We're shutting down the channel.

KAI

(dramatically)

Whhaaaat?

RIVER

Thank you for that, Kai. Yeah. we'll be stepping away
from all our social media channels. We, uh . . .

(struggling)

SARANG

We haven't been honest in our videos. This isn't us,
it's not Bingsu for Two, and performing has started to
take a toll on everyone involved. Some of us have been
targeted. Some of us have had to make hard choices.

(glances at River)

Some of us have also had to lie—to ourselves and to
you all.

A moment of heavy silence clings to the room. River and
Sarang lock eyes awkwardly. River makes an "Are You Going
to Say It, or Should I?" face, which is impressive for
just a raise of his eyebrows.

SARANG

Me and River only pretended to be a couple for views. I
hated lying, but . . . it was for the store. That's what
I kept telling myself.

(quieter, staring at her lap)

Lying got easier. To myself and to all of you. We
were never dating, and our breakup earlier wasn't
real, either.

RIVER

Everyone wanted us to be together, so we went along
with it to save the cafe. I'm sorry we lied, but . . .

Hesitating, he glances over at Sarang, who's already
watching him with wide, curious eyes.

RIVER

I don't regret it.

The camera doesn't catch Sarang's reaction—it's there and
gone, a flash of something only River seems to see. It
makes him smile.

Dario clears his throat.

DARIO

Another reason we're getting rid of the socials is
because of safety reasons. We weren't going to address
this, but it's fucked up, and deserves to be called
out. Somebody attacked Kai and framed him online, then
tried to turn us against each other.

(he looks at River)

Did you want to . . . ?

RIVER

(consideringly)

Actually, no. I won't out who it was that threatened us.
I don't want to add fuel to the fire they started. I'd
just like to move on and forget about them. She—*they*—
don't mean anything to me anymore.

Is that okay, Kai? It's up to you if you want to call
them out. You're the one they hurt.

KAI

You know what? I think I'll give "being the bigger person" a try. I don't give a shit what they have to say about me, or what the internet believes I did.
I know I didn't. That's enough.

(*pausing*)

Whoa, this feels weird.

SARANG

It's very weird. No one holds a grudge better than you, usually.

DARIO

(*grumbling*)

True.

RIVER

That's partly why we're cutting the channel. But we want to thank all of you who've been watching and supporting us this whole time. We never thought we'd do so well online—

ISABETTE (O.S.)

You didn't intend for that original video to blow up, right?

RIVER

(*flustered*)

Yeah, that was an accident.

VANNA

Oh yeah, you posted it to your fandom account, didn't you?

RIVER

Aren't we getting off topic here?

SARANG

I think your fanboy tendencies should always be the
topic. Especially when they make you squirm.

KAI

(sincerely)

Wait, guys, I want to say something, seriously.
Bingsu for Two is only still around because of
the followers and all of you watching. This cafe
is like a second home to me, especially since my
family isn't always around. So, thanks for
keeping it alive.

*Dario tilts his head up, his eyes roaming up and down the
side of Kai's face. A small smile worms its way on his
mouth, and he bites his lips to stop it.*

DARIO

Working here means a lot to me, too. I don't know what
I'd do if we closed.

VANNA

I'd be screwed if this place wasn't around. I *was*
screwed, until Mr. Cho gave me a job.

(wincing)

I'm glad some strangers on the internet found
us entertaining enough to keep us in business.
Thank you. Everyone that works here is
my family.

With just River and Sarang left, they turn toward each
other in unison. Sarang blinks, expression pinched as if
unsure what to say, or how to say it.

SARANG

I was against all this at first. The internet stuff. It
seemed disingenuous. But the support everyone's shown
for Bingsu for Two—that was real. I felt it every
single day, with each new customer that came in. Thank
you. This cafe means everything to me.

River is transfixed. Once Sarang finishes speaking, she
ducks her head and stares at her knees, and River con-
tinues to watch her. His shoulders tighten. Then, still
looking at her turned face, he speaks.

RIVER

(somberly)

This is the first time I've felt like I belonged
somewhere. Like I wanted to *be* somewhere. I was in a
weird place before coming here, and I never imagined
I'd ever feel . . . so whole. I had a purpose here that
I'd been looking for elsewhere and never found. It was
because of you, the followers.

(He twists around to look at Vanna,

Dario, and Kai.)

And because of you guys, too.

KAI

Awww.

VANNA

My frozen heart is thawing a bit.

RIVER

I mean it. Thank you. I don't know where I'd be or *who*
I'd be if I'd never come to work here.

*Finally, Sarang lifts her head and meets River's intense
gaze. He grins, and it softens his eyes. Her expression
smooths into something quiet, a private realization. She
turns to the camera, giving a genuine smile to the internet for the first time.*

SARANG

This is it. Our last video. We know uploading this will
be a risk. I'm not sure what this will do to Bingsu for
Two's business. So, please come visit us at the cafe.
We—*I'd* love to meet everyone who's supported us, so I
can say thank you in person.

Isabette cuts. Someone says something about editing and posting the video, but I'm not paying attention to them. All I'm focused
on is Sarang. She notices my gaze. Without a word, she reaches over
and grabs my hand, giving it a painful squeeze.

She trusted me with this decision. She trusted me all along.

I hope to God I don't let her down.

33. YOU'RE TELLING ME MY ACTIONS HAVE [CHECKS WRITING ON HAND] CONSEQUENCES?

I wake up to rain drumming on the windows and the crazy urge to piss. It's a pain to crack my eyes open. I raise a hand to shield them from the glaring rays of the sun, before realizing that it isn't the sun. It's a fluorescent ceiling light. Where the hell am I?

The events of last night trickle into my brain. I don't remember falling asleep. After we recorded the video and uploaded it, I was in such an adrenaline-infused near-hypothermic state that the rest of the night was a blur, but I vaguely recall sliding down to sit on the floor, and someone joining me at my side.

A weight sprawled over my legs shifts then. I look down to find Sarang fast asleep, with her head resting on my lap and her green hair splayed in an untamed halo across my thighs. Her nose scrunches, and she grumbles in her sleep before scooting closer and nuzzling my stomach. Holy *fucking* shit. That's adorable.

God, I have to pee.

Another noise joins the pelleting of rain against the roof. My sleep-fogged brain doesn't realize what it is until the bell above the front door chimes and in walk a rain-drenched Haneul and

Mr. Cho. They freeze in place once they spot the six of us fast asleep on the floor.

I jump, accidentally startling Sarang. "Stop it," she mumbles into my lap.

Haneul crosses the dining room, stopping in front of us with a snort. I want to *die*.

"How sickeningly cute," she drawls. "Now will you get your lazy ass up and open the store?"

Sarang's eyes fly open. She sits up so fast she nearly headbutts me in the chin. Mr. Cho joins us then, smiling at the six of us with amusement. I can't meet his gaze.

"I'm glad you weren't stuck in the storm alone, Sarang" is all he says, mercifully.

The others wake, shifting and moaning from their rigid places on the floor. Kai and Dario untangle themselves, having somehow migrated under one of the tables in the middle of the night. Isabette sits up on the couch behind me. Vanna, tucked behind her, stretches and lets out an inappropriately loud yawn.

Haneul kicks Sarang's calf, then mine. "It's almost six. Hurry, or else you won't be able to open in time for the customers."

"We're not getting any customers," Kai grumbles. He's given up trying to stand, and collapses face-first to the ground. "Not after that video we posted."

"I saw the video," says Mr. Cho. "I thought it was very nice. And clearly so did the customers outside."

Dario quickly sits up and knocks his head against the table. "*Ow*—customers?"

Any trace of sleep is gone from Sarang's voice. "What customers?"

Mr. Cho walks over to the window and peels back a corner of the curtains we'd drawn last night to conserve heat. There are people outside. And a *lot* of them, even in the pouring rain and slush. A girl with dyed-red wavy hair notices us and waves cheerfully. Mr. Cho waves back before sliding the curtains in place.

"Holy shit," Vanna says, hopping over Isabette and the arm of the couch. "Wait, how do we still have customers? I thought they'd be boycotting our asses."

"Are we sure they're not an angry mob?" Kai asks.

Isabette taps my shoulder. Sitting on the floor, I roll my head back on the couch to look at her. Her upside-down face is smiling with pride.

"You were right. It worked."

Something bright blooms in my core. I glance at Sarang, who's watching me with fondness I never would've expected could be directed at me, and the brightness turns into joy behind my lungs.

Grinning, I lean toward her. "Don't look so surprised."

"Smugness is not a good look on you."

"Sure, sweetheart."

Outside, somebody knocks on the covered windows and says, "It's six!" followed by muffled sounds of scuffling.

Pushing on my shoulder for leverage, Sarang stands. "We're *late*. We've never been late except for that one time Dario slept through his opening shift."

"Get over that already, I had a late game the night before," he mumbles.

She's gone, already hurrying toward the counter to start the cleaning cycle on the espresso machine. "Why are you still talking and not working? Go! Dario and Kai, clean up the living room. Vanna, restock the fridges. River, finish setting up the front while I throw the pastries in the oven."

Isabette raises her hand. "Can I help?"

Vanna offers her hand to Isabette, who accepts it and stands. "Usually I'd tell you not to worry your pretty little head, but you can look pretty *and* help me, right?"

As the others scurry to their tasks and Haneul helps Mr. Cho upstairs, I make a quick run to the bathroom, then join a frazzled Sarang behind the counter.

"Hey," I say, holding her chin in my palm to tilt her my way. I swipe my thumb over a spot of nothing at the corner of her lips, letting my fingers linger. "You've got drool all over your face, you toddler."

"What? I don't *drool*." She furiously rubs her mouth.

"You do. A lot. It was all over my pants. You should probably get that checked out by a medical professional, it can't be healthy."

"Shut up, bastard. Go get your knobby knees checked out, they were digging into my stomach all night." With a shove that doesn't even make me budge, Sarang stomps to the kitchen in a huff. I grin, watching her disappear behind the curtains. I'm glad she's still *Sarang* after everything.

We open at record speed. It usually takes a half hour to do it myself, but with everybody helping, we're ready ten minutes later.

The six of us stand in front of the door in collective silence. I've thrown my apron on and washed my face, yet I still feel like a mess. Last night's eyeliner is smudged in a dark shadow beneath Sarang's eyes, but it looks hot on her, so she can get away with it. She runs her hands over her hair and smooths her apron down, fidgeting.

Dario rubs his arm. "I don't know what to expect."

"I'm nervous," Kai mutters.

Vanna claps them both on the back, leaning forward and inserting herself between them. "What's the worst that can happen?"

Kai counts on his fingers. "They barge in and set the place on fire, rob us, punch Dario in the face, break the espresso machine, hold us at gunpoint to restart the YouTube account—"

"Okay, all right, plenty of bad things could happen. You got me there."

Sarang lets out a shuddering breath at my side. I look down at her, taken aback by the nervous pallor of her face. With a quick glance over to make sure the others aren't looking back at us, I wrap an arm around her shoulders to turn her toward me and place a kiss on her forehead. Her wide eyes lock with mine.

"Don't worry," I say quietly, smiling. "Whatever happens, you won't be facing it alone."

She blinks. Then, quick as a flash, she stands on her tiptoes and drags me down into a kiss, fitting her lips against mine. Before I can register anything other than *holy shit, she's kissing me, this is great* and Vanna's whistling, Sarang pulls back. Her face is flushed and full of life again, and her grin is steady this time.

"All right. Let's get this over with."

Sarang walks away, flips the Closed sign over, then pushes the door open. I brace myself—

Only to be greeted by cheering.

She freezes halfway out the door, gaping at the line of customers. Kai runs over to the dining area and pulls back the curtains all the way, revealing the alleyway packed with people pumping their fists and whooping like they're in line for a concert and not a latte.

"What the hell?" Vanna says.

The first dozen people crowd into the lobby, lining up at the register. I hurry behind the counter to take the first three teenagers' orders.

"Good morning," the girl with dyed-red hair and kind, dark brown eyes greets me cheerfully. "No offense, but you all kind of look like shit. Are you okay?"

"*Anahita*, you can't say 'no offense' and then offend someone," her tall friend chastises. He turns to me with an apologetic smile. "Ignore her."

"Sorry! I didn't mean *shit* as in bad, just like they haven't slept in ten years."

"Are you trying to get them to spit in our coffee?"

Kai leans around me. "We spit in all our coffee regardless. It's store policy."

Their third friend speaks up. "We watched your guys' video last night. You're not really ending the channel, are you?"

"It's true." I say with a half-smile.

They lean back, twisting their face. "That's a bummer. We've been following along since the beginning when that first video went viral. Big fans. Those videos are hilarious."

I go to apologize, but the tall friend interrupts.

"It's not a huge deal; the store's not closing or anything."

Vanna slides up next to me. "That's right. So please, come by whenever. Just make sure to *order*."

The girl, Anahita, laughs sheepishly. "Can we please get a fruit bingsu to split and three iced lattes?"

It's a similar conversation with the rest of the customers: they're all disappointed that we're done with the videos, but that they've come to love the cafe because of them, and they'll keep coming back. The only outliers are the handful of our regular customers who work nearby and just want their lattes and one of Sarang's pastries before they head to their jobs and have no idea why it's so busy today. Maybe it's because I'm tired and the last twenty-four hours have been an emotional roller coaster, but by the fifteenth customer who beams and tells me how much they've enjoyed watching our content, I have to blink harder to keep back the wetness in my eyes.

The line never ends, but it doesn't make me want to die today. I've never enjoyed a shift at work so much. Vanna runs the food out with Isabette, while the rest of us crowd behind the counter, bumping into one another as we try to keep up with all the orders. Occasionally, Sarang will brush by my side, or her shoe will tap mine—so brief I'm sure it's an accident. But then I meet her eyes and see the glint in them as she smiles with false innocence, and my heart rockets into my throat.

"You're looking a little red, River," she says as she starts making a peppermint mocha. "Something getting you worked up?"

"*Something's* getting worked up, yeah," I shoot back without thinking. Both Dario and Kai freeze in the middle of what they were doing and whip around with identical expressions of disgust. The steaming wand screams as it's forgotten in a pitcher of milk.

"It's eleven in the morning," Dario says.

"Dick jokes are only funny past three," Kai agrees. "Have some self-respect."

"I didn't *mean* it!"

Sarang runs her hand down her burning, crimson face. "Are you always going to be like this?"

I hook my finger through her dainty chain necklace and tug gently to pull her toward me. Leaning down, I whisper into her ear, "Always for you."

She pushes my face away and I burst out laughing against her palm.

The next customer to wiggle through the door sports a familiar mess of shaggy brown hair and a split lip that makes my heart sink at the sight of. Jace looks around, then lights up when he spots me.

"River!"

I barely have time to step out from behind the counter and ask what he's doing here before he launches himself at me in a flurry of limbs. It takes a moment to process that Jace is hugging me, cheek mushed against my apron and arms wrapped so tightly around my torso it hurts.

"Jace," I start, hands hovering uncertainly above his back. He hasn't hugged me since he was a kid, and it makes alarm bells ring in my mind. "What's—"

"I thought you might be dead," he mumbles into my chest quietly.

I blink. Then hug him harder, uncaring of anyone else in the store.

Not a second later, Jace pulls away and punches me straight in my solar plexus, making me wheeze. "You didn't answer your phone all night! Umma thought you froze to death out in the snow! We were all worried!"

"River—!"

Squeezing through the doorway is Umma, and right behind her, Dad. Both their twisted faces relax the instant they land on me. Umma runs over and pulls me in, cradling my head to her shoulder.

"다행이야,"[9] she says in relief, running her hand over my hair. "Thank God. Why—we didn't know where you went after you stormed out. It was so cold. We called all your friends—even Cecelia. She had no idea where you were. She kept crying. I thought—"

They called Cecelia? "My phone died last night, and then so much happened this morning and I got caught up in . . ."

Dad's shoes shuffle into my line of sight behind Umma. I glance up at him, dread creaking in my bones. The lines of regret creasing his forehead are foreign, and I nearly miss the tight purse of his lips hidden beneath his beard.

"River," he starts.

I steel myself.

"I'm sorry."

Wait—what?

Dad continues, rubbing his goatee and having a hard time meeting my eyes. "The stress of opening a new store has been taking a toll on me for months and . . . I realize now that I took that out on you and the family. It wasn't fair to you. No matter how angry I was about you lying and working here, kicking you out was wrong, especially in a snowstorm."

---

9.   Thank God

I don't know what to say. A lump forms in my throat.

Umma speaks up. "It makes me sad that you hid your feelings about Cafe Gong for so long, but I see we didn't exactly make it easy for you to come to us. We should have *asked* if you wanted to be manager, instead of making you."

"Yes," Dad says. He winces, and pauses before mustering up the strength to say, "I'll admit, it hurt when you quit. It hurt worse when you went to work for a different family, like what we gave to you wasn't good enough. It felt like you were drifting away from us."

My throat tightens. I *really* wish we weren't doing this in front of a crowd, but it might be our only opportunity. We're not an open family, exactly. "I know, and I'm sorry for that. I was scared to disappoint you guys, or make you think I'm useless and not grateful for all you've done. But I couldn't take it, being in a place that didn't feel like our family's business anymore. Getting the management position because you knew I didn't have a chance elsewhere was the final straw. I knew it, everyone else at Cafe Gong knew it—"

"River," Umma interrupts. "That's not why we made you manager."

"Come on."

There's a knit between Dad's thick brows. "No, it isn't. We could've hired somebody older and with more experience if we wanted to—but we wanted *you* because it was special. The cafe is the product of everything your mom and I worked for, but you and Jace are at the heart of it all. Cafe Gong means the world to us. That's why we wanted to give that to you. Not because we thought you needed our help, but because—" He struggles to tap into a mostly dry well of emotional vulnerability. "It was the best way we could say we love you, and we're proud of you, and that we trust you."

It's only when my fingers start cramping that I realize I'd been clutching the fabric of my apron so hard the bones in my hand are stiff when I let go. My face is hot. A tight band around my chest has me wondering if Jace is still hugging me, but no, it isn't him squeezing the air from my lungs.

"I—" I have to stop, clear my throat. "I never knew that. I always thought I was disappointing you guys."

"Never," Umma says. "Sure, maybe we don't always understand where you're coming from at first, but there is so much about you to be proud of. Look around." Her head turns, scanning the wall of customers outside and the crowd in every inch of the cafe. My smile turns watery.

Dad approaches and squeezes my shoulder. "Just so you know, even after all of this, there will always be a spot for you at Cafe Gong. If you'd like."

I stand up straighter, rolling my shoulders back. Despite everyone's eyes on me, the only pair I can feel on my skin belong to Sarang. I chew over the words that have taken me a long time to formulate—even longer to accept.

"Thanks, Dad, but I'm happy here. It's not anyone's fault, but at Cafe Gong, nothing felt right. I was doing everything I was supposed to, and it still wasn't enough. Trying to convince myself that it's what I wanted was terrible. But here . . ." I gesture around. "This feels right. It feels like something I want to keep doing."

"I'm glad, because it'd be a shame if we were to lose you."

My body twists around at the unexpected voice. Mr. Cho steps out of the kitchen, Haneul following behind, holding the curtains to the side. He walks straight to my parents, and on the way, smiles at me, eyes crinkling the same way Sarang's do. He offers a hand for Dad and Umma to shake then bows.

"**만나서 반갑습니다.**[10] Because of your son, the store my wife and I started can live on. As another family business owner and a parent, thank you. River is one of the most dedicated people I've met, and I'm grateful that this is a place he decided was worth his passion and skills."

Haneul gives me an up-and-down scan with an amused expression. "He came and *begged* to work here, and then never stopped working hard to prove his place."

"River's done so much for us," Kai adds on, leaning halfway over the handoff counter. "It was a wreck before he got here, we were close to shutting down business. He helped save us."

Dario pulls Kai off the counter and back onto his feet. He clears his throat. "It was his idea to make videos for the cafe. He really stepped up." Next to him, Vanna nods in agreement, shooting me a wink.

My throat tightens. *Don't betray me now, body.* Sarang steps around the counter to stand by her father, looking between my parents and me.

"River cares so much about our store. **심성이 좋나요,**"[11] she says, meeting my eye. She smiles like it's a secret, just for me. "I used to think he wasn't a good fit, but he proved me wrong over and over again. He makes Bingsu for Two feel like home."

---

10.   Nice to meet you.

11.   He has a good heart

My body *does* betray me, and I curse internally when heat prickles behind my eyes. I have to clench my fists and curl my toes to keep myself rooted in place so I don't cross the distance between us and do something embarrassing in front of everyone.

I can't believe I hated her at one point. That I ever thought there wasn't anything beyond her thick skin and sharp words speared by black-painted lips. I didn't see her then. I didn't know who she was and didn't bother to find out. Now I do.

If I make Bingsu for Two feel like home to her, Sarang makes it a home worth coming back to every day.

Oh, fuck. Am I in that deep already?

Strangely, the thought doesn't scare me.

Dad clears his throat. A mesh of emotions plays across his features, from surprise to confusion. "That's very high praise." He gives Mr. Cho an awkward white-person bow. "Thanks for taking care of him."

"Our pleasure," Mr. Cho replies. Then he turns his attention to me and places a soft touch on my shoulder as he speaks. "It's because of you and your efforts that my wife's dream was saved. Thank you, River. It doesn't feel like very long ago, but you've changed a lot since you came to me asking to be manager. What happened?"

Guiltily, my eyes flicker to Sarang, then away. Mr. Cho catches it.

He turns to Umma and speaks in Korean with a smile, something about kids. Umma laughs and replies, "네, 아이들은 빨리 자라니까."[12]

Mr. Cho gives my shoulder a squeeze, recentering my attention. "I can tell you love this place now, like it's your family's. Did

---

12.   Yes, they grow up fast

you mean it when you said this feels like something you want to keep doing?"

I nod so hard my glasses slide down. "Yes."

"How does a promotion sound, then?"

The wind knocks out of me like Jace has punched me again. "Are you serious?"

"The management position is yours. As long as my daughter doesn't mind me passing it to you, of course."

First, my eyes flicker over to Vanna as I hold my breath. But all she does is give me a nod and a steady, confident smile. The nerves knotting in my stomach lessen, and I smile back at her.

Then I look at Sarang, who's as still as a marble bust. Slowly, realization loosens her shocked-stiff features, animating them and making her eyes sparkle. She laughs. The sound tugs a laugh out of my own lungs. And then she's in front of me, beaming and twisting my hand in hers.

"You sure you can handle it?" she asks with a teasing lilt, but a stain of honesty colors the rich onyx of her eyes. It's a genuine question. There isn't a right answer; she's not waiting for me to say what she wants to hear.

You should be making decisions for yourself. It's your life.

I squeeze her hand. She doesn't need to worry. This is for me as much as it is for her. "What, like it's hard? Given the previous manager's example, I think I'll be fine."

"I can hear you, brat," Haneul pipes up dully.

Somebody claps my back. I turn around. Dad's smiling more genuinely than he has in a long time. It's been a while since I've seen him look like that—wholly, genuinely proud, and not just halfway there.

"You'll do good," he tells me. "You were a great manager at Cafe Gong. You'll be an even better one here."

Sarang barks out a laugh, bright and disbelieving. She hooks her hands into the collar of my shirt and drags me down. From this close, I go cross-eyed, but the strain is worth looking at her smile.

"Manager," Sarang says under her breath.

I hold her waist, grinning back. "Johns Hopkins."

Moisture glistens in her eyes. Her smile wobbles. She wraps her arms around my neck, and I squeeze her back in a hug.

Like the encouraging idiots they are, Jace and Kai start whooping and clapping obnoxiously, which of course inspires the customers inside the store to start doing the same. I think I'd be mortified in any other situation, but Sarang is a good distraction. It's hard to think of anything else when she's near.

It's always been like that, hasn't it? Even when I despised her guts, I couldn't get her out of my mind. I've always tilted toward her instead of the sun.

I doubt that will change when she leaves. But that's a thought for another time. For now, I focus on how she feels under my hands, the way her soft puffs of laughter brush the shell of my ear, and how the stirring of warmth she ignites in me now is so, so far away from the cold brew of hate it used to be.

34. ONE YEAR, SIX MONTHS, AND FIVE DAYS LATER. YES, I COUNTED, BUT DON'T TELL HER THAT.

"Hey—*Kai!* Watch it, man, you made me mess up."

The late-afternoon summer sun shutters through the windows of the cafe, lighting the empty dining area up like fire. We closed early today, so the only sounds filling the restaurant are of dishes clattering together as Kai, Vanna, and Isabette close up around me. I'd help, but I'm busy working on our menu board in the corner of the cafe. Also, I don't want to.

Instead of getting back to work, Kai peeks over my shoulder. "What are you doing?"

"Making some changes to the menu."

"Okay . . . why?"

Smirking, I say, "Because Sarang will *flip* when she sees it. It's a sweet welcome-back gesture, right?"

Kai shakes his head, muttering, "And they say romance is dead," as he goes back to sweeping.

"Hey," Vanna shouts from the counter. "Are you just going to sit your lazy ass there while the rest of us work?"

"Yeah, pretty much. Manager privileges, remember?"

"Co-manager," she corrects.

Isabette steps out of the kitchen, wiping her hands on her black apron as she retrieves more dirty dishes.

"You should take advantage of being a manager, too," she says to Vanna, loud enough that I can hear. "Like . . . by calling out tomorrow so River has to cover while you, me, and your sister finally try out that new ice-cream shop on Alki Beach."

Vanna twists around to pull Isabette down and plant a wet kiss on her cheek. It's *obnoxiously* loud, and I know they're doing it on purpose. "I'm so lucky you're my girlfriend."

"We *get it*. You're in love," Kai says.

I sit back, tuning them out to admire my chalkboard. I can't wait to see Sarang's face when she gets a look at this.

WELCOME TO CHUCK E. CHEESE! HOME OF THE CHUCK AND THE CHEESE!

EXPRESSO

- AFFOGATO BUT WITHOUT THE SHOT $3.25
- AMERICAN €8.00
- LATTE WITH OXIDIZED SHOTS $14.75
- JUST MILK $12.99
- WE DON'T SELL COFFEE HERE

NON-COFFEE & TEA

- MORNING WAKE-UP SLAP $23.95
- A CUP FULL OF DISHWATER $2.75
- 3 MINUTES OF STARING INTO KAI'S DREAMY EYES $9.99
- LITERALLY ALL THE CASH IN OUR REGISTER $.99

SNOW CONES

- TARO 과일 $8.00
- FRUIT 오레오 $10.00
- OREO 타로 $10.00
- PURE ICE $10.00
- EXTRA CONE, HOLD THE SNOW $2.25

TAIYAKI

- PLAIN, BUT VANNA WILL SPIT ON IT
  $1.25
- YOU DON'T WANT TO KNOW $1.25

- SALMON $3.45
- WHATEVER IS LEFT IN THE KNOCK BOX $1.25

BRUNCH/DESSERT

- NOTHING. STARVE.

ENTREES

- A WHOLE LIVE OCTOPUS $9.95
- A WHOLE LIVE MAN $7.50
- AN EVERYTHING BAGEL BUT NO BAGEL
  $6.50

Then I notice the clock. Panic shoots through me. "*Shit.* It's already five! Why didn't any of you say anything?"

"What? It's five?" Kai yells. He drops the milk cartons he was restocking into the fridge and throws his apron across the dining room. "We're going to be late, their planes arrive at five twenty! I've got to get my poster."

We rush to close, not caring that the dishes are in the wrong spot and there's still a huge puddle of caramel syrup on the floor. Then we all set off for my family's apartment, where my car is parked.

On our way there, we inevitably pass Cafe Gong's busy storefront. Well, what used to be Cafe Gong. After this location went out of business, the *other* giant corporate coffee chain in Seattle took over the store. I think that's what stung Dad the most about the whole situation, but he and Umma have plans to open another store sometime next year, so hopefully he'll get over it by then.

I glance through the window, then blink in surprise to see Cecelia on the other side, wiping down a table. Her eyebrows shoot up. She grimaces and waves hesitantly. I wave back politely, concealing my own wince.

We haven't kept in touch—matter of fact, the last time I heard anything about her was from Umma, who mentioned that she got a part-time job here to cover her tuition at UW Bothell after getting rejected from UPenn and losing her scholarships. Someone ratted her out about being behind the online scandal with Kai to the college board, apparently. It wasn't me, but frankly, I don't care who it was. I've moved past it all.

But it's always awkward running into your ex.

We round up on my beat-up car in the parking lot. Kai takes the passenger seat, Vanna and Isabette situate themselves in the back, and I get behind the wheel. Nervous from both anticipation and having to drive in rush-hour traffic, I head toward SeaTac Airport.

As we're driving on the freeway, Kai asks me, "Oh yeah. Did Sarang lose your guys' bet?"

I grin, fingers tightening around the wheel. "Obviously."

"Figures. You think she'll wear the shirt?"

"She better if she wants a ride home."

Isabette pokes her head between our seats. "What bet?"

"When she left for the start of the school year, I bet her that she couldn't go a week without asking how the cafe was doing, and she bet I couldn't last a week without bringing up Son of Sin. If I lost, I had to give her an hour-by-hour update on the store for two weeks, and if she did, she'd have to wear one of my really obnoxious fandom shirts today."

Vanna snorts. "How long did she last?"

"Two days before she cracked and tried to find out through Haneul if we'd burned the store to the ground yet."

"But Haneul's in California?"

"I know. She was desperate."

The exit is coming up. I start the grueling process of merging across five lanes.

"Wait," Isabette says. "How would Sarang have your shirt?"

I barely manage to swerve out of the way of a minivan trying to cross into my lane. Oops. "Uh," I drag out, pulling onto the exit. "I accidentally left it in her dorm when I visited over spring break."

Vanna perches her chin on my seat. The back of my neck sweats. "Ah, yes, that trip you took to visit her. Alone. The one you refuse to tell us *anything* about. How interesting."

I wet my lips, trying to focus on not crashing—or thinking about that week with Sarang. "Yep. Good times. Anyway, wow, look at that, we're already here."

It's 5:43 p.m. when we get through the terminal, find parking, and run inside. Dario's and Sarang's gates are near each other, conveniently. The four of us make it to the baggage pickup area just as a sea of people toting carry-on bags and looking two inches from death descends the escalators.

Kai stands on his tiptoes to try to get a look over the incoming crowd. "It could be either one of their planes. Oh, shoot, my poster."

He holds it up. Written in crayon on a flattened cardboard box he scavenged from the dumpster in the alley, it says:

SORRY I ELOPED WITH UR OLD COACH. WELCOME HOME, ~~DAVID~~ DARIO!

Vanna nods approvingly. "Nice, Coach Sampson. Good pick."

"Thanks. I was deciding between him or the gym teacher, Mrs. Newman."

A deep voice speaks from behind us. "Mrs. Newman has had four ex-husbands. You really think you're in her league?"

Kai shrugs. "They were all bald. She might go for someone young and with a full head of—"

He whips around, the poster flopping and smacking the top of some poor stranger's head. Standing there is Dario, taller and more muscled than he was when he left, with his hair grown out and a wicked grin on his face. His eyes flick up to the poster.

"Really? Coach Sampson?" He scoffs. "The man is like, five years away from retire—*oof!*"

Kai launches himself at Dario, who catches him with one arm while still holding onto his bag. The sound of Dario's bright, booming laugh cuts through the chatter of the terminal and the people around us. He drops his bag to hug Kai fully, lifting him off the ground.

Between cackles, Kai says, "I didn't actually elope with your old basketball coach."

"No more talking about that old fart. I missed you," Dario says, in a rush to pull Kai back in and kiss him.

I avert my eyes to the ceiling. "Come on, too much tongue," I complain.

Vanna reaches up to cover Isabette's eyes. "Not in front of the baby."

"I think they're cute," Isabette says.

I glance back—nope, they're not done. *Okay.* I turn around to search the crowd, and my pulse jumps when I spot a familiar crown of green hair.

My feet move on their own, forgetting my friends and everyone around me. I'm hot with anticipation; I've been waiting for this moment for what feels like forever. Will she complain about my clammy palms? Probably, but that doesn't mean she won't still hold them.

The group of tourists with their oversized suitcases in front of me move, and I catch another glimpse of bright, shocking green. I nudge two people out of the way, tripping over my own feet.

And there she is.

It's only been three months since I visited her at college, and I FaceTimed her last night for Christ's sake, but seeing her right now is like seeing her for the first time all over again. Her round, rosy cheeks, dimpled and squished from smiling so hard. Her thin, sparkling eyes pinning me in place, with dark eyeshadow smudges at their corners. Her hair—shoulder length now—with black roots she made me promise to help her bleach tonight. Her.

Sarang is unsuccessfully trying to smother her grin. She waddles over, weighed down by her huge backpack and an overstuffed tote bag. "You are so embarrassing, holy crap. Everyone was staring at me because of this shirt!"

I grab her hand, interlocking our fingers and holding them against my chest. Around Sarang, my lungs have to work overtime.

"You wore it," I say, looking her up and down. That shirt is at least ten years old, a novelty one I got at the premiere of the first *Son of Sin* movie. I used to wear that thing religiously and it shows, with its dozen moth holes, frayed hemming, and the print design so faded it resembles a stubborn food stain. Somehow, she still makes it look good, which would be annoying if it didn't make me so light-headed. I snake my other hand around her waist to pull her in close. Sarang gasps, blinking rapidly before glaring at me again.

"Fair's fair," she grumbles, and reaches up with her free hand to cup the back of my neck. Her glower smooths out as she runs her fingers through my hair. "It's longer now."

"Want me to cut it?"

"Nah." She grins, roughly tugging the strands. "I like it. Something to hold on to."

Jesus.

"You're as insufferable as ever," I grind out.

"Pretend all you want. You love me."

"I do. I love you."

Surprise still flits across her expression no matter how often I tell her—which is *often.* I savor the bleeding of a blush across her skin, the way her nose scrunches, how she tries to suppress the smile tugging at her mouth. Sarang lets go of my hand to interlock hers behind my neck. I bend down when she pulls me. Like a magnet. An orbiting planet chasing after its sun.

As my lips graze hers, she pauses.

So quietly that I feel her speak more than I hear her, Sarang whispers, "I love you, too, River."

I capture her words between my lips before they can escape too far from hers.

Sarang's mouth parts under mine. The easy action of it is like a reflex, like we've grown to meld with one another rather than around. Her teeth nip at my bottom lip as she cups the side of my face, thumb brushing the shell of my ear, and I sigh into the kiss. I missed her.

"I love you," I mumble against her mouth.

"You said that already."

"Want me to stop?"

"Obviously not."

An idle, fleeting thought trickles into my mind then, with Sarang's touch as its harbinger. I finally *know*. Know how I feel, what I want, and who I am. Her love turned me brave enough to ask the question, and the answer all along has been her. The realization makes me ache in ways that are quiet and intense all at once.

She makes me feel real.

THE END

ACKNOWLEDGMENTS

I wrote this book as a nineteen-year-old in college who desperately needed a break from classes and internships and the budding horrors of adulthood, so I'd first like to thank this story for being my happy reprieve from school. *Bingsu for Two* was for me—but only at first.

Second and more importantly, thank you to everybody who picked up this book. I never thought it'd leave the light of my laptop, but now it exists in heads besides my own, so from the bottom of my heart, thank you. You made my biggest dream come true. I hope River and Sarang's story brought you joy.

Thank you Mom and Dad, for everything, but especially for supporting me as I pursued my dreams of becoming an author. My love for stories is thanks to my mom, who read me books from a young age in a language that wasn't hers (and in funny voices, too), and my dad, who encouraged this hobby and was my first-ever reader. I love you both so much. 사랑해요.

Thank you to my wonderful agent Maeve MacLysaght, who took a chance on me with this silly little story and helped turn it into something legible. You're the reason this book is here today and why I'm able to do what I love. Thank you for every perfect suggestion, brainstorming session, reassuring email, and for answering my panicked calls on weekends.

There are a million hands who must touch a book before a reader can pick it up, and I'm grateful for every single person who helped along the way. My first editor, Laura Schreiber, whose enthusiasm for this story uplifted me throughout the entire process—I won the author lottery working with you. My other editor, Stefanie Chin, who is an angel sent via email. Thank you both for your tireless work on this and for making me feel heard every step of the way. Marcie Lawrence and Jen Keenan for their beautiful work on the interior and the cover. All the copy editors and proofreaders who, because of them, I now know that "shithole" is one word per Merriam-Webster. Thank you to the entire marketing and publicity department who champion this book more than I know. The entire team at Union Square & Co. will forever have my gratitude.

I have the best friends in the entire world, which is just objective truth. Kylina Nhem-Lim, whose endless kindness, humor, and friendship got me through the grueling process of middle and high school, life, and everything in between. Keyona Pine, who is not only one of the best people I know and one of my closest friends, but also my college roommate. I wrote most of this book late at night in the dorms, so thank you for putting up with the clacking of my keys (and me) for almost four years. I love both of you and I count myself lucky every day that you're in my life.

Ben Frizzell. I wouldn't be a romance author if I hadn't met you. I only know how to write about love because you showed me what it feels like. You were here with me for every single milestone of this book, and I could not imagine doing it (or anything else) without you by my side. Thank you for being my best friend, my favorite person, and for calming me down after every single book-related breakdown. No one was more excited for this story than you. There are no words to describe how much you mean to me, which really sucks because I'm supposed to be good at words, but you already know that. Every thread of love I wove into this story is borrowed from you.

A million thank-yous to my writing best friend, Anahita Karthik, for keeping me sane through my publishing journey. You inspire me every day with your talent, encouragement, and passion, and I'm always going to be rooting for you.

To Bella Zulueta, Kimmy Nguyen, and countless other friends for being great constants in my life. To the dozens of people in the writing community who helped me in more ways than they'll ever know: Nancy, Nelita, Emma, Briana, Helen, Chloe, Steph, Ry, Sydney, Anna, Ashley, Amanda, Elise. The 2024 Debut group chat. My amazing agent siblings. And the entirety of the Bingsu street team, whose enthusiasm for this story reminded me why I love doing this.

Finally, thank you to the shitty customer service jobs I worked as a teen. You were awful, but man, you did give me great material for this book.

Never again, though.

ABOUT THE AUTHOR

Sujin Witherspoon is a Korean American author, artist, and lover of words she can't pronounce. She gravitates toward stories that will either plague her nightmares or make her stomach hurt from laughter—no in between. Having earned her degree in English from the University of Washington, she spends her time writing, thinking about writing, or exploring Seattle. You can find her online at sujinwitherspoon.com.